To Thee I

Sing

C.L. Howland

To Thee I Sing

Copyright © 2018 by C. L. Howland

For information contact:

http://www.clhowland.com

Cover design by John Doppler

Publisher's Cataloging-in-Publication Data
Names: Howland, C. L., author.
Title: To thee I sing / C. L. Howland.
Description: Santa Monica, CA : Random Tangent Press, 2018.
Identifiers: LCCN 2018935464 | ISBN 978-1-947957-05-3 (paperback) | ISBN 978-1-947957-03-9 (ebook)
Subjects: LCSH: Man-woman relationships--Fiction. | Organized crime--United States--Fiction. | New Jersey--History--20th century--Fiction. | Pearl Harbor (Hawaii), Attack on, 1941--Fiction. | Women--Fiction. | Historical fiction. | BISAC: FICTION / Women. | FICTION / Historical / World War II.
Classification: LCC PS3608.O95727 T68 2018 (print) | LCC PS3608.O95727 (ebook) | DDC 813/.6--dc23.

First Edition: November 2018

Dedication

To my darlings, Christian and Charlotte—your goodness and light guide my steps.

And to those who've served their country—your sacrifices are what have allowed our children to grow up in goodness and light. Thank you.

Acknowledgements

As always, first I'd like to thank God for my many blessings.

To my critique partners, Carol J. Bova, CJ Alfonso and Helen Lane—thanks, ladies, for your support and insights.

Thanks to my betas for their feedback: Lydia Hill, Stephanie Lewis, Ellen Bagley and Jenna Ditcheos.

I'd like to thank John Doppler from Random Tangent Press for his continued grace and patience in assisting me to bring stories to the world. You're a good man, John, and you do great work!

Also, a shout out to Clare McAfee at wiggoddess.com for my fabulous photos.

Chapter 1

Hawaii at Christmas time, who would've thought? A cool ocean breeze washed over Elizabeth Wellman as she dug her feet into the sand and leaned her head back to catch the early morning rays of the sun.

"I said I'd take care of it, and I will."

Elizabeth started as her sister's raised voice carried through the open doors from inside the large bungalow.

Oh no, they're at it again. Elizabeth rose, picked up the worn leather case by her side and climbed the wide steps.

Her sister, Katherine, huffed out onto the porch, her arms crossed. "Why does she insist I have to go to college? Because she marched in a few parades and carried a sign? Big deal."

"Women getting the vote was a big deal. You don't know the whole—" Elizabeth stopped. "Mother just wants us to have the opportunities she didn't."

Her sister paced back and forth. "If that was the case, she'd help me find an apartment in Hollywood while I establish my career." Katherine stopped and narrowed her gaze on Elizabeth. "Besides, that's easy for you to say. You always do what she wants."

"Career?" Bernice Wellman joined her daughters on the porch. "Singing a few monotone notes into a microphone does not a career make. And don't belittle your sister for the good choices she's made."

"I'm not, but I don't want to be like her. All she cares about are books. It's not normal. Look at her. She has nice dresses; I've seen them in her closet." Katherine paused. "Lizzie, when was the last time you put on something ironed?"

Elizabeth flushed and tried to smooth down the wrinkled cotton jumper she'd grabbed from her suitcase.

"Or went to the beauty parlor for a decent styling? Pigtails? Seriously?"

A few wisps of hair had escaped Elizabeth's loose braids. She resisted the urge to smooth her hair and shrugged instead.

"Katherine, leave your sister out of this. This has nothing to do with her." Bernice turned to give Elizabeth a wan smile. "Good morning, dear."

"Good morning, Mother."

Her mother *tsked*. "Elizabeth, you really should wear a hat. Look at your nose. You just got done peeling, and it's red again. We're going to have to put another milk soak on it."

"See? That's what I mean—she doesn't care." Katherine shook her head. "Lizzie, you look like Rudolph. We won't need to put up Christmas decorations; we'll just stand you on the porch."

"That's not funny." Bernice laid a hand on Elizabeth's shoulder. "Wear a hat when you go out again, all right?"

Elizabeth nodded. "I will."

"Is that more seashells?" Katherine eyed the case her sister held. "Don't you dare bring them into our bedroom—it already stinks to high heaven from the others you've dragged in!"

"Katherine, enough. We'll discuss school later. Right now, breakfast is ready." Bernice led the way to the airy dining room and took a seat at one end of the table, laying a napkin across her lap. The girls settled into chairs flanking her. "Your father's off golfing with your brother again." A small dark-skinned woman set plates in front of each of them, fruit laid out in an artistic arrangement. "Thank you, Lalli."

"Teddy was here?" Elizabeth asked, a chunk of pineapple halfway to her mouth, disappointment etching her features.

"Yes, you missed him."

"Again," Katherine added to her mother's sentence. "You might see him if you ever took your nose out of a book. You know, Mother, she's missing out on everything. There are a lot of available officers stationed here; even she could have her pick."

Thanks, Katherine.

"Has it occurred to you that maybe your sister isn't ready to start a serious relationship?"

"Geez, Mother, it's not like anyone's asking her to marry them, but Teddy's arranged several outings." Katherine pointed her fork at Elizabeth. "And Lizzie hasn't gone on one of them. He won't say it, but I think he's disappointed we came all this way and she doesn't want to spend time with him."

Elizabeth straightened in her chair. "That's not true! It's just…"

"Just what?"

Elizabeth ignored the challenging tone in her sister's voice. "There are always so many people around him."

Katherine snorted. "So what? It's not like anyone is going to bite you." The maid set a plate of ham and eggs in front of her.

"That's enough." Bernice took a sip of her tea. "What events has he arranged? Perhaps your father and I should join in."

Oh no. Elizabeth waited for her sister's answer. On more than one occasion Katherine had come home late reeking of alcohol and spent half the next day in bed.

Katherine shrugged. "Nothing too elaborate. A couple of beach parties." She grinned. "A tour of the harbor. At midnight. In a PT boat. Well, he didn't actually arrange that one," she amended at her mother's shocked expression. "Someone else did, but the point is, I think Teddy feels Lizzie cares more for her books than him."

Katherine, you don't play fair. "That's not true."

Bernice directed her attention to Elizabeth. "Of course it's not, dear, but you should try to attend Teddy's next outing. Promise me?"

I suppose I could endure a few hours of silliness if it makes Mother—and Teddy happy. Elizabeth nodded.

Katherine hooted. "Great, because it's tonight."

Elizabeth scowled at her sister.

"Wonderful." Bernice smiled as she cut a piece of ham. "What is it?"

Katherine took a sip of her juice before answering. "Remember, I told you? After the luau?" She leveled her gaze on Elizabeth over the rim of her glass.

"No."

"C'mon, Lizzie."

Not this again. "No."

"Mother, she promised, and this is the next outing. Besides, it won't work unless she does it with us."

"Oh, that again. Katherine, this may be too much for your sister. She isn't like you."

"Well, actually, Mother, she's just like me."

"No need to be fresh, young woman." Bernice glanced at Elizabeth, whose eyes were on her plate of untouched food. "You may be twins, but no two girls could be more different. Your sister may not fix up as much as you—by the way, that red lipstick is too bright for this time of day, but she has just completed her second degree."

"So what're you saying? She's smart and I'm not?"

"Absolutely not. I have no doubt you're every bit as intelligent as Elizabeth and will prove that as soon as you decide to apply yourself. I don't want another row, but the paperwork for school—did you send it in? Classes start in January."

"I told you I'd take care of it."

"When do you plan to do it?"

Katherine pushed a piece of ham around her plate. "It's done. I just need to mail it."

"That's exactly what I'm talking about. That paperwork should've been mailed last month." Bernice laid her fork on the china plate with such care it didn't make a sound. "Katherine, must I remind you again, how fortunate you are to have the opportunity for education?"

"I know. I know. I've heard the suffragette story a hundred times, but that was a long time ago, Mother. Things have changed. You can stop fighting. You won the battle."

Oh, Katherine, if you only knew. Elizabeth glimpsed the hurt look in her mother's eyes for just a moment before the woman straightened in the chair, her carriage erect.

"I wanted nothing more than to go to a university, and here you've squandered the opportunity—at several different institutions. This may be your last chance, and only because I persuaded your father to make a large donation to get you in."

"What? No." Katherine set her glass on the table with a thunk. "Mother, do you hear yourself? You wanted to go. You! Not me. I'm twenty-five years old. There are so many other things I could do that I don't need a college education for. Daddy couldn't care less if I go back. He's always saying why waste money on educating girls—they're just going to end up married and never use it."

"Your father has some very old-fashioned ideas despite the fact it's 1941. He may be ambivalent about women getting an education, but I'm not."

"Really, Mother, I don't know where you get your notions sometimes." Katherine picked up her fork. "Besides, look at Elizabeth. For all her education, she's yet to get a job."

Elizabeth's cheeks warmed. "That's not true. I had a job every year I was at Bennington, during Winter Field term."

"Yes, at Daddy's factory. If I remember correctly, Mother told him it'd give you a better appreciation of how hard your husband worked when you married." Katherine shook her head. "Besides, it's not exactly like we have to work. I want to sing. I don't need a piece of paper from some college for that."

"Money has never been an issue, but it's more than that. I want you girls to be able to fend for yourselves without having to rely on a man like I—" Bernice stopped and cleared her throat. "Look, finish college, then you'll have the freedom to pursue whatever hobbies you choose."

"Hobbies? Like Teddy, you mean? Why is it music has to be a hobby?"

Elizabeth winced. *This is not going to be good.*

"Katherine, once your brother is back home from the service, things will be different. He'll have more freedom to do whatever he wants about his music, play, compose—"

"No, he won't. You know Daddy expects him to come into the business with him."

"I won't deny your father would like him to join the company, but time will tell. Now, enough of this. How about we go shopping today at—"

Katherine interrupted her mother again. "You know, I just had a thought. Since Elizabeth's always hanging out around the factory anyway, why doesn't she go to work with Daddy?"

Elizabeth perked up. *I wouldn't mind working there.*

"I doubt that will happen, my dear." Bernice responded to Elizabeth's crestfallen look by patting her hand. "Oh, I have every confidence you could do it, but your father would never hear of it. Actually, Elizabeth, I think you'd make an excellent teacher."

"A teacher? Really?" Elizabeth hadn't thought of that, but the idea was appealing. She smiled. "Thank you."

Her mother returned the smile. "You're welcome. And now, please forgive me, but I'm going to hold you to your promise."

Elizabeth's smile disappeared. "What? What are you talking about?"

"I want you to go with Katherine and Teddy tonight."

"What? Mother, I can't. You know I hate doing things like—"

Bernice held a hand up to stop her. Katherine applauded, which drew her mother's attention. "Just a minute, Katherine, I'm not done. If Elizabeth does this, then you're back in classes in January and will stick with it this time until you graduate."

"What?" Katherine slammed her palm on the table and jumped up. "I have to tie myself down for the next year or so, just to get Lizzie's cooperation for a couple of hours? Mother, that hardly seems fair."

"Sit down, young lady. I think it's time you learned life isn't always fair, Katherine. That's my offer."

Katherine dropped back into her seat.

Relax. She'll say no. Elizabeth's stomach churned. *She needs her education, but I can't do this.*

Silence prevailed for almost a minute. Katherine didn't like being bested. Elizabeth held her breath. *Say no.*

"Fine."

What?

"You'll go to classes and use the tutors we hire?"

Katherine nodded.

"No more drinking and sneaking men into your dormitory?"

"Mother, that only happened once, and I've told you a hundred times nothing happened."

"Regardless, is it a deal?"

Please say no. Please.

Katherine gave an exaggerated sigh. "Yes, fine. Fine. Boy, I hope Teddy appreciates this—he's going to owe me."

"Good." Bernice turned to Elizabeth. "It'll only be for a few hours. You'll do it? For me, please?"

No! But Katherine's education depends on it. Elizabeth pushed her plate away and nodded, her throat too dry to speak at the thought of the coming hours.

Katherine jumped up from the table. "Great! There's so much to do and very little time to do it. Could you two hurry up and finish breakfast? I'm going to change. We need to go shopping," she called over her shoulder as she left the room.

Bernice Wellman didn't move, her gaze on the blue ocean through the open doors. "She's right. I have pushed you girls."

"With good reason. I think you should tell Kat what Grandfather did."

Her mother shook her head. "No. I don't want her to know. And you wouldn't know either if I'd burnt that foolish diary years ago."

"But I do know, Mother. You were brave to fight for what you believed in."

"How brave was I, really? I gave in to my father's demands." Bernice dabbed at her eyes with her napkin.

"An arranged marriage or a lunatic asylum? What kind of choice is that?"

"Not much of one, I admit, but I could name a half dozen other young women from our social set faced with the same option. There was this heinous doctor at my father's club who put the idea—"

Katherine's voice broke in from the hall. "Mother. Elizabeth. You need to get ready. I have a lot to do."

"It was a long time ago, and for the most part, I've made a good life with your father. And I have three lovely children." Bernice sniffed and swiped at her eyes once more before dropping the napkin on the table. "Hopefully, three lovely, college-educated children."

Chapter 2

That evening the park hummed with life from the crowd attending the luau. Elizabeth dropped her fork to her plate, too nervous to eat any of the delicious food the locals had been cooking all day.

"Are you ready?" Katherine whispered in her ear.

"Now? I've barely had time to eat." Elizabeth snatched up her fork, speared a piece of pork and brought it to her lips. It was no use. She released the utensil. "What's the rush?" She indicated the outdoor stage. "The Polynesian dancers are about to start. I'd like to watch them for a few minutes."

"Forget it. You've seen them twice already. We need to get ready."

"Ready? What do you mean?"

"You'll see. C'mon." Katherine pulled Elizabeth to her feet. "Let's go." They picked their way through the crowd.

Almost an hour later, Elizabeth stood off to the side of the platform stage watching the dancers, feeling overheated. *I don't know how that could be. It's definitely not because I'm overdressed.* She glanced down at the outfit matching Katherine's. A sarong. A snug red sarong yet, with a variety of flowers printed on the cloth. Her hair was down in a draping wave on one side in the Veronica Lake style Katherine preferred, while the other side was held back with a large red hibiscus blossom tucked behind her ear. Makeup and red lipstick completed the get up.

"Here, have some more punch." Katherine offered her a tall glass and then took a sip from the glass in her other hand.

"Thanks. It's certainly hot enough tonight." Elizabeth fanned herself with her free hand.

"Yeah, it sure is." Katherine grinned. "Drink up. You don't want to get dehydrated."

Her smile gave Elizabeth pause. "What's in this, anyway?"

"Oh, fruit juice, pineapple, other stuff. I don't know what else." Katherine set her own glass down. "Criminy! Relax, will you? Look what I've got." She produced two sets of black high heels. "Nice, huh?"

Elizabeth shook her head. "No. I am not wearing those."

"I suppose your socks and oxfords look better?"

Elizabeth glanced at her feet and then shrugged. "I won't be able to walk in those things. I'd rather go barefoot, for goodness sakes."

"That's a great idea." Katherine slipped off the heels she wore. "C'mon, hurry up."

"I was kidding."

"I'm not. Let's go."

Elizabeth handed her drink over and reluctantly followed her sister's lead, wiggling her freed toes for a moment. "You know,

Mother and Father aren't going to be happy when they get a look at these outfits."

"Relax. They're gone. Mother arranged for the Nelsons to invite them over for coffee. Here, finish your punch, but don't smudge your lipstick."

"Kat, I'm not sure I can do this."

"Of course you can. We've done this a hundred times."

"Yes, but not in front of a crowd like this—dressed like this."

A low whistle sounded behind them. Both girls turned at once.

"Holy smokes! There's two of them!"

"Man, they're gorgeous!"

"Hello, ladies."

"Wow, they're gonna go crazy over this!"

Elizabeth's face flamed while Katherine grinned at the uniformed men.

"Knock it off, you meat heads! You're talking about my sisters."

Teddy. Theodore Stone Wellman, III stood taller than most of the other men.

The group advanced to where the two women stood. "I heard you had two sisters, but no one mentioned twins. Identical twins? Yowza!" The man next to Teddy looked from Katherine to Elizabeth and back to Katherine again, returning her smile as she nodded. "You girls are knockouts. Old Wellman's been holding out on us."

"Ignore them; they're harmless." Teddy stepped closer to Elizabeth. "Hi, Lizzie."

"Hi, Teddy."

"You look great."

She gave him a slight smile. "Thanks, I guess. It's not exactly my style."

"I know. Thanks for doing this."

Katherine's finely arched eyebrows formed a scowl. "What're you thanking her for? It's me that's going to have to rot in boring classes."

Teddy laughed. "If I know you, Katie, you'll make the best of it. As usual. Anyway, I'm thankful we're going to get to do this." He squeezed Elizabeth's hand. "I know you're nervous, don't be. You'll be great." He handed her a piece of paper. "Here's the order. It's all stuff we've done, except for a couple playing on the radio that you've probably heard a hundred times. I think you can handle them."

She looked at the list, nodded and took a sip of her drink.

"What have you got there?"

"Fruit punch."

"Fruit punch? Really? Mind if I have a sip?"

She handed the glass over.

"Where'd you get this?" he asked after taking a taste.

"Katherine. I'm sure she'll get you one too. Kat, Teddy would—"

"No, that's fine. I'll get my own. Take it easy on that stuff, okay?"

Elizabeth nodded, using the paper to fan herself. "It's so hot tonight, I might melt," she joked.

"I doubt it, but I bet you two will melt a few hearts. Look, these guys are a long way from home. I know they'll appreciate this, and it'll be great for morale."

The troupe of dancers passed them, leaving the stage. Teddy turned to the others in the band. "You guys ready?"

The men nodded. Some turned to open instrument cases.

"Okay, girls. They've got the stage set up. Are you ready?"

"Let me at 'em," Katherine said with a grin. Elizabeth gave her brother a weak smile.

"We'll go first, and then I'll introduce you. Let's go." Teddy led the group out, and as they took their places, he stepped up to the microphone at the right side of the stage. "Hi, folks. How are you all tonight?" Thunderous applause met his question. "Every once in a while, the guys behind me get together for the fun of it, and we thought maybe you wouldn't mind listening in tonight." More applause. "I can see we have some regular patrons here. I hope you folks don't mind, but we've invited the boys from the harbor in, and they promised to be on their best behavior. Right, boys?" More applause and hoots. "There may be a few more coming, but we're going to get started." He walked to the piano at the middle of the stage, adjusting the microphone as he sat down. He looked to the men around him. One man pulled a bass cello closer as several others raised brass horns of various types. Another man sat at the ready behind a set of drums. Teddy counted and the band swung into a Glen Miller tune to warm up the crowd.

The cheers were loud even off stage. Elizabeth tapped her bare foot against the wood floor in time to the music.

After a few minutes, Teddy raised his hand and spoke into the microphone. "Tonight, we have two special guests from the mainland."

"Are you ready? Let me check you." Katherine smoothed down Elizabeth's hair. "Here, have one last sip. There's more on a stand on the stage if your throat feels dry. Do I have lipstick on my teeth?" She bared her teeth.

Elizabeth shook her head.

"Good. Don't freeze up, okay? We're doing this for Teddy and all the boys over here. Remember that."

"I'll try not to."

"It's my pleasure to introduce the Hula Dolls."

"The Hula Dolls?" Elizabeth questioned. "Where'd that come from?"

"I made it up. You go first. When you get to the microphone, I'll come out," Katherine instructed. "Don't forget to smile and wave." With that, she shoved Elizabeth onto the stage. A mass of humanity spread out before her, though she couldn't make out any faces through the glare of the floodlights. The roar of the crowd was deafening as Elizabeth worked her way across the stage, remembering to wave just before she got to the microphone. She turned to see Katherine waiting off stage and signaled for her to come out. *What's she doing?* But Elizabeth already knew the answer. Her sister loved playing the twin card, as much as Elizabeth hated it. *Remember, you're doing this for Teddy.* She pasted a smile on her face. Without looking, Elizabeth knew exactly when her sister stepped onto the stage. The crowd went crazy. Katherine blew kisses as she took her time getting to the other side of the stage and put an arm around Elizabeth's waist. "For goodness sake, smile would you?" Katherine hissed through painted lips. Elizabeth did her best, and it was several minutes before Teddy or the band could be heard.

"Well now, that's a welcome! And you haven't even heard them sing yet."

Someone from the crowd yelled, "Who cares if they can sing?" Laughter and more applause followed.

The three Wellman siblings had been harmonizing for years, so although that part came naturally, it took several songs and just as many sips of punch for Elizabeth to relax enough to be able to really look at the crowd. As far as she could see, most everyone wore a uniform—marines, soldiers and sailors, all smiling and clapping. The audience spread out to the sides, way past the stage, and more were coming. She glanced down to see a sailor smile and wave to her. He reminded her of Teddy when he'd been a teenager. She gave him a small smile, and his grin got even wider. How old were these servicemen? She glanced at other faces and saw many looked to be young—how young? Nineteen, twenty maybe?

Engrossed in the harmonic intricacies of the songs, Elizabeth loosened up a little, but was glad when Teddy finally announced a short intermission. Without the singing to concentrate on, her discomfort grew as she became even more aware of eyes on her, lots of eyes. It didn't seem that way for Katherine. She laughed and chatted with the men pressing close to the stage.

"Miss?"

Elizabeth felt a tentative touch on the top of her bare foot and jumped back.

"Sorry. I didn't mean to scare you."

She looked down. It was the young sailor she'd spotted earlier.

He snatched the white cap off his head and gave her a shy smile. "Can I get your autograph? On this?" He held up the cap.

"Ohh. Ahh, I'm sorry. I don't have a pen."

He looked crestfallen—just like Teddy, the time someone had run over his dog Juniper.

"Hold on a second." Elizabeth turned to the group on stage. "Does anyone have a pen? No?" She thought for a moment and then bent down, holding out her hand. She took the hat and pressed it to her mouth. It came away with the imprint of full red lips. "How about this?" Someone handed her a pen. "Oh. Thanks." She rested the cap across her bent knee. "What's your name?"

"George. George Simpson. From Pennsylvania."

"Really? I'm from Vermont. A little town called Northam. To George, from Elizabeth," she said aloud as she attempted to sign the material without blotting the ink from the fountain pen. "How old are you, George?"

He leaned in a little closer. "The truth?" His voice was low.

She continued to work without looking at him. "Yes, of course."

"I'm seventeen. I lied and nobody checked too close, so here I am."

"What about your parents? They must be worried."

"I ain't got any, not that I know of at least. I was brought up in an orphanage. And trust me, it's not only the chow that's better here."

She glanced at him. *He's serious.* "Well, George, I'm glad things are better for you now."

"Yes, miss, being in the Navy is swell. Can I request a—" Someone pushed him from behind. "Hey, knock it off."

"You're hoggin' all the lady's time, and some of the rest of us were hoping for a word with her," a burly soldier piped up.

"Gentleman, I'll be glad to talk to you as soon as George finishes asking his question. George?"

"Well, I know there's no snow or nothin', but do you think maybe you could do a Christmas song?"

"I'll talk to the band leader." She pressed the cap into his hand. "Merry Christmas, George."

"Thank you, miss. Merry Christmas to you too," he said before being swallowed up by the surging crowd.

Elizabeth was relieved when Teddy came over a few minutes later to say intermission was over. Though Katherine seemed to be genuinely enjoying the banter, Elizabeth had run out of polite excuses for declining date offers and rubbed the tight spot just above her right temple, the usual sign a headache was coming on. She managed to speak to Teddy for a moment before returning to her spot on the stage.

They worked their way through the rest of the song list, and after two encores, Teddy raised his hand for quiet as he walked toward Elizabeth and Katherine, coming to stand between them in front of the microphone. "You've been a great audience. I mean that, the best. Now, we'd like to close the show with a special request." He reached out for the girls' hands and gave each a squeeze. In perfect unison, the three sang *Silent Night.* No instruments, just their voices. His rich tenor in combination with their soprano and alto filled the night air and carried over the silent crowd in a wave. "Please sing with us." Teddy urged into the microphone, before continuing with the lyrics a second time. And everyone did.

It was a memory Elizabeth would keep the rest of her life. The sky was a canopy of stars, sheltering hundreds, maybe thousands of men singing the simple words in quiet reverence. She scanned the edge of the stage, and sure enough, there was George Simpson, staring right back at her, his face aglow as he sang, the folded hat peeking out of the pocket of his uniform shirt. She smiled at him as they finished the song. For several moments, no one moved as the sound died away.

"Good night. Thanks for coming." Teddy, still holding the girls' hands turned to walk off stage. The audience slowly came to life. Claps, whistles and cheers followed them into the wings.

"Wasn't that great?" Katherine gushed. "That was so much fun. I could do that every day. How about you, Teddy?"

Teddy grinned and nodded his agreement.

Elizabeth shook her head. "Not me. I was too nervous."

"You did great." Teddy gave her a squeeze. "I'm really proud of you. Both of you. And I can tell you this, the guys really enjoyed it, so thank you. Oh, damn."

Elizabeth heard her brother's muttered oath, but had no time to ask what was wrong before his right hand snapped into a sharp salute.

"At ease, Lieutenant Wellman."

"Yessir. Thank you, sir." Teddy dropped his hand, but looked neither left nor right, his frame still as erect as a ramrod.

"I was having dinner nearby and heard all the noise. That was quite a show." The older man removed his hat. "And may I say, you ladies are lovely."

Both girls murmured, "Thank you."

"I'm sorry if we disturbed you, sir."

"Nonsense, son. It did my heart good to hear the boys enjoying themselves. I'm sure it'll be the topic of conversation around here for months. In fact, I think we need to get together and talk about something like this on a more regular basis. Can we count on you ladies?"

Teddy cleared his throat. "Ahh, I don't think that will be possible, sir. They're visiting over Christmas, from the mainland."

"I see. Well, you're lucky you've got a girl willing to come all this way to visit you. Which one?"

"I beg your pardon, sir?"

"Which one is your girl? And how do you tell them apart?"

"Neither is my girl, sir."

"What? Then why would they bother coming all this way? Surely they're pretty enough to find someone closer to home?"

"Yes, sir...no, sir. What I mean is, they're my sisters, sir. This is Miss Elizabeth Wellman," Teddy paused.

Unsure of protocol, Elizabeth extended her hand to the older man who clasped it gently.

"And this is my other sister, Miss Katherine Wellman."

Katherine stepped forward, laying a hand on the man's sleeve. "It's nice to meet you, sir." She smiled up at him. "So, did you like the show?"

What's she up to?

"Yes, indeed."

"Our parents are here as well. Maybe they can be persuaded to allow me to extend my stay to help Teddy—Lieutenant Wellman with the show."

"Excellent idea. I'd love to talk to them. Wellman, why don't you bring your parents and these lovely ladies aboard tomorrow morning? O-eight-hundred?" He fit his cap back on his head and adjusted it at a slight angle. "We'll have breakfast and a tour of the ship."

"Yessir." Teddy saluted again.

"Until tomorrow, ladies." The man touched the bill of his cap, turned and left.

Teddy exhaled in a huge gust. "He wants to talk about a regular show? Am I dreaming?"

Katherine grinned and saluted him. "No, sir, you're not."

Teddy laughed at her antics.

"And I'm going to get to stay and help. I can't wait."

"Katherine, you can't, you promised Mother you'd go back to school. It's the only reason I agreed to this."

"Oh, Elizabeth, stop being such a wet blanket. I'm sure once Teddy's commander talks to Mother, she won't dare to disagree. Besides, I bet Daddy will think it's a great idea."

"Regardless of what Daddy thinks, do you think Mother's going to give in on the subject of your education because someone she doesn't even know, commanding officer or not, asks her?"

"We'll see." Katherine's smile was smug.

"Yes, we will."

"Okay, you two. I'm beat, and it seems we all have an early morning. Let's go. We need to let Mother and Father know they've been invited to breakfast with the CO. That'll be a feather in Dad's cap."

"I'm not the least bit tired. I could stay up for hours," Katherine said, even as a yawn stretched her happy features. "Okay, maybe I'm a little tired."

Elizabeth grimaced as she slipped her dirty feet into her socks and oxfords. "I'm exhausted, and I'm getting a headache."

Teddy shook his head. "I think you can thank Katie for that."

She turned to Katherine. "What's he talking about?"

Katherine shrugged. "Well, the punch you were drinking may have had a touch of rum in it."

"What?"

"I was trying to help you relax. Honest."

"Don't ever do that again."

"I promise I won't. But it did help. We were pretty good tonight. What do you think, Teddy?"

He nodded and grinned. "We were. And the guys in the band were great too. " He headed toward the exit. "I'm with Katie on this one. I could do this every day."

"Maybe you'll get your chance after all."

"Yeah, maybe you're right, Katie." Teddy's grin faded. "But I'm not getting my hopes up. My CO had a couple of drinks under his belt tonight; we'll see what he has to say in the morning. Besides, that's not my job here." He closed the car door after them, went around to the driver's side and climbed in. "And as Dad is so fond of reminding me, I'll have the rest of my life to play music after I'm done here."

Chapter 3

The Wellman family traveled the street heading toward the harbor in the early quiet of Sunday morning. "Teddy's CO inviting us to breakfast—that's a good sign for the boy. He's going places. Why he might even end up an admiral," Theodore Wellman crowed from the front seat of the four-door Buick convertible he'd borrowed from the Nelsons.

He hit a bump in the road, and Elizabeth groaned. Katherine had lied. Sunglasses did nothing to alleviate the pounding headache and nausea she woke up with this morning. "I thought you said these would help," she whispered to Katherine next to her in the back seat.

Katherine looked at her over the top of her own dark glasses. "They are. They're hiding your bloodshot eyes."

"I don't think Teddy wants to be an admiral," Bernice Wellman reminded her husband.

"Nonsense. Of course he does. Why, I'd even hire someone to help me run the business if that was the case."

"Really? You're getting a little ahead of yourself, don't you think, Theodore?"

Elizabeth detected the slight sarcasm in her mother's voice, but as usual, her father missed it, or chose to ignore it.

"Not at all. It'll take a while to find the right man for the job."

"Man? What about a woman?" The sarcasm was less veiled this time.

"Have you gone daft? A woman couldn't run the company."

"I bet Elizabeth could."

"Elizabeth?" He glanced at her in the rear view mirror. "Is that before or after she recovers from her hangover?"

Elizabeth's cheeks flushed.

"Either, I'll wager."

"Wager? As if you had anything to wager. Besides, the board would never go for it. Look, we're almost there, so for once—" He broke off as he glanced at several planes overhead. "What in blazes? Early for maneuvers, I'd think." He returned his attention to his wife. "For once, do you think you could keep your cockamamie ideas about women working to yourself?" He looked up again as more planes roared over. "Holy Christ, those are—" He never got to finish.

What sounded like a jackhammer went off behind them. Elizabeth turned in time to see pieces of pavement fly into the air a ways back from the car.

Her father slammed on the brakes. "Out. Everyone out. Now!"

Both girls scrambled out of the car, leaving the doors wide open.

"Theodore, what is going on?"

Bullets ripped through the trunk.

Theodore Wellman threw his considerable bulk against the door. "Jesus, woman, get out of—" he stopped abruptly as bullets riddled his body causing it to convulse before ending up laid over the seat, half of his body in the back.

"Mother, get out of the car," Elizabeth screamed and started toward her.

Her mother didn't move at first. "Theodore? Oh my god. Oh my god."

Bernice was half out of the car when another hail of bullets rained down, driving Elizabeth back to the pavement and causing the older woman to do the same macabre dance as her husband had before she collapsed on the ground.

"Mother." Elizabeth rushed to her. Katherine sobbed somewhere behind her. "Check Father." The sobbing continued. She turned to find Katherine curled in a fetal position under a concrete bench. "Katherine, now!" Elizabeth ordered before gently rolling the woman over. A bullet had parted her mother's otherwise perfectly coiffed hair, then dug a shallow trough down her cheek before lodging in her breast. It was not her only injury. Blood seeped through several holes in her dress, staining the material, and Elizabeth knew even before she felt for a pulse what she would find.

"I can't tell. I can't tell."

As Elizabeth turned to her sister, she registered the distant hum of plane engines. *This is crazy. Who's doing it?* She hurried to the other side of the car and glanced into the back seat. There was no way her father could have survived that head wound.

"Is he okay?" Katherine paced and sobbed at the same time.

I have to be sure. Elizabeth steeled herself and slid her fingers over what was left of his neck.

"Well? Daddy's okay, isn't he?"

"No, he's gone." Numb, Elizabeth tried to wipe the blood from her hand on the seat upholstery.

"No, that can't be. He has to be okay. Where's Mother?"

Katherine started around the car, but Elizabeth grabbed her by the collar of her dress and yanked her back.

"Kat, they're both gone." She could see the planes now. "We have to get out of here."

But there was no time. The now familiar spray of bullets was already on them. Elizabeth grabbed her sister and pushed her back under the bench, laying on top of her. She felt gouging pain along the back of her torso and cried out, but didn't move. In a few minutes, it was quiet again. Elizabeth crawled out on her hands and knees. When she twisted to check on Katherine, she felt something running down her back. "C'mon. We're not that far from the harbor. We can make it. We have to find Teddy. He'll know what to do."

Katherine didn't move. *Oh Lord, no.* "No. No." Elizabeth pulled her sister out from under the bench. "Katherine?"

Her sister stared at her, tears slipping from the corners of her eyes into her hair. Her nose was running and bloody at the same time and blood smeared across her cheek. "I can't do it."

"Yes, you can. Come on." Elizabeth dragged the woman to her feet. She'd lost a shoe. "Katherine, take your shoe off."

"But I love these shoes."

"Kick your shoe off, Kat. We'll come back for them later." She put an arm around her sister and steered her away from their mother's body, her face almost unrecognizable from the last round of bullets. They walked down the street, Elizabeth attuned for the sound of more planes. "Look over there, Kat. There's the harbor and Teddy's ship. We're safe." The words had no more than left her mouth than the very ship she had pointed to exploded into a fireball. Even at this distance, the repercussion knocked them down. Several attempts to get up were fruitless as one explosion after another decimated the ships in the harbor.

"What's happening?" Katherine screamed, covering her ears at the same time. "I want to go home. I want to go home."

Elizabeth hugged her sister. "We will. We will. Soon." The spot where Teddy's ship had been anchored was now a burning hulk with plumes of black smoke reaching hundreds of feet into the air. *Oh, Teddy, please be all right.*

Suddenly Elizabeth could feel the vibration of a rumble in the pavement under her knees. "Get up. Get up. We've got to move."

They'd made it as far as the sidewalk when a large truck turned the corner and rolled to a stop in front of them. There were a couple of men and several women in the back. One of the women called down, "You okay?"

"Yes. No. I don't know." Elizabeth shook her head, hoping to clear it. "They killed our parents." She pointed in the general direction of the car, "and we were trying to get to our brother at the harbor."

"You can't do any good there right now. You'd be more help at the hospital. There's going to be wounded." Another ship in the harbor exploded. "Lots of wounded. Either of you gals nurses?"

Katherine shook her head.

"Ahh, I have a degree in nursing, but I haven't had much practical experience," Elizabeth admitted. Another explosion rocked the ground under their feet.

"Well, after today, I'm thinking you're going to have plenty of experience. Climb on board."

"Wait, my parents—"

"We'll come back for them. We gotta go. We're sitting ducks here."

Elizabeth nodded and guided Katherine to the back of the truck. Several hands helped to pull them in, and Elizabeth avoided looking back.

"Elizabeth, look at your arms and legs." Katherine gasped. "They're all blood. You're hurt."

"It's just pieces of pavement. I'll take care of it later. It'll be okay."

"But your back is all bloody too."

"I said I'm okay; don't worry."

"Let me look."

Elizabeth shook her head. "Not now."

The truck pulled into the hospital parking lot, and everyone piled out. Elizabeth half dragged her sister inside. "Katherine, listen to me. Don't leave the building. I'm going to try to help where I can."

An explosion nearby shook the building and shattered the window right behind their heads, showering them with glass. Elizabeth shoved Katherine into a small utility closet and leaned her against the wall. "Don't leave, okay?"

Katherine slid down the wall to sit next to a bucket of dirty mop water, oblivious to the strong bleach odor as she huddled in the corner. "Okay. Please try to find out about Teddy."

Hours passed. So many bodies, some could be helped. More couldn't. Elizabeth kept working, wondering if it would ever end. The standard hospital smell of rubbing alcohol she'd noticed upon entering was no longer detectable. The odors of blood, burnt flesh and offal now presided over the building. Others, battling to save lives, stood as Elizabeth did, reduced to wearing blood soaked street clothes amid mounds of discarded gory bandages and gauze. But even their shouted orders and the constant metallic bangs of instrument trays and stretchers being shoved around couldn't drown out the screams and moans of pain and desperation.

"Elizabeth."

It was barely above a whisper. She turned and saw a hand lift before falling back on the stretcher. She moved closer. The man was covered in black from head to foot. Most of his uniform was gone, revealing huge burns on his legs and torso. His hands had no skin left, but his head was much worse. Most of his nose and some of his upper lip had been burnt away, along with his hair. One ear was gone. *Oh, no, please don't let this be Teddy.* But who else could it be? No one knew her here. "Teddy?"

He stared at her with unblinking green eyes. His eyelids were gone too. *Wait, Teddy has blue eyes.* Elizabeth had all she could do not to sigh out loud in relief. *Who is he?* It didn't matter, he wasn't Teddy. "You rest now. Have you had some morphine?"

"Yes. Hurts though."

His breathing was labored and his whole body shook. It was beyond her how he could get those few words out. "Please don't

try to talk anymore. I'll see if I can get you some more morphine."
She turned to leave.

"Thanks for...song."

Elizabeth stopped and turned to face him again. *It can't be.* She
glanced at what was left of his shirt. Sure enough, a tiny piece of
pocket with an even tinier scrap of white and a spot of red.
"George?" *It can't be, he's only seventeen.* She wanted to comfort
him somehow, but there was no place she could touch him without
causing more pain.

"Yes." The single word came out as a sigh.

"Oh no, George. Hang on. I'll get you something for the pain."
She grabbed the nurse who'd spoken to her on the truck and turned
her toward the stretcher. "Morphine. He needs morphine."

"We ran out of morphine hours ago." She sighed when
Elizabeth stood wringing her hands. "Okay, let me take a look at
him and see what I can do." She bent over George for a second
before straightening up. "He's beyond morphine or anything this
world has to offer, honey. He's gone. Hey, you, don't leave that
cart there, we need the room." She stepped around Elizabeth and
hurried after the orderly.

Elizabeth stared at George, his unseeing eyes wide open. And
she wept. For her father, her mother, for Teddy wherever he was
and for George, the child who thought this was a swell life.

Chapter 4

May 1943

"Good morning, everyone. Let's get attendance out of the way." Elizabeth Wellman waited for the rustling to die down before she continued. She read the names on the English class list and received a "Here" or "Yup" in response.

"Frank Flynn." No answer. She looked up. "Frankie?" His seat was empty. "Is Frankie sick?"

Sam O'Hearn spoke up. "Naw. He enlisted yesterday. His old man threw him out for filching some change out of his pocket."

"Oh. Well, perhaps if I talked to Mr. Flynn and Frankie returned the money, we could straighten—"

Sam cut her off. "He's already gone. Left on the train last night."

"I see." *Another one gone? Over a few coins?* "I'm sorry to hear that."

The boy snorted. "Why? He'll get three squares a day and less beatings, I bet ya."

Elizabeth said nothing more on the subject, just finished attendance. "Please get your books out and read chapter 8. It begins on page 92." She retrieved the stack of papers she'd been correcting earlier. *If he needed money, I would've given it to him. That makes fourteen boys from this one school. Will this nightmare never end?* With a deep sigh she refocused on the top sheet of paper, scanning the answers and marking each. 100%. *Of course, Nicolina Moretti.* Her grades were outstanding. When Elizabeth mentioned college, Nicolina had laughed, saying she'd probably end up married like her three older sisters if her mother had any say in it.

Elizabeth finished the papers and rose to write on the blackboard. "Okay everyone, homework. Finish reading this chapter, and there's a handout on the corner of my desk. Please pick one up on your way out. It'll be due when we come back on Monday."

The bell rang, dispelling the quiet in the classroom as students trooped by her desk to retrieve the handout.

"Sam, don't forget the homework." She gave him a slight smile. "Again."

"Yeah, yeah. Sorry." The boy rolled the papers into a tube and tucked them into the back pocket of his pants.

Only sorry that you got caught. Elizabeth shook her head.

A group of girls approached the desk.

"Oh, Nicolina, do you have a minute? I'd like to talk to you."

Nicolina rested her books on the corner of the desk and told the other girls, "I'll catch up." She turned to Elizabeth. "Did I do something wrong, Miss Wellman?"

"Oh no, of course not. In fact," Elizabeth handed her the graded paper. "You're doing a wonderful job."

Nicolina grinned. "Thanks."

"Which is why I'd like to talk to you about college again."

The girl's smile faded a bit. "Look, Miss Wellman, I really appreciate what you're doing and all, but I don't think it'll work out. My parents can't afford it."

"What if money weren't an issue?"

"Huh? I don't know about your family, but money is always an issue with my family."

Elizabeth nodded. "I understand. But most schools have scholarship funds available."

The girl shrugged. "I have no idea how to go about doing that."

"Well, you have another year to think it over, and I can help you figure it out."

"That's mighty nice of you." Nicolina hesitated. "Can I be honest?"

"Of course."

"I mean no offense by this, but that sounds like charity and my parents, especially Mama, wouldn't take kindly to that. Besides, we're really busy right now. My whole family. It's kind of a project."

To hide her disappointment, Elizabeth got up to erase the blackboard.

"Maybe you'd be interested. Do you want to hear about it?"

Elizabeth moved the felt eraser across the slate and tried not to inhale the chalk dust as she kept her eyes on the board. "Yes. Of course."

"On Sundays, after church we go to Port Johnson. We have picnics and play games."

"That sounds nice."

"It is. Mama and the other ladies always make so much food. My mama loves it when the boys eat. It's a fun day." A pause. "What are you doing this Sunday? Maybe you'd like to come?"

"I don't think," Elizabeth stopped. *Nicolina's mother will be there? Maybe if I could talk to her about college?* She turned to smile at Nicolina. "Actually, I believe I am free this Sunday."

"Great. It'll be fun..." The girl's words trailed off as her gaze landed on the blackboard.

Elizabeth's hand still rested on the eraser. The sleeve of her sweater had ridden up from the exertion of rubbing and exposed a bit of the skin on her forearm dappled with small pockmarks. She dropped the eraser and yanked her sleeve down, then slid her arm behind her back. "What should I bring?"

"Huh?"

"Should I bring some food to share?'

"Oh, no." The girl gave a slight shake of her head. "Sorry. No, there'll be plenty there."

"Okay. I'll see you then."

On Sunday, Elizabeth got off the bus and sat on the bench at the stop to wait for Nicolina. *Why would people have a picnic here?* The

surrounding buildings were commercial businesses, if the signs were any indication. An old truck approached and came to a stop right in front of her. There were three adults and two toddlers jammed into the cab, and at least a dozen people of all sizes wedged in the back.

"Let me out." Someone dropped the tailgate, and Nicolina jumped off the back of the truck. "Hi, Miss Wellman. Are you ready?"

"Ahh, yes." Elizabeth didn't move.

"Okay. Are you coming?"

Elizabeth stood as curious eyes watched her. "Umm, are we walking?"

"No. C'mon." Nicolina rounded the truck and plunked down on the open tailgate before tapping the spot next to her. "Plenty of room. I saved a seat for you."

Still under scrutiny, Elizabeth settled onto the rusty metal.

"Are you all set?"

At Elizabeth's nod, someone banged on the roof of the truck and it lurched forward, the engine whining.

"I'll introduce you to everybody when we get inside." The truck slammed to a stop after what seemed like only a few feet. Nicolina grabbed the chain holding the tailgate up. "Whoa. Hang on."

"Is something wrong?" Elizabeth grasped the edge of the pickup body with one hand and clutched her purse with the other, afraid she'd lose it.

"No. We have to stop at the gate house and sign in to visit the soldiers."

Soldiers? Unease crept up the back of Elizabeth's neck like a wayward spider.

The truck started up again, gears grinding as they passed through a brick archway. Several sets of legs pressed against Elizabeth's back as the truck jerked its way along a dirt road, surrounded on either side by rows of long one-story buildings. Rolled barbed wire topped the walls. At each corner a small tower of matching brick overlooked the area—like a guard tower. A silhouette moved, and Elizabeth saw the distinct outline of a gun barrel. *It is a guard tower.* "Nicolina, where are we? Is this safe?"

The truck ground to a halt. Nicolina held out a hand. "C'mon. We have to get out to let the others out."

People milled around in a large open grassed area. Elizabeth held her purse shield-like as she turned in a circle. Beyond the buildings at one end, she glimpsed water. "What is this place?"

"Miss Wellman? Are you okay? You look pale."

"What's over there on the other side of those buildings?"

"The harbor."

Harbor? Elizabeth squeezed her purse a little tighter to stop her gloved hands from shaking. *I have to get out of here.* She stood rooted in place.

"Yes, I told you. Remember? Port Johnson?"

"I thought you were talking about a park."

"No, Port Johnson is a POW camp."

"What? A prisoner of war camp? Japanese?" Elizabeth couldn't hide the tremor in her voice.

"No. No. Italians. That's why we come and visit. Look, I'm sorry. I should've explained it better to you. Why don't you sit down for a minute?" The girl tugged on Elizabeth's arm. "Miss Wellman? Are you okay?"

Elizabeth's mouth was so dry, she had to swallow before she could answer. "Yes. Yes, I'm fine. Maybe I should sit down. Do you think perhaps I could have a glass of water?"

"Of course. We have several blankets laid out to sit on. You have a seat, and I'll find you a drink."

Elizabeth lowered herself onto a brightly colored quilt and kept a firm grip on her purse. It was the only thing keeping her from hurtling back down the road to escape.

Breathe. Take a breath. Relax. Breathe. She inhaled deep breaths through her nose and exhaled through her mouth. After repeating the ritual several times, Elizabeth felt calm enough to take a tentative glance around the area. Several old ladies dressed in black sat in a cluster of straight-back wooden chairs and watched her with interest. *They look like crows.* All around, small knots of men and women stood in groups talking and laughing. Every group held several men in dark blue uniforms. *Are those POWs? Why are these people fraternizing with the enemy?*

Elizabeth jumped when someone tapped her on the shoulder. She turned, expecting to find Nicolina, but instead it was a man, in his mid-thirties maybe, his pleasant features arranged in a slight smile.

"Good afternoon. Nicolina asked me to let you know she'll be right back with your drink." He extended his hand. "I'm Dante Montenari."

"Elizabeth—" It came out as a croak. Elizabeth cleared her throat. "Sorry. Elizabeth Wellman."

"Yes, I know. How are you?"

"Fine." *Who is this?*

The man pulled a vacant chair to the edge of the blanket and sat, before stretching his legs out. "It's a beautiful day." He lifted his face to the sky, bringing his Adam's apple into prominence. "Feel that sun."

Does he have an accent? Is he a POW? She took the opportunity to study him. Clean-shaven, his black hair was curly, but instead of a uniform he was dressed in dark pants, a white shirt and a tie. "Yes. It's lovely." Elizabeth waited a moment, but he didn't move or speak again. "Are you a prisoner of war?" It was out before she had time to think about it.

His smile was rueful as he leveled his gaze on her. "No. I'm a tailor."

"I'm sorry. That was rude."

He must've read her look of confusion. "My mother and father were from Italy, but I was born here."

"For a moment I thought I heard an accent..."

He shrugged. "Maybe. Sometimes. It comes from living in the neighborhood. We're Americans with accents, but Americans nonetheless."

"I apologize. I guess I'm nervous."

"There's nothing to be nervous about. Everyone here is friendly." He glanced around the clearing. "They're just curious about you, that's all."

"Why?"

"Why? Well, because you're different, and you're a teacher, a position respected by the elders."

"Oh." Elizabeth looked around the group again. Several old people nodded and gave her a smile. She smiled back. "Wait, how do you all know I'm a teacher?"

"Well, Nicolina told me. I'm sure she told her mother too, and her mother probably told Mrs. Carapetti, and Mrs. Carapetti told Mrs. Cammareri and so on." He grinned. "No one needs a telephone in our neighborhood when you have a front stoop."

"Why did Nicolina invite me here? I'm not Italian."

"Why did you accept? You're not Italian." Despite the serious tone of the question, a slight smile played across Dante Montenari's lips.

Elizabeth flushed. "I had an ulterior motive."

"So does she—what's yours?"

Elizabeth studied him a moment. Without knowing why, she felt she could trust him. "I wanted to talk to her mother about Nicolina going to college."

He nodded. "She's a smart girl, but I doubt *Zia* Rosa will approve."

"Who's *Zia* Rosa?"

"My Aunt Rosa, Nicolina's mother."

"You're Nicolina's cousin?"

"*Sì.* Our mothers are sisters."

"What's Nicolina's motive?"

He lifted his head. "Here she comes now. Why don't you ask her?"

"Here you go, Miss Wellman." Nicolina handed Elizabeth a cup and dropped to her knees on the blanket in front of them. "Ask me what?"

Dante smiled. "Miss Wellman was wondering why you invited her here."

Nicolina smoothed her full skirt. "Well, I thought she might enjoy an outing. She never mentions having a boyfriend or going out, so I thought maybe she'd—"

"Wait," Elizabeth cut her off. "Nicolina, my personal life is none of your concern."

"I know." The girl exhaled in a gust. "Boy, this seemed easier when I thought about it in my head. Okay, the truth. I thought if I brought you here, and you met a few of the fellas, you might be interested in..." The girl hesitated.

Oh, my word. Is she trying to fix me up with a POW? "Nicolina, thank you for thinking of me, but I'm not interested in dating one of these gentlemen."

"Dating? What? No."

Dante burst out laughing.

"Shut up, Dante. No, Miss Wellman, I didn't mean dating—well, I guess you could if you wanted to, but I thought you might be willing to teach them English. Stop laughing!" Nicolina reached over and slapped Dante's leg. "*Zitto, idiota!*"

His laughter turned to an immediate groan. "*Figlio di una cagna!*"

"Oh, jeez. I'm sorry, Dante. I forgot."

He shook his head and sucked breath in through his teeth for a few seconds before biting out, "It's okay." But clearly it wasn't if his grimace and sudden pale skin were any indication.

"What's wrong?"

Dante shook his head. "Nothing to worry about, Miss Wellman."

Nicolina scrambled to her feet as he levered himself to a standing position. "I'm really sorry, Dante."

"I know you didn't mean it. It's fine." He gave his cousin's arm a gentle pat.

"Will you still be able to interpret later? Do you want me to find someone else?"

"I'll be fine. I just need a few moments to myself. Miss Wellman, it was nice to make your acquaintance. I'll talk to you later. Enjoy yourself." With that, he limped off.

Nicolina dropped to the blanket again. "I'm such an idiot. I forgot about his leg."

"What happened?'

"He got hurt in the war."

Elizabeth's heartbeat quickened again. "Pearl Harbor?"

"No, no. That was bad, but I guess this was pretty bad too. He was on a Navy ship in the Coral Ocean, or something like that. There was fighting with the Japanese."

"The Battle of the Coral Sea," Elizabeth murmured.

"Yeah, that was it. I heard my aunt talking to my mother about it once. He got a lot of shrapnel in his leg, and they couldn't get it all out. I guess he almost died from an infection. I don't really know much more about it, other than he's in a lot of pain; he doesn't talk about it."

I can understand that. Elizabeth watched the man disappear into the crowd.

"I didn't mean to hurt him. Honest. I just forgot." Nicolina picked at the embroidery on her skirt for a moment. "So, will you do it?"

"Do what?" She turned her gaze back to the girl.

"Teach the POWs English."

"Nicolina, what kind of prison camp is this?" Elizabeth looked over the groups again now she was a little calmer. People were not only talking, there were small tables set under a large tree where several card games were in progress, as well as a game of horseshoes over by the wall. "It looks more like a family reunion."

The girl shrugged. "It is, kinda. A couple of people have relatives here. Some are from the same town in Italy, and lots of people just like to talk about the old country."

"But these prisoners probably killed some of our soldiers."

"I know, but some of our soldiers killed them too."

Elizabeth shook her head. "I can't do this."

"Look, Miss Wellman, before you say no, would you at least meet some of them?"

"I don't know."

"Please. I know for a fact not all of them killed people. Alessio didn't shoot anyone. He was drafted into the Italian Army, and he thought that was okay, 'cause his family didn't have enough to feed them all, but being in the army was worse. He was happy to surrender. His whole group was starving—lots of them died. Even now, although they're prisoners a long way from home, they think it's paradise. They love everything American, including a few of the girls here."

"What? Would you be one of those girls?"

The girl blushed under Elizabeth's scrutiny. "Maybe."

"Nicolina Moretti, does your mother know about this?"

"Sure she does. And she doesn't mind. She thinks Alessio is a wonderful boy."

Another obstacle to getting this girl into college. Well, I might as well meet my competition—Mrs. Moretti and the wonderful Alessio.

Later, with Dante acting as her interpreter, Elizabeth moved among the groups, speaking to most of the uniformed men. Alessio did indeed seem to be a nice man, as were most of the others, and all were very young. *As young as the boys at Pearl.*

It took only a few minutes for Elizabeth to realize she had nothing to fear. The prisoners were more nervous than her. Most smiled and shyly shook her hand, using what few words of English they knew to greet her.

At dinner, everyone sat outdoors at long tables. Dante sat on one side of her, Nicolina on the other, with Alessio next to her. Dante's mother, Maria, and Nicolina's parents, Rosa and Basili, sat across the way. Dante's mother seemed quiet, but Rosa Moretti was a miniature general ordering people around one minute, and the next minute, jumping up to fill someone's glass, fill the bread basket, whatever needed taking care of. Even with Dante's help, Elizabeth hadn't gotten far in her quest about college since it seemed neither Mr. nor Mrs. Moretti understood what she was trying to tell them.

The sun was low in the sky when Elizabeth stood. "Thank you so much for inviting me. The food was wonderful, and I'm absolutely stuffed." She laid a hand against her flat abdomen. Dante interpreted. Several people chuckled. "It was wonderful meeting you all. I had a lovely day." Everyone nodded and smiled. "Thank you again. I need to go now." She stepped over the bench and started to back away with a wave.

Several people called, "*Arrivederci.*"

"*Arrivederci.*" Elizabeth smiled and turned to leave. It was a ways to the gate, and she'd need to hurry to make the last bus.

"Miss Wellman."

She turned. It was Dante Montenari. "If you need a ride, I can give you one."

"Oh no, that's fine. I'm going to take the bus."

"All right, but I'll give you a ride to the bus stop at least. Otherwise, you'll miss the bus."

She hesitated for a moment.

"If you think we should have a chaperone, I can ask Nicolina, or my mother."

She smiled. "No, that won't be necessary."

He limped to a black sedan and held the door for her before lowering himself onto the driver's side seat. They were back through the gate in what felt like half the time it took to get there this afternoon. He parked the car near the bus stop.

Elizabeth grasped the door handle. "Thank you very much. I appreciate it."

"One second." He came around to her side and opened the door.

"Thank you." They walked to the bus stop.

"I should wait until you get on the bus. Do you mind?"

She shook her head and sat down.

He sat next to her. "Are you going to do it?"

"Do what?" But she knew what he was talking about.

"Teach the boys."

"I don't know." She sighed. "Can I be honest with you?"

"Please do."

"Well, in a way, I'd like to because I love teaching, and it's obvious they want to learn in the worst way. But then I think of our soldiers, and I feel like I'm being—I don't know, what's the word I want to use?"

"Disloyal?"

"Yes, something like that."

"I understand, believe me. I guess only you can make that decision."

A low rumble signaled the bus's approach. "Well, Mr. Montenari, it was a pleasure to meet you." She extended her hand.

He clasped and held her hand for the briefest of moments. "The pleasure was mine."

She blushed and turned toward the bus, hoping he hadn't noticed.

Chapter 5

"So, Mr. Romano," Dante pulled open a small wooden file drawer, extracted a packet of index cards held by a thick rubber band and set it on the counter. "You were here a few months ago and ordered two suits. Is there something wrong that you needed to come back so soon?"

"Naw...I, ahh...," the rotund man hesitated. "I just felt like another suit. How about we do blue this time? Yeah, that's it. I feel like a blue suit."

Blue? Dante shuffled through the group of cards. Benito Romano had been getting his suits made here for twenty-five years, all in black. "Blue?"

"Yeah, that's it. Blue, but the darkest blue you got. Okay?"

"Sure, Mr. Romano. Sure." Dante reached for some samples. "How about something like this?"

"Yeah, yeah. That looks almost black, don't it?"

Dante nodded. "Okay. I think we're all set then." He put the samples away. "Since you were just here I have your measurements."

"Yeah, about that." The man cleared his throat. "Dante, you do good work—almost as good as your old man, but last time I think you made the vest a little too tight."

"Really? I'd better re-measure you then."

The squat man removed his suit coat. One of the vest buttons was missing and the rest were strained.

"I apologize, Mr. Romano. That vest is a bit snug."

"No problem, Dante. It just makes it hard to work sometimes."

Benito "Bennie the Hammer" Romano worked for the Salucci crime family. Dante's father had warned him years ago to never ask questions, so Dante didn't, but he'd gotten a good indication of Mr. Romano's occupation when he found a set of bloody brass knuckles in the pocket of a suit coat dropped off for mending. Dante pulled out a blank card and started a new set of measurements, stretching the tape measure across the back of the man's broad shoulders.

"So, Dante, did you hear about Russo's?"

"Yes. That was unfortunate."

"Unfortunate, my ass! Everybody knows the micks did it, they been tryin' to take back this neighborhood for almost twenty-five years now. It won't never happen. We'll make sure of that."

We? The Salucci family, of course. The Irish gangs had run this whole section of town before Don Salucci appeared. Now, most of the Irish populated a small adjacent neighborhood dubbed Irish Town. Over the years, the Italian and Irish mobs had continued to war against each other and sometimes amongst themselves. Dante knew all too well the tragedy created by these territorial skirmishes, but said nothing as he finished recording measurements on the card. He compared the two sets of measurements. *That can't be right.*

"We've got a pretty good idea who did it. That smelly bastard, Flanagan. He been around here?"

"No." Dante looked at the two cards again. "Mr. Romano, I need one more measurement."

"Sure, sure, kid." The man patted his substantial paunch. "I want you to get it right. You let us know if he shows up." The man raised his arms a bit.

Dante drew the tape around his customer's considerable girth.

"You hear me, boy?"

Dante swallowed his irritation at the man's address and nodded. "Yes."

"Good. The Don would have my ass if anything happened."

"The Don?"

The man shrugged. "Yeah. He protects his people. Now, did you figure out what you did wrong last time?" Romano tugged on his vest.

"It seems my waist measurements were two inches too small. Would you like me to alter this vest?"

"Maybe next time. I got an appointment." Romano gave Dante a sheepish grin as he tugged on his vest again. "Some of it might be my fault too. I been eating too much lately."

"I can understand. Your wife is a good cook."

"Yeah, my Rose Marie cooks good, but I got a new piece of tail down on the other side of town. The girl's great in the sack, and she can cook. And I like to eat almost as much as I like to fu—"

The bell over Dante's front door interrupted the man.

"Excuse me a moment, Mr. Romano. I'll be right back to help you with your coat." Dante looped the tape measure around his neck and stepped through the doorway to the front of the shop. His cousin, Nicolina, hurried toward him.

"Hi, Nico, what're you up to?"

"Well, two things actually. Mama sent me with a pair of Papa's pants and guess what?"

"I have no idea." Dante heard Mr. Romano clear his throat. "Look, I have to finish with this customer. Then we can talk. I got a shipment of material in this morning, maybe you could put some of it away for me?"

She nodded. "Sure."

Dante limped back to Mr. Romano and held up his suit jacket as the man worked his way back into it. Dante ushered him to the door. "It should be ready for a final fitting in two weeks at the latest. I'll let you know if it's ready earlier."

The chunky man's head bobbed on his shoulders. "Good. Good." He paused and spoke in a low voice, "Don't forget—you come see us if one of those micks comes callin'."

Dante nodded. "Give Mrs. Romano my regards." He closed the door and leaned against it for a moment to relieve the pain in his leg. *Damn thing.* He sighed and used one of the counters lining the walls to support his weight as he worked his way toward the storeroom at the back of the shop. Nicolina had turned on the radio he'd bought Mama last Christmas and sang along with the latest Judy Garland song. He came to lean on the door frame. "Okay, how about you turn that thing down a little, and tell me again what you're doing here? Are you looking for a job?"

"No. At least not yet." She turned down the radio. "Where's *Zia* Maria? She's not working?"

He shook his head. "I made her stay home today. She works too hard for a woman of her age."

Nicolina gave a snort. "Yeah, right. Like that would stop her. When you get upstairs, she'll have been cooking all day. If she makes cannoli, you'd better call me this time."

Dante just smiled.

"I'm serious."

"Fine. Now, what'd you need?"

"Oh, yeah. Mama wants to know if you can make Papa a pair of new pants. He's got this pair, but there's a big tear in the leg where he caught it."

"Sure, I'll get to it as soon as I can."

"She said no hurry. His other pair is in good shape."

He nodded. "Is that it?"

She snapped her fingers. "Jeepers, I can't believe I almost forgot. Miss Wellman finally agreed to teach the men at Port Johnson. Isn't that great?"

"Really? You didn't pester her, did you?"

"No, I swear. It's been forever since she came out, and I've been dying to ask, but I didn't. Honest. It took her so long to decide, I thought for sure the answer was going to be no."

"I thought so too. Did she say why she decided to do it?"

"Yeah, sort of. Miss Wellman said her mother fought for her to be educated, and now it was her turn to fight for the POWs since no one else would. She said it's what her mother would've done."

Interesting. The woman was an enigma. One moment, she fought for the POWs' rights, and the next she was—what?

Standoffish is the word that came to mind. The image was further enhanced by her dowdy way of dressing, but even her plain clothes and hair scraped back in a bun couldn't hide the fact she was an attractive woman, if a little thin. He wondered why she dressed like that. *It's not your business, Montenari. Just forget it. You've got enough problems.*

The bell rang again and Dante turned to see who entered the shop. One of the problems he'd expected to show up any day now pushed open the front door. *Burt Flanagan.* As if discussing the man with Benito Romano had called him in. "You stay back here," Dante ordered his cousin before reaching into the desk drawer. He straightened his vest as he met the broad man halfway up the aisle. "Good afternoon. What can I do for you?" He tried to ignore the odor of perspiration emanating from the man.

"Are you Montenari?"

Dante nodded.

"Good. I'm Burt Flanagan." The man pushed back his overcoat, resting meaty fists on his hips and displaying pants and a matching vest in a garish gold and brown plaid as he studied the dark wood and high ceilings of the shop. "Nice place you got here. Real nice. I been thinkin' about a new suit." The man stroked his chin for a moment and then picked up several swatches of silk laying on a counter top nearby. He rubbed his fingers back and forth over the material. "This is fancy. It's silk, ain't it?"

Dante nodded and tried to ignore the dirty finger prints smudged across the fine fabric.

"I thought so. I know quality goods." The man tossed the material back on the counter. "How about plaid? I like plaid, you got any plaids?"

"No, I'm afraid not."

"What? Why not?" The man narrowed his eyes. "You got something against plaid?"

Dante shook his head. "Right now, I only keep small amounts of plaids for vests and the like."

"Oh. Okay, fine then. I take it you'll be orderin' some soon?"

"I'll look into it."

"Thanks." The man strolled at leisure around the shop, glancing into the fitting room off to the side. "Yeah, it's a real nice place you got here." He touched several more pieces of fabric and with studied nonchalance pulled open several drawers to examine the contents as he meandered toward the front of the shop. "I'll be back later then." Flanagan reached for the door knob, but stopped, holding up his index finger. "Oh, there is one more thing. You know, this neighborhood is gettin' pretty unruly. Why just last week, only a few blocks from here, nearer to Irish Town, someone trashed Russo's Market in the middle of the night. That's a shame, ain't it?"

Dante said nothing.

"You know," Flanagan's tone was conversational, "It never hurts to have a little protection. Me and my boys could do that for you." The burly man studied his dirty fingernails a moment. "I'll even knock the price down a wee bit seein' how you're a veteran and crippled." Flanagan grinned. "Just doin' my part for the war effort. It'll be hardly nothin' for a successful business man like you."

Dante cleared his throat. "I appreciate the offer, but I think we're all right for now." The sound of footsteps overhead echoed through the quiet shop. *Mama.*

Flanagan glanced up. "Are you sure? You can never be too careful." The man splayed a hand flat against his chest, his gratuitous smile revealed a missing front tooth while the rest were black with decay. "I'd hate to see someone you care about get hurt in an unfortunate accident."

Bastard. Dante's smile tightened as he crossed his arms, his hand finding its way to the comfort of cold steel. *Relax.* "That's true, Mr. Flanagan. But as intelligent men like us know, it may not be the wisest move to do anything like that around here, especially in Don Salucci's territory. Don't you agree?" The Irishman reached into his pocket. Dante's hand tightened on the butt of the gun.

Flanagan produced a handkerchief and mopped his furrowed brow. "Shit, it's hot. I'll never get used to it." Several moments more passed before his face eased into a smile again. "But I'm thinkin' a smart man like you'd want extra protection, ya know." He pointed toward the ceiling. "For your family."

"Hmm, that may be true." Dante paused as if considering it. "But out of respect, I should ask the Don first. You understand? He'll be in next week for a fitting. I'll ask then and let you know."

"What?" The man's ruddy complexion paled a bit. "The Don gets his suits made here?"

"He has frequented my establishment in the past."

"You dagos and your respect talk. Always kissin' Salucci's ass." Flanagan shook his head and edged to the door. "Your Don don't need to know nothin' about this. Keep it to yourself, you hear, boy-o? Otherwise," he pointed toward the ceiling with his index finger and then drew it across his throat in one motion. "Got it?"

Dante wrapped his finger around the trigger, but made no other movement, not taking his eyes off the man as Flanagan banged the door shut on his way out.

He sagged against the counter in relief.

"Who was that guy?" Nicolina came to stand next to Dante, waving her hand in front of her nose. "Phew, he stinks. He ever hear of soap?"

"Flanagan? He's trouble. If you see him coming, you run, do you understand me?" When she didn't answer, Dante grabbed her arm. "Do you understand me?"

"Yeah, Yeah. I get it. Do you mind?"

Dante let her go. "Sorry, Nico. But this is no joke."

"Okay, I get it. Relax. Since when does Don Salucci get his suits made here?"

"He doesn't, but it wasn't quite a lie. The Don has been here. Once. When I got home from the war. He came in by himself one afternoon. I thought it was about tribute, but he said he was glad I made it home and left. It was strange."

"Do you pay tribute?"

Dante shook his head. "No. My mother told me once my father wanted to, but the Don wouldn't hear of it. I guess it was because the Don and Mama are *paisans*, from the same place in the old country. Flanagan doesn't know that though." He straightened up. "Hopefully, he doesn't figure it out any time soon."

"And if he does?"

Dante shrugged. "I hear it takes nothing to provoke him, so I'll just have to watch my back." *And carry a gun.* "No sense worrying about something until it happens." *Change the subject.* "So, Miss Wellman is going to work with the boys. That's great." He turned and headed back to the store room. "What do you know about her?"

"Not much. She doesn't talk about herself, but I can tell she's real smart. And she's a good teacher, maybe the best at the high school. The kids all like her. Much better than old lady Henderson, who's either sleeping or whacking someone for disturbing her nap."

Dante laughed. "Mrs. Henderson was there when I went to school."

"She's an old bat. You know, there's something about Miss Wellman though. I don't know if I can explain it. She seems kind of sad, but every once in a while, when she smiles, she looks real pretty, or I bet she would be if she dolled up a little." Nicolina shrugged. "Except for her arm."

"Her arm?"

"Yeah, I saw it once. It reminded me of *Zio* Enzo's face, remember?"

"Uncle Enzo had smallpox when he was young. I doubt Miss Wellman had smallpox."

"I can't help it; that's what it looked like."

"Hmm. I don't know."

"I'm a little nervous for her, Dante. She plans on going out to Port Johnson twice a week by herself. Do you think it'll be safe?"

"She should be fine." *Who are you kidding? In that neighborhood?*

"Good. It's kind of a long walk out to the Rec hall, especially at night."

She'd be easy prey. Just forget it, it's not your problem.

"Maybe I should go with her."

That's all I'd need is for something to happen to Nico. Dante sighed. "No. It wouldn't be right. I'll go with Miss Wellman."

"You will? Great! Thanks. As much as I'd like to see Alessio, that place is so big, it kind of gives me the creeps."

"On one condition. Since I'm taking one night a week away from the business, you're going to help me out by coming down here on Saturday mornings and work."

"What? You know I'm no good at sewing."

"No sewing. Dust, sweep, write up invoices—whatever needs to be done."

"Okay, I can do that."

He nodded. "Good. Now, I have to finish putting that stock away. Why don't you help me, and then we'll go upstairs and see if your *Zia* Maria made cannoli after all."

When Elizabeth Wellman got off the bus near Port Johnson on Wednesday, Dante was there to meet her.

"Hello, Miss Wellman."

Surprise registered on her features. "Mr. Montenari, what are you doing here?"

"Nicolina was in my shop the other day and told me you'd agreed to teach. We talked it over and decided it'd be best if you had someone with you."

"Mr. Montenari, that's incredibly nice of you, but I couldn't possibly put you out like this, every week."

"It's no bother. My car's right here." He held the door for her. "Besides, unless your Italian has improved dramatically in the last few weeks, you're going to need an interpreter—for a while at least."

"No, it hasn't, but I have been studying."

He closed the car door after her.

"*Grazie.*" She paused. "How was that?"

He smiled. "*Perfecto.*"

"Perfect? Really?" At his nod, a satisfied smile passed her lips.

Neither said anything else on the ride to the Rec hall. He shut off the engine.

Elizabeth took a breath.

"Are you ready?"

She nodded, and they headed toward the building. "What if no one shows up?"

"Then you're off the hook." He pulled open the door. "But I don't think that's going to be the case."

The room was packed, every chair taken, with a few men lined up against the wall. All eyes were on Elizabeth.

"Oh, my goodness, I can't do this. There's too many of them."

She started to back out, but he stepped behind her and touched her arm. She stiffened. Dante chose to ignore it and instead leaned forward to whisper in her ear, "You'll be fine. Take a deep breath. Relax. It'll be fine." With his hand lightly riding her elbow, Dante propelled her to the front of the room. "It's only for a couple of hours. I'll be here with you."

Elizabeth nodded and sat her bag on the little table one of the men pointed out. Dandelion blossoms sat in a small jar of water, next to it a shiny red apple. A large chalkboard on wheels stood off to the side.

She studied the items on the makeshift desk, took another deep breath and stepped around to the front of the table. The room was silent.

"Good afternoon, gentlemen. Ahh, *buon pomeriggio, signori.* Correct?"

Dante nodded and came to stand beside her.

"*Buon pomeriggio, Signorina* Wellman."

She smiled at the chorus of voices. "Good. Mr. Montenari, would you please translate?" Elizabeth pulled a stack of large cards out of her bag. "I'm going to teach you English, but you all also have a job. Your job is to teach me to speak Italian. *Sì?*" She glanced around the room. "Good. First, we're going to look at some pictures. You're going to tell me the word in Italian, and then we'll learn it in English." She put up the first card. The immediate response was "*cane*". She nodded. "Dog." She turned and wrote it on the board in large letters, working her way through the stack this way. "That's it."

"*Di Più.*"

She looked at Dante. "What does that mean?"

"More."

"More? Hmm, okay." She handed him one of the cards. "Would you write these new words down on the back, please?" She walked to the window and pointed. That started another round of her moving around the room to point to as many different objects as she could. She stopped when the chalkboard was full and dusted off her hands. "How do you say finished?"

"*Finito.*"

"*Finito,* everyone."

The room got loud with protests.

"Just for this week." She put an index finger to her lips. "Shh."

The men quieted down.

"Okay. When I come on Sunday, we'll review our words."

"I wish I had a way to make them some practice sheets. I'll have to think about that," she said later as they walked toward Dante's car.

"Why don't you make some up? I have a friend who's a printer. He'll do it if I ask."

"That'd be wonderful. I'd pay him, of course."

"I'll take care of it."

"Mr. Montenari, as much as I appreciate the offer, this is my responsibility."

"Are you always this stubborn, Miss Wellman?"

She blushed. "No, just independent, I guess."

"Hmm. Mind if I ask you something? Why are you doing this?"

"At first I didn't want to." She hesitated. "I've adjusted to my school routine, but I'm not always comfortable in new situations." Elizabeth sighed. "I guess what it comes down to is I'm a teacher, and they want to learn, so I couldn't say no."

"Of course you could have. This is taking a lot of your free time."

"I don't really socialize much." Her voice was quiet.

"Still, it's your time. Do you know why a lot of them want to learn to speak English?"

Elizabeth shook her head.

"They want to talk to American girls."

"Regardless of the motivation, they want to learn, that's what's important."

He started the car, and they rode in silence for a few minutes.

"Look, since we'll be spending some time together, maybe we should get to know each other, so we'll have something to talk about." Dante glanced over to see her reaction. She sat unmoving on the other side of the car. "Okay, I'll start. I'm an only child, and I still live in the building I grew up in. What about you, where'd you grow up?"

No response.

"Miss Wellman?"

She cleared her throat. "Northam."

"Where's that?"

"Vermont." It was barely above a whisper.

"No kidding? I went there once, well, through there—we were going to Canada. It's beautiful."

Nothing.

"And you came to New Jersey? Why?" He parked across from the bus stop. "What about your family? Are they still in Vermont?"

"I have to go. My bus will be here any minute." She pushed against the door.

"Wait. I'll get that for you."

"That's not necessary, Mr. Montenari. Thank you for the ride. Good night." Elizabeth closed the door and ran across the street.

She's a strange woman. What's she hiding? She paced back and forth in front of the bus stop. A long black car crept by, cutting off his view of her for several seconds. Something about the car wasn't right. *Flanagan? One of his men?* Dante twisted to get out, but his leg protested. "Damn it." By the time he rounded the front of his car, she'd taken a seat on the bus. He glimpsed the car just before it turned the corner. A Mercedes-Benz. Too rich for Flanagan. Too rich for most people in town, except one man—*Don Salucci. What's he doing around here?* It could be a coincidence. *Or he thinks you're in cahoots with Flanagan.* Dante hadn't gone to the Don about the Irishman. He had to keep his family safe, and it looked like Miss Wellman had just been added to the list.

Chapter 6

August 1943

Several months passed, and Dante Montenari hadn't tried to question her again, much to Elizabeth's relief. They'd settled into a routine of sorts. He picked her up at the bus stop on Wednesdays and Sundays and took her back too, most of the time without a word spoken between them.

Sundays were informal, as far as lessons, with the advent of warmer weather. The blackboard appeared outside, and as the group went over words Elizabeth noticed several young men crane their necks every time a vehicle pulled up. They'd collect their practice sheets and be gone. Like young men the world over, they were interested in the young women who visited the camp.

After class, Elizabeth visited with families and shared a meal. Several times she'd attempted to engage Mrs. Moretti in a conversation about Nicolina and each time had come away frustrated. The gray haired woman would listen and then say, "*Mi dispiace, non capisco,*" before moving on to something else. "I'm sorry, I don't understand." Today was no different. Elizabeth dropped onto the bench at one of the tables.

"She's scared."

Elizabeth looked up to find Maria Montenari seated across from her. She too had gray hair, but overall lacked the sharp edges of her sister. Instead of the severe knot of hair Mrs. Moretti wore at the nape of her neck, Maria's hair was pinned up in a loose bun with several tendrils trailing down. And unlike her sibling, the only lines on her face were at the corners of her eyes when she smiled. *She must've been beautiful when she was young. She's still beautiful.*

"My sister understands what you're saying. She just doesn't want to offend you."

"She won't offend me, but I don't understand. Why wouldn't she want Nicolina to further her education?"

"I think she does, but it is not her decision. Nicolina's father decides."

I've been talking to the wrong parent?

"Plus, you should know, I don't believe Nicolina wants to go to college."

"Why? She's very intelligent, she'd do well."

"Miss Wellman, if I'm not mistaken, I believe Nicolina is in love." Maria pointed a finger over Elizabeth's shoulder.

Elizabeth turned. Nicolina and the POW, Alessio, sat close together on a blanket, oblivious to others as they chatted. "But she should really go to college first."

"No offense, but I disagree. If someone is lucky enough to find love, they shouldn't wait. Look at my son."

"Dante?"

Maria nodded. "I don't know if he'd approve of me telling you, but I believe you will keep this between us. He was in love once, a long time ago. A local girl. Luciana. Dante had the opportunity to go to college and took it, thinking he'd make a better life for them, and she waited for him. He graduated and they were planning their wedding when she was shot, right in her father's restaurant, an innocent bystander in a war between two of the local families."

"Oh, I'm so sorry, that's terrible. Why would families fight like that? Did they get arrested?"

"No, my dear. No one was ever arrested. They were *Cosa Nostra*...mafia."

"Here?"

The woman nodded.

"I didn't realize. Is anyone here?" Elizabeth looked around.

"No, most of the people here are just hard working families."

"What did Dante do?"

"He went crazy. Drinking and fighting, always pushing the wrong people, until one night someone beat him and left him for dead in an alley." Maria shook her head. "He lay in the hospital for weeks, hardly talking. He'd been out of the hospital two days when he came home and announced he'd joined the Navy as an officer and shipped out the next day. Just like that, he was gone, but to tell you the truth, I was relieved. I thought he'd be safer. After he was hurt, he came back here—for me. I told him not to. He tries to hide it, but I know he's not happy." Maria sighed. "The point is, Miss Wellman, I can tell you from experience when happiness comes around, you should grab it, like a greedy child would a cookie. It could be gone tomorrow."

"I agree."

"You do?"

"What are you ladies talking about?" Dante came to stand next to his mother. "Mama, can I get you anything?"

She shook her head. "No, thank you, son."

"Miss Wellman?"

"Actually, some cold water would be nice. It's really hot today."

"Coming right up." He placed a hand on his mother's shoulder. "Mama, are you sure I can't get you something?"

Maria patted his hand. "I'm fine."

Someone had left a newspaper on the table. Elizabeth picked it up to fan herself.

"It's not my business, but perhaps you should be wearing lighter clothes. It's very warm today."

"I'm fine, Mrs. Montenari. Honest." Elizabeth set the paper aside, and smoothed down her long sleeves as she watched Dante leave. *He's been through so much.* For the rest of the day she found herself watching Dante Montenari with covert glances. He joked with the POWs. He stopped to converse with the elders, and for the first time Elizabeth noticed several women approach him throughout the day. Most were quite pretty in flowery summer dresses. *Oh, to wear a cool sun dress again in public.* He'd chat for a few minutes, but then excuse himself.

Later, Maria came back to sit with her for dinner.

"Mrs. Montenari, does Dante have someone," Elizabeth searched for the right words. "After his fiancé, was he able to move on and find someone special?"

Maria shook her head. "Not that I know of. I wish he would. He's only thirty-four. He should be married and starting a family by now. He's a handsome man, si?"

"Yes." And he was. Lean in a tailored white shirt, its rolled up sleeves exposed the dark skin of Dante's forearms. His curly black hair shone in the summer sun. "Yes, he is."

"He's had a lot of opportunities to be with someone, but he's refused them."

"He must have loved his fiancé very much."

"Luciana? Yes, he did. A long time ago. Now, I think he uses it as an excuse not to get involved. We've talked about it a few times. After being wounded, Dante thinks he's damaged. I've seen the scars on his leg. They're not pretty, but they're not who he is. Do you know what I mean?"

Elizabeth nodded. "I do. But sometimes it's hard to convince yourself of that, when the rest of the world often only sees your scars."

"That's funny—Dante says that same sort of thing sometimes." Maria studied Elizabeth for a moment. "Has he talked to you about his wounds?"

"No, no. It was just an educated guess."

"I believe you're a smart woman as well as educated. I like you."

Elizabeth returned the woman's smile. "I like you too."

During dinner, Dante came to join them and sat at the end of the table next to Elizabeth. She looked at the unfamiliar food on her plate and leaned toward him. "What's this?"

"Trust me, it's good."

"Okay." She took a bite and chewed. "This is really good." She took another mouthful. "Mmm. Really good. What's it called?"

Dante smiled. "*Lasagne.*"

"Well, it's delicious." Elizabeth smiled in pleasure. "Did you make this, Mrs. Montenari?"

Maria nodded.

"It's wonderful." Elizabeth glanced at Dante. "Oh, wait, you have a little something." She took her napkin and brushed it against his cheek. "There." She gave him a quick smile before turning to his mother. "Mrs. Montenari, could I have this recipe please? I have to try to make this."

"Of course." Maria glanced at her son. A slight smile touched his lips as he studied the woman next to him.

After dinner, one of the POWs approached their table. "*Buona sera.* Good evening."

"Good evening, Roberto. How are you?"

The young man smiled and nodded. "Good, Miss Wellman. Ahh, I want tell you, ahh," he stopped. "Difficult, the words. Umm, *Signor* Montenari, translate please?"

"Yeah, sure."

The young man spoke in rapid Italian for a few moments and waited.

Dante shook his head.

"What? What's he need? Help with his homework?" Elizabeth looked from Dante to the POW and back to Dante again. "Mr. Montenari?"

"No. A girl brought a portable phonograph and some records, and there's going to be dancing in the Rec hall."

"That's nice. Go ahead, Roberto. It'll be fun." She gave him an encouraging smile, and he smiled back.

"Ahh, that's not all." Dante cleared his throat. "He wanted to know if you'd like to go too—with him."

"What?" Elizabeth looked up, and the soldier nodded. "What? Oh, dear. What do I say? How do I tell him no?"

"Shh. Don't worry. I'll take care of it." Dante spoke in Italian, and Roberto's smile dimmed as he listened. "Okay. Okay. Another time. Good bye." He turned and left.

"What'd you tell him?"

"That unfortunately you couldn't stay. You had to go teach a group of orphans after this."

"Orphans? That's silly." But Elizabeth couldn't help laughing. "Orphans?" She shook her head.

"What? I had to think of something, so the boy wouldn't feel too bad."

"Thank you. I think. Well, I need to get going to make the bus. I can't keep the orphans waiting. Mrs. Montenari, it was very nice to see you today."

The older woman's smile was warm. "It was nice to see you too, dear."

"I'll be looking for that *lasagne* recipe next time."

"Yes, I was thinking about that. You know, I don't have anything written down, it would be easier to show you. Why don't you come over Wednesday after class? We'll make it and then have dinner."

Go to their house? Elizabeth glanced at Dante, but his eyes were on his mother, a questioning look on his face. "Thank you for the invitation, but I don't want to put you out."

"It's no bother."

"Okay, thank you. How far is the bus stop? I'll need to catch the bus home."

"Nonsense. Dante will drive you. You don't mind, do you?" Maria met her son's gaze with a nod.

"No, no problem." Dante finally looked in Elizabeth's direction. "It's not a problem."

"Oh, that's not necessary. I'm sure there's a bus. Anyway, it was nice to see you again."

"It was nice to see you too, and I insist Dante drive you." The woman smiled. "We'll see you on Wednesday night."

Elizabeth and Dante arrived at the bus stop a few minutes early and walked over to sit on the bench. As usual, no words had passed between them since climbing into the car.

"Mr. Montenari, I apologize."

"Miss Wellman, I'm sorry."

They both spoke at the same time and then laughed.

"Ladies first."

"I'm sorry about the whole dinner thing. I just wanted the recipe, but I couldn't say no to your mother; she's such a nice lady."

Dante smiled. "She is. And I know you said you don't socialize much, so I want to thank you for agreeing to come. She'll be happy to have someone to teach."

She nodded. Neither spoke for a few moments, but for the first time the silence didn't feel as uncomfortable to Elizabeth.

"Tell me, Miss Wellman, what have you been doing with your days, now that school is out for the summer?"

"Well, I've been painting some of the rooms in my house. I read a lot, and I tend my gardens."

"Why doesn't your landlord do the painting?"

"I don't have a landlord. I own the house." She shrugged. "It's not grand, by any means—in fact, it's tiny, but it's mine."

He nodded. "We own the building we live in too. The shop is on the first floor. My mother has an apartment on the second floor, and when I came home from the service, I built an apartment on the third floor. Most of the time it's okay, but at this time of the year, it gets hot up there."

"Well, it's starting to cool down a little, so maybe it won't be too bad tonight." Elizabeth leaned back. "What a gorgeous evening. Look at that sunset." The sky was awash with pink, lavender and orange.

"Yes, it is. And the weather's getting warmer every day. If we don't get some rain pretty soon there won't be a place to escape it unless you go to the beach. Do you like the beach?"

"I used to, but not so much anymore. My backyard has several shade trees and is actually quite cool."

"That sounds nice." The bus pulled up and the door opened.

"Goodnight, Mr. Montenari." Elizabeth climbed the steps and sat near the front, giving a wave of her hand as the bus pulled back onto the street. He raised his hand.

After the bus left, he noticed a car parked across the street. He made eye contact with the guy sitting in the front before the man lifted a newspaper in front of his face. "Who the hell are you guys?" Dante made for his car, snatching his gun out of the dashboard and started across the street. He hesitated when another man came out of a nearby building and approached the same car.

"Thanks for pickin' me up, Ernie. It's too friggin' hot. Let's get that beer I promised you."

The car took off and left Dante standing in the middle of the street. "You're a paranoid bastard." He shook his head and climbed into his car. "*Idiota*," he muttered as he pulled away from the curb, never seeing the two cars pull out of the lot across the street. One car trailed him at a distance, while the other followed the route the bus had taken.

Chapter 7

The warmth of the afternoon intensified the scent of roses perfuming the garden.

"Hello, Elizabeth."

Elizabeth turned to the voice. "Mother?" Sure enough, her mother sat in the lawn chair across from her, wearing her favorite burgundy dress, the one they buried her in. "It can't be."

"Why not? I'm here, aren't I?"

"Yes, and I'm so happy to see you. Where's Daddy? He's going to be upset, but I have to tell you—we don't have the business anymore, and I sold the house. We had to get out. They wouldn't leave us alone."

"I understand."

"But you loved that house."

Her mother nodded. "But I love you more."

"I brought some of your roses with me." Elizabeth hesitated. "Katherine didn't go back to college. She went off to sing. I'm sorry."

"We each have to pick our path."

"But you were right about me. I love teaching."

"I'm glad."

Elizabeth returned her mother's calm smile. "I have a little house, maybe you and Daddy can come here."

"Darling, I think we both know that's not possible."

"Why not? Mother, I'm so lonely."

"I know. I'm sorry, my dear. But know we're at peace now. You need to move on with your life."

"How can I do that?"

"You've always been a smart girl. You'll find a way."

"I don't think that's possible. Besides," Elizabeth stopped. "What's that noise? Do you hear it?"

Her mother shook her head.

"It's planes. Hear the engines? Run, Mother. This time you've got to run! Run!" She screamed and reached for her mother.

Elizabeth hit the ground hard, landing on her knees. "What?" She glanced at the chair. Her mother wasn't there. *The planes? Where are they?* She crouched near the chaise lounge. It took a few moments to register the noise wasn't an airplane, but the loud hum of her neighbor's fancy new gasoline mower. Elizabeth crawled back onto the chaise and lay there. Her heart pounded against her ribs, and her breath came in short pants. Sweat not only poured down her face, it drenched her whole body.

Relax, you've got to relax. Do your breathing. She clamped her mouth shut, inhaling deeply through her nose. It took at least five minutes of this exercise before she was able to sit up. Elizabeth exhaled in a gust and pushed back the perspiration soaked tendrils clinging to her temples as she fought the sense of disorientation. *I must've fallen asleep from the heat.* Earlier, the house had been so hot, she'd come out to the garden to stay cool and relax before class.

Class? "Oh no, I have class this afternoon. What time is it?" She bolted through the back door and into the kitchen, glancing at the clock. "I'm going to be late for the bus. I need to change. This dress is too hot." She glanced at the clock again. "Oh, I can't, I don't have time." She grabbed her hat and tucked it in her bag, locked the front door and hurried down the street at almost a run. Several minutes later, Elizabeth skidded to a stop as the bus driver reached for the handle to close the doors. "Thank you," she huffed, climbing the steps to drop into a seat a few rows back.

The run, in combination with the magnification of the sun through the bus windows soon had rivulets of perspiration trickling through her hair and down her temples. *I should've changed. Favorite dress or not, it's too heavy for this time of year.*

Elizabeth opened her bag to retrieve a small cotton handkerchief, dabbed at her face and fanned herself as nausea churned in the pit of her stomach. *I need some fresh air, it's so hot in here.* She laid her head against the back of the seat, closed her eyes and prayed she could hold out.

The bus rolled to a stop. Elizabeth hurried to the front and down the steps. *I need to get in the shade.*

"Miss Wellman? Are you all right?"

"Yes, of course, Mr. Montenari." Elizabeth mopped her face with the now soggy handkerchief still clutched in her hand. "I believe the heat has me a little fatigued."

"This isn't like Vermont. It gets hot here and stays hot. It's 110 degrees today and you're wearing long sleeves?"

"I'm fine." She attempted to smooth the wrinkles from her dress, but gave up after a few moments. "I'll be fine, I just need to cool down. Shall we?" She headed toward the car and climbed in without waiting for him.

He limped to the driver's side and opened the door. "Would you like me to get you something to drink? A pop maybe? There's a store around the corner."

She shook her head, but didn't look at him. "No, thank you. I'm fine. Can we go, please? I don't want to be late."

He started the car, and they rode in silence. Both windows were open and Elizabeth's hair blew everywhere. She reached in her bag for her hat, only to find she'd lost it in her rush. By the time they got to the Rec hall her bun had loosened and stray wisps of hair hung in her face. She repositioned some of her hair pins. It wasn't much of a success if her reflection in the back seat window was any indication. She gave up and headed toward the building, trying to ignore the trickles of sweat running between her shoulder blades.

Without the benefit of a breeze, oppressive heat and body odor clogged the large room despite the open windows. After forty-five minutes of sluggishness and yawning by the POWs, Elizabeth's heat induced irritation won out, and she called a halt to the class. "Gentleman, it's too hot. Class is dismissed early." For once, no one lingered, impatient to get out into the air. She erased the board and shoved a stack of papers in her bag. *I could use some air myself.*

Dante spoke as they headed out of the gate. "My mother is looking forward to tonight."

"Tonight? I'm sorry?" She pushed hair out of her eyes again, thankful now for the air blowing around the inside of the car.

"It's Wednesday. You're supposed to come to dinner?" He glanced over at her. "Look, Miss Wellman, if you're not feeling well, that's fine. We can do this another time."

"No. No. I just forgot for a moment. That's why I wore this dress, it's the one I save for special occasions."

"You look a little pale. Are you sure you're all right?"

"Yes, of course. I had an unsettling afternoon with the heat and all, I'll be fine." She made another attempt to smooth back her unwieldy hair. "I'm looking forward to it."

He nodded, and they continued on past the bus stop. Soon, they were in a section of town Elizabeth had never visited. She studied the lit signs on the store fronts, mostly Italian names.

Dante pulled the car over to the curb. "Here we are."

Elizabeth waited for him to open the door. Her dress clung to her back, soaked with perspiration from pressing against the seat. The words, Montenari & Son were lettered in gold on the window in front of her. Several other large windows dominated the darkened first floor of the brick building.

"This way." He led her around to the side and up a staircase attached to the outside of the structure. He opened a door at the top, and then stepped back to let her enter first. "That's my place." Dante pointed to a set of stairs off to the right. "This is my mother's apartment." He opened the heavy door. "After you."

Warm air hit Elizabeth full force as she stepped into the entryway. Dizzy, she faltered for a second.

"Mama? Miss Wellman and I are here."

She followed Dante through rooms long lived in, filled with dark, heavy furnishings, finally landing in the kitchen.

"That's odd. There's nothing out to start dinner. Excuse me for a second." He left the room.

Elizabeth collapsed onto a chair. It was either that or fall down as the room swirled. She was soaked in sweat right through to her nylon full slip and brassiere. *Maybe I should have Mr. Montenari take me home.* She'd misplaced her handkerchief, so Elizabeth patted her forehead with her sleeve and caught the slight hint of body odor as she raised her arm. She quickly dropped her arm at Dante's voice.

"Ma, where are you?"

"Stop shouting. I'm right here, of course. I was in my bedroom." Maria Montenari glided into the kitchen. "Hello, Miss Wellman."

"Good evening."

"You don't look so well."

Elizabeth resisted the urge to use her sleeve again. "It's the heat. I guess I'm not used to it."

"Mama, have you forgotten you invited Miss Wellman over tonight?"

"No, of course not."

Dante glanced at the empty counter top. "Did you already make the *lasagne*?"

"No. I decided it was too hot to light the oven. I was thinking maybe it would be better to go to the picture show. It's nice and cool there." Maria turned to Elizabeth. "Miss Wellman, would you like to go to a movie?"

The idea of sitting in air conditioning sounded like heaven to Elizabeth. "Yes, I wouldn't mind. I haven't been to a movie in a long time."

"I'm not sure what's play—"

Dante's mother cut him off. "*So Proudly We Hail* with Claudette Colbert is at the Imperial, and *Coney Island* with Betty Grable is at the Grand."

His grin was wry. "Well, it looks like you've done your homework. Miss Wellman, since you're our guest, do you have a preference?"

"I don't like war movies."

"*Coney Island*, it is then. Mama, maybe you should go get your purse before Miss Wellman melts."

"Not me." Maria picked up a fan and snapped it open. "I'm going over and sit on Mrs. Tessio's new porch and visit. We'll do *lasagne* when it cools down. You two have a good time. Good night, Miss Wellman." With that, she was gone.

A drop of sweat found its way into Elizabeth's eye. She blinked several times to alleviate the sting. "Mr. Montenari, please don't feel you have to go to the movies."

"I don't mind. It'll be cool, and by the time we come out, hopefully the temperature will have dropped a little. Shall we go?"

Chapter 8

The theater was filling up fast with people trying to escape the heat. Dante stopped at a row midway down the aisle and indicated the two end seats. "Is this okay?"

Elizabeth nodded and stepped into the row to sit down.

He followed. "It feels good in here."

"It does." She sighed, leaned her head back and closed her eyes. "Nice and cool." She sighed again, but didn't lift her head after several minutes.

"Miss Wellman, are you falling asleep?" He touched her sleeve and felt the heat rising off her body right through the heavy material of her dress. "Miss Wellman?" Dante could see beads of perspiration on her forehead, even in the dim light. He'd left his suit jacket behind and had rolled up his shirt sleeves, but wasn't faring much better.

She lifted her head. "I'm sorry. I was drifting, I guess." She shivered and licked dry lips. "I think I may be a little dehydrated. Would you mind getting me a drink?"

"I think we could both use a drink. Are you going to be all right 'til I get back?"

"Of course." She looked around. "There are a lot of people here. I'm going to lay my head back and enjoy the coolness until the picture starts."

Dante nodded. "That's a good idea. The usher said they're playing a short before the feature. It should be starting any minute. I'll be right back." Elizabeth's eyes were already closed. He headed out, the pain in his leg flared as he attempted to sidestep people still pouring into the darkened cavernous room. A click and a whir signaled the start of the projector. "Your War and Navy Department presents December 7th," came over the speakers as the theater doors shut behind him.

After several minutes in line, Dante stepped up to the counter. "Could I have a—," he stopped as a chunky man barreled out the theater door.

"Somebody's gotta help. There's a woman goin' crazy in there."

An usher stepped up to the man. "Sir, you'll have to keep your voice down, so others can enjoy—"

Another man and a woman came careening out of the theater, the double doors opened just long enough to let a high pitched wailing escape before banging closed again. The usher headed toward the doors with his flashlight in hand.

What's going on? "Never mind." Dante moved away from the counter. *I'd better get her out of there.* Miss Wellman had been acting a little strange all afternoon. Who knew what a screaming woman would do to her? Dante fought his way back in against the throng of people exiting the theater, checking for Elizabeth as he went. The woman still screamed, wherever she was. *Where's Miss Wellman?* He broke through the crowd and glanced to where he'd left her. *She's gone. I didn't pass her on the way out.* He scanned the fast emptying room and spotted the usher down near the front. *Maybe he saw her.* Dante headed that way. The film continued to run, the screen lit by exploding ships and Japanese planes.

"Lady, you gotta stop screaming, or I'm gonna have to call the police." The beam of the usher's flashlight landed on a woman crouched against the wall, her hair disheveled and her hands covering her ears. "You hear me? Lady?"

Dante stopped short.

"Mister, you might want to stay back, I don't know what's wrong with her. Lady, stop it! I'm gettin' the manager. He can call the cops."

Dante put a hand on the teenager's sleeve. "Wait just a minute. Please." He walked closer to the woman. "Miss Wellman?"

Her wailing didn't stop. He moved closer. "Elizabeth? It's me, Dante." He touched her arm. She flinched. *What the hell is wrong with her?* "Elizabeth," he shouted over her screaming. When that didn't work he grabbed her arm and yanked her up, wrapping his arms around her. His clothes were damp from sweat, but she was soaked. She tried to pull away. He hung on, and kept repeating, "It's me, Dante." After several minutes, her screams turned to wails and then to sobs. "Shh, shh. It's going to be all right," he crooned as he stroked her hair, free of most of its pins.

"Not. Again."

She wilted, and Dante tightened his hold.

"Get. Me. Out," Elizabeth gasped against his neck between sobs.

"Okay, *cara mia*. Hang on." He looked at the usher. "Do you have a side door?"

"Sure, right over there." The teenager pointed it out with the beam of his flashlight. "I don't know about this though. Maybe we should report it."

"There's nothing to report." Dante dug in his pocket, pulled out some cash and shoved it in the kid's hand as he passed him.

He led Elizabeth to the car behind the theater and put her in on the passenger's side. By the time he started the car, she'd curled into a ball, her back to him. Sobs wracked her body.

"You need to tell me where you live." He waited. "Miss Wellman?" Her crying was so mournful, it tore at Dante's gut. "You know what, we'll just drive around for a while."

He drove up one street and down another for who knows how long before he found himself traveling the overgrown dirt road to the place he always ended up when he couldn't sleep. The small lake he'd been coming to since he was a kid. It belonged to a friend of his mother, but nobody else ever came as far as Dante knew. The car headlights shone on the water. Dante switched off the ignition, but left the headlights on. He stepped out. The cool breeze gave him pause for a moment. It felt good.

He pulled open the other door. At least she'd stopped crying. "Miss Wellman?"

No response. He leaned into the car. She'd slumped to the side of the seat. He touched her cheek. *She's burning up.* "Miss Wellman, can you hear me?" She muttered something. It sounded like "All burnt," but Dante couldn't be sure. A shudder jerked her body so hard he heard her teeth click together. The involuntary movement brought back a memory from his Navy days. "Damn!" He swung her legs around and slipped her shoes off before pulling her out of the car. Her body jerked several more times before drooping against him. She would've fallen if he hadn't held her upright. "Miss Wellman, you're sick. We have to get you cooled off. Do you understand?" She mumbled something unintelligible. "You need to get out of this dress. I'm going to reach back and unzip it." He did, and as the dress fell from her shoulders, she blindly reached out to pull it back up. Dante dragged it from her grip and let it drop to the ground. He kicked off his shoes, scooped her up and plowed into the water up to his waist, ignoring the stab of pain in his leg from the resistance of the water and her added weight.

The minute her feet touched the water Elizabeth gasped and stiffened. Dante almost lost his grip on her from the sudden movement. "I'm trying to help you, stop fighting me." His shout must have gotten through. She went limp in his arms again. He dropped into the water in one movement, and they both went under, to resurface a moment later.

Her body spasmed in coughs for a minute or so, probably from inhaling a bit of water. Dante cradled her weightless form and pushed her hair back from where it lay matted to the side of her face. Her limp arm bobbed on top of the water, but other than an occasional shiver, she didn't move.

"Miss Wellman? Elizabeth? Please speak to me." He waited several minutes more. *Is the water working?* "Miss Wellman?" She rolled her head toward him until her cheek touched his chest and murmured something he couldn't quite make out. Dante felt her forehead with the side of his jaw for a moment. *It's a lot cooler. Thank goodness.* He continued to let her float in his arms. His fingers brushed her arm. The skin surface felt uneven. *Is this what Nico was talking about?* He shifted just a fraction, moving into the light from the headlamps. It cast shadows across them both, but couldn't hide the scars on her arm. Though each indentation was small, they were numerous. Dante's eyes traced the marks up her arm to her shoulder. Turning again for a bit more light, he could see faint scars spread across her chest, right to the lace edge of the full slip she wore. *What happened? Did somebody do this to her?* That might explain her standoffish manner. It certainly explained her long sleeves all the time. *But what was that all about in the movie theater?*

She sighed, and Dante shivered in reaction to her warm breath against his neck.

Is she asleep? "Elizabeth?"

She stirred. "Teddy?"

A boyfriend? "No, it's Dante Montenari."

"Mr. Montenari?" Her eyelids fluttered, but didn't open. "I'm dreaming again, aren't I? I don't have many nice dreams. Today, I dreamed of my mother, but this is lovely too." Her lips curved into a smile. "The water is so cool. Why isn't Teddy here? He loves to swim." She spoke just above a whisper and then shuddered. "I'm cold."

"I think we need to get you out of the water and get you something to drink. Do you understand?"

She moved her head against his chest in the slightest nod, but it was several more moments before she spoke. "Yes. This isn't a dream, is it?"

"No. Hang on." Dante stood up in the water. His bad leg screamed in protest at being in one position for so long. "Son of a bitch." Nausea welled up. He groaned. After a few deep breaths, he forced himself to take a step. It hurt, but he managed to get to shore. Elizabeth clung to him, shaking in earnest now. "Cold," was all she could get out between chattering teeth.

He lowered her to a large boulder on the shore. "Hold on, I have a couple of blankets in the trunk." Dante wrapped one around her and helped her to the car. He took his dress shirt off and wrung it out. His sleeveless undershirt would have to do for now. He folded the other blanket up and laid it on his seat. After gathering their discarded items and tossing them in the back seat, he headed the car out. "I think we need to get you to the hospital."

"No."

"I think I should take—"

"No. Home. Please."

"Fine. Can you tell me your address?" She eventually got the whole thing out and twenty minutes later he turned off a quiet street into a driveway alongside of a small white house, complete with a front porch and flowers. He glanced over at her. Slumped in the seat, her head hung down and her chin almost touched her chest. "How are you doing?"

Elizabeth didn't lift her head. "I'm so sorry. I can't believe I embarrassed myself that way."

"You don't need to be embarrassed. Heat stroke is dangerous. I saw it happen to a sailor on board ship once. They stripped him and doused him with sea water. It worked to cool him down and stopped the seizures." He cleared his throat. "That's why I removed your dress."

She nodded. "I understand. Thank you."

"I really think I should take you to the hospital to be checked out."

"Thank you for offering, but it'll lead to questions I don't want to answer. I'm tired. I just want to lay down."

She did sound tired. "Let's get you inside." He came around to her side and helped her out of the car.

"Around the back, please. I don't want my neighbors to see me like this."

They rounded the corner of the house and worked their way to the back door.

"Hold on a second." She reached down behind a flower pot and stood again. "Whoa. I'm a little dizzy." She grabbed the door frame to steady herself.

He stepped closer.

"I'm okay. I left my book bag in your car. It has my other keys in it." She turned the spare key in the lock. "Please come in."

Dante closed the door behind him and waited for his eyes to adjust to the darkness. He could hear her moving around in another room. The click of a lamp switch flooded the archway ahead of him with light. He glanced around the room. The kitchen. Everything neat and in order.

"Come in and have a seat. I'll be right back."

"Wait. I think you should have—" By the time he got to the living room she was gone. He got a large glass of water from the kitchen and waited for her to return. Dante didn't want to sit on her furniture and tried to ignore the throbbing in his leg and the clammy feel of his wet pants.

Though not large the living room was neat. Built-in shelves lined the walls, every one filled with books. More books were stacked on the side tables. She did say she read a lot. *She couldn't have read all these books, could she?* Another book sat on the coffee table. *Introduction to Italian.* A baby grand piano sat at an angle by the bay window; a vase of roses and several framed photos rested atop a paisley shawl draped over the lid. The roses filled the room with a heady fragrance. Dante stepped closer. A large photo in a gold frame showed a well-dressed man and woman in a formal pose. The woman was much heavier than Elizabeth, but there was a resemblance. *Her parents?* The next picture was a lanky young man in uniform, a friendly grin spread across his face. Dante recognized the uniform he wore as the same one he'd spent several years in—the man was a naval officer. *Is this her boyfriend? Where is he?* He glanced at the next photo and did a double take. It was Elizabeth Wellman, but not the woman he knew. Long auburn hair parted on the side curved in waves past her shoulders. Red lipstick emphasized her bright smile, but it was her eyes that drew his attention. Sultry. *She's beautiful. What happened to her?* A loud thump down the hall and an unladylike curse word caught his attention. "Miss Wellman?" He flipped a switch near the hall entrance and an overhead light came on. Shelves lined each side of the hallway. More books. "Are you okay?"

"No. Yes. I bumped my head, that's all."

"Where are you?"

"I'm right here."

He stopped at the first room on the right. The light from the hall dimly illuminated the space. Elizabeth Wellman sat on the floor, her back against the bed, her head resting in her hand.

"What happened?"

"I put my nightgown on and reached for my robe and everything started to spin. I think I hit my head on the edge of my nightstand."

"Let's have a look." Dante sat the glass on the nightstand and lifted her to the edge of the bed before he turned her face toward the light. His fingers were gentle as he touched a spot on her forehead. She flinched. "You're going to have a goose egg, but the skin's not broken. I think a cold compress will help. I brought you some water. Please try to drink, but take small sips or you'll be sick."

She nodded. "I think I need to take some aspirin. My head is pounding. It'll just take me a minute to get it."

"Sit still and drink the water. I assume the aspirin is in the medicine cabinet?"

"Yes. In the bathroom at the end of the hall."

He returned a couple of seconds later and handed her the pills.

"Thank you." She took several sips of the water and set it down.

"You're going to have to drink more than that."

"Yes, I will." She cleared her throat. "Mr. Montenari, thank you for helping me. I should be fine now. I don't want to take up any more of your time."

"You're not fine, and I'm not going anywhere yet."

She reached for the robe at the foot of the bed and held it in front of her plain white cotton nightgown. "This is not exactly proper. If you insist on staying, maybe we should move to the living room."

"You're staying put. You need to rest. I'll stand right here."

"Stand? Why? Did you hurt yourself? Did I hurt you?"

He was in pain and had swallowed several of the aspirin himself, but Dante wasn't going to tell her that. "No, it's my pants; they're still damp. I don't want to ruin your furniture."

"Oh. Oh, I see." She was silent for a few minutes. "You can't stay in wet clothing. You'll get sick."

"I'll be fine."

"No, you won't. In the next bedroom, you'll find some men's clothing in the bottom drawer of the dresser. Please change, at least until your trousers dry. Otherwise, you'll just have to go home."

He recognized her teacher voice and without another word went into the next room. He pulled a tissue wrapped bundle from the drawer and tugged on the string to open it. *Pajamas?* He removed straight pins to separate the top from the bottom. *Well, at least they're new.* A few minutes later, after putting on the bottoms and laying his pants over the edge of the tub, he returned to where Elizabeth still sat on the edge of the bed. He pulled back the covers. "Now, how about you get comfortable? I've got a cold cloth."

She acquiesced and leaned against the pillows he'd fluffed up. Her hair had dried in a wild array in the heat and hung down to somewhere near her waist. *She looks like a teenager—a pretty teenager.* Dante stared at her; he couldn't help it. It was like she was two different people—three, if you counted the photograph in the living room. *Enough. Let it alone.* "Here you go." He laid the wet cloth against her forehead.

"Thank you, that feels like heaven."

"You're welcome." He handed her the glass. "You need to drink more."

She took a couple of more sips and studied the glass for a moment. "I owe you an explanation."

Dante shook his head. "You don't owe me anything."

"But I do. It's something I've never talked about."

"And you don't have to now. I just hope whoever did that to your arms paid for it."

"If only it were that easy." She sighed. "Since it seems propriety has already gone out the window tonight, have a seat." Elizabeth tapped the bed. "Mr. Montenari, you have the wrong impression. No one person did this to me."

"Were you in an accident?"

She shook her head. "No. It was deliberate." She set the compress aside. "This is hard for me to talk about." Elizabeth ran her fingers through her hair. "You saw some of my scars."

He nodded.

"Well, there's more. A lot more. Some on my legs, the worst are on my back."

"Miss Wellman, you're not making sense. No one did it, but it was deliberate?"

She held up her hand. "Please, give me a minute. The scars are from flying debris—pavement, cement, glass, you name it. Some were superficial wounds, but it took four surgeries to get the rest of it out, which made the scars even worse."

"I'm sorry you had to go through that."

"Don't be. I was lucky."

"How can you say that?"

She tugged at a string on the chenille bedspread. "Because I'm alive. Many aren't." Elizabeth continued to pluck the string without looking up. "My parents surprised Katherine and me with a trip to Hawaii to visit Teddy during Thanksgiving and Christmas. He was a lieutenant in the Navy. It was so beautiful there. I walked the beach every day. We even did a show for the military. That was Teddy's idea, of course."

"You mentioned him earlier when you," he hesitated a moment, "weren't feeling well. Is he your boyfriend?"

She smiled. "No, my brother. The best brother a girl could have, I might add." She said nothing more for a few seconds, then exhaled in a long breath. "Anyway, we were on our way to the harbor to meet his commanding officer when the planes came." A single tear slid from the corner of her eye.

Hawaii? Planes? It can't be. "When did this happen?'

"December 7th..." she trailed off.

"1941," he finished. "You were at Pearl Harbor?"

She nodded as tears continued to slip down her face.

"No wonder you were upset in the movies tonight. I'm sorry, I'm so sorry."

"It's not your fault." A sob caught in her throat.

What are you doing? This was the third time Elizabeth Wellman had ended up in Dante's arms tonight. But it felt like the right thing to do as she soaked the front of his undershirt with tears until there was nothing left. She continued to rest her head on his shoulder.

"What happened to your family?" His voice was quiet.

She took a shuddering breath. "My parents died in the first wave of the attack. That's where my injuries came from. Teddy was on his ship when the bombing began. His body was never found."

"Your whole family is gone?"

She shook her head. "I still have my sister Katherine. I worried about her after the attack, but I think she's doing better. I got a postcard from her last week. She's in England. She finally got a spot as a singer with Mr. Hope's troupe. I hope it makes her happy."

"And what about you? Are you happy?"

"I have my teaching. I'm thankful for that."

"I didn't ask if you were thankful; I asked if you were happy."

Elizabeth pulled back. "Well, as happy as I can be, I suppose. My life didn't quite turn out as I thought it would."

"And how is that?"

She shrugged. "My father used to tell me to forget about a husband. He said no man wants a wife who thinks she's smarter than him. Still, I thought maybe someday I'd marry and have a child."

"You still can."

Elizabeth shook her head. "No, Mr. Montenari, look at me. I'm disfigured. Scarred. And after tonight I know I'm scarred on the inside too. Why would anyone want that?"

"Miss Wellman, any man who can't see past a few marks on your skin is a stupid man and would make a stupid husband. Don't underestimate yourself. I'm sure you were as courageous as any serviceman there that day. Your scars are your medal of honor. You shouldn't be afraid to show them."

"I could never do that. People would stare and ask questions."

"So, let them stare. You have nothing to hide."

She yawned. "Oh, sorry. I think the night is catching up with me. What about you?" She shifted onto her side and hugged the pillow.

"What about me? I don't follow you."

"Why aren't you married?" She yawned again. "Whew, sorry. Where was I? Oh yes, you're young and women are interested, I've seen them at the picnics."

"It's not the same. I have other responsibilities. The business, my mother, lots of things." *Not to mention Flanagan and probably Don Salucci.*

"Really?" She closed her eyes. "I think you're underestimating yourself because of a few scars on your leg. None of those women at the picnic are stupid. Take a closer look next time."

He smiled. "Okay, I'll think about it."

"Good..." her voice trailed off.

Half an hour later he stood by the bed watching her sleep. Her hair fanned out over the pillow, her delicate features calm in repose despite the bruise on her forehead. He leaned down and brushed a light kiss against her cheek. *I'm not a stupid man either.* But she'd been through enough already. Dante would never again make the mistake of exposing a woman to someone like Flanagan or Salucci.

"Miss Wellman?" He kept his voice low.

"Hmm?" She didn't open her eyes.

"I left another glass of water on the night stand. I'm going now."

"Good night, Dante." She rolled over and burrowed further down in the bed.

He resisted the urge to kiss the scarred shoulder she presented with the movement. "Good night, Elizabeth."

Dante locked the door and turned to leave when he caught a movement from a second story window of the house next door. He looked up. No one was there. *Probably my imagination. Again.* Just the same, he eased out of the driveway and quietly motored down the street.

Chapter 9

Elizabeth locked her front door and started down the walkway, her step light. It was still cool, but promised to be a beautiful day without the humidity of late. She had plenty of time to get to the bus stop. *Admit it, you're looking forward to seeing Dante Montenari.* A smile touched her lips at the thought. It was nice to have a person in her life she didn't have to hide anything from.

Doris Sargent, her neighbor, stood at her mailbox, the ever present cigarette clutched between her fingers. When Elizabeth moved in, the woman had arrived with half a loaf of stale bread and a dose of neighborhood gossip. Uncomfortable with the woman's prying questions and snide comments about other neighbors, it wasn't long before Elizabeth stopped answering the door. "Good morning, Mrs. Sargent."

"Mornin'." The woman stepped onto the sidewalk and looked Elizabeth up and down. "That a new dress?"

As much as Elizabeth wanted to brush past the woman, she stopped. "No. I just haven't worn it in a long time." She glanced down at her outfit. She'd pulled it out from the back of her closet yesterday and debated since she got up this morning whether to wear it or not. The A-line dress was light blue rayon with small white polka dots, a simple rounded neckline and loose, bell shaped long sleeves.

"A little fancy for church, isn't it? I assume that's where you go on Sunday mornings. Probably a good thing."

"What?"

The woman continued on as if Elizabeth hadn't spoken. "Hmm. Nice black and blue you got there."

Elizabeth touched her forehead. "Yes, I fell."

"You also gotta little somethin' on your neck. What is that? It's a red mark. Is that a hickey?" The woman squinted and touched a bony finger to the base of her own throat. "Right there."

Elizabeth didn't bother to touch her neck. "It's a scar."

"Really? How'd you get that?"

"I'd rather not talk about it."

"That new boyfriend of yours been roughin' you up?"

"What?"

"I saw him leaving your house the other night. Kinda late for visitin'."

"Mrs. Sargent, you have the wrong idea. I was sick. He's my," Elizabeth hesitated. *I hate to tell this woman anything, but I can't have her spreading lies all over the neighborhood.* "He's my interpreter."

"Interpreter?" The woman snorted and took a drag off the cigarette, blowing smoke in Elizabeth's general direction.

Elizabeth took a step back to avoid the cloud. "He is. I'm teaching English—to the POWs at Port Johnson."

"You're teachin' them I-talians?"

Elizabeth nodded.

"What? Why would you do that? You can't do that. My younger sister lost her boy over there in North Africa. Those I-talians should be lined up and shot."

The vehemence in the woman's voice took Elizabeth by surprise. "I understand how you feel, I was opposed to it at—"

"You've got no idea. My sister, Sally, went crazy after Danny died. They had to take her to the State Hospital at Trenton. Two weeks later, she got another patient to help her hang herself." The woman pointed the two fingers that held the cigarette at Elizabeth and made a jabbing motion with each word she spoke. "So, don't tell me how to feel about those guineas." She let the cigarette drop and ground it into the sidewalk.

Elizabeth took another step back. "Mrs. Sargent, I'm sorry for your loss. I do understand."

"Like hell you do." The woman glanced over Elizabeth's shoulder. "It looks like your interpreter is back. I'll tell you this, missy, people don't take kindly to loose women around here, or traitors either, for that matter. You might want to think that over." Mrs. Sargent huffed up the steps to her own porch and dropped into a chair.

Not sure which way to turn, Elizabeth stood frozen in the middle of the sidewalk.

"Elizabeth?"

She turned. Dante stood there, a questioning look on his face. "What are you doing here?"

"Since we're early, Mama thought it would be nice to stop by and offer you a ride. Is that okay?"

Elizabeth glanced at her neighbor's porch. The woman sat there, a glare on her face.

Dante followed her line of vision. "Is something the matter?"

Elizabeth shook her head and turned toward his car. "No. No, not at all. Thank you for thinking of me." He opened the car door, and she settled into the back seat, reaching forward to rest a hand on Maria's shoulder for a moment. "Good morning."

Maria patted her hand. "Good morning. How are you feeling?"

"I'm fine," Elizabeth stammered.

Dante started the car and glanced at her in the rear view mirror. "I told Mama about you slipping at the movie theater the other night and hitting your head."

"Yes. Yes, but I'm better now. Thank you." They pulled away from the curb, and though Elizabeth knew her neighbor watched, she refused to look in her direction.

"Okay, gentleman, that's it. *Finito* for today," Elizabeth addressed the group of men sitting on the grass in front of her.

"Miss Wellman, you look *bella* today."

"*Bella? Bella?*"

"Beautiful," Dante supplied.

Elizabeth blushed. "Thank you, Roberto. That's sweet."

The man turned to Dante and spoke a few words in Italian, then touched his forehead.

"He says you shouldn't let your man do this."

Elizabeth's face turned bright red. "No. No. I bumped it." She pantomimed a fall and pretended to cry.

The men laughed, and she laughed along with them for a moment. Everyone gathered their papers and drifted off toward the gathering in the main field. *Could one of these boys have killed Mrs. Sargent's nephew?* Elizabeth knew anything was possible, especially in war. *Am I a traitor?*

"Everything okay?"

She smiled at Dante. "Yes, of course."

They walked toward the crowd.

"He's right. You do look beautiful today."

Elizabeth blushed again. "Thank you. I don't want another episode of heat stroke." She paused. "And I've been thinking about what you said the other night about my scars. I doubt I'll ever wear a bathing suit again, but I do have a few dresses I can wear where it isn't too noticeable."

"I don't see the need to worry about it, but it would be an easy matter to make up a few dresses."

"I'm not much of a hand with a needle. Are you offering, Dante?"

"I make men's clothes, Elizabeth. There are plenty of good seamstresses around."

"I don't know if I would feel comfortable doing that."

He shrugged. "Think about it. If you decide to, I can give you some names."

"Thank you." She walked at a slow pace to accommodate Dante's shortened stride. "Do you think I'm a traitor for teaching these men?"

"Where'd that come from?"

"My neighbor. She saw you the other night and assumed you were my boyfriend."

"What'd you tell her?"

"The truth. I had to. She's such a gossip. Sadly, she lost a family member fighting the Italians. In hindsight, maybe I should've let her think I was a fallen woman."

"A fallen woman?" Dante's laugh was rueful as he gave her shoulders a quick squeeze. "Forget it. It sounds to me like you wouldn't have won with this woman either way."

She gave him a slight smile. "You may be right. I'll just stay out of her way. By next week, she'll be on to someone else." *I hope.*

One of the women Elizabeth had seen approach Dante in the past strolled over to them. "Good afternoon, Dante."

"Hello, Connie."

"How are you? You're lookin' good." The woman smiled, showing slightly yellowed teeth.

Dante didn't respond.

What's wrong with him?

The woman reached into her purse and pulled out a pack of Chesterfield cigarettes, extracting one for herself before offering one to Dante. "That's right, you don't smoke. How about you?" She turned the pack in Elizabeth's direction, and then dropped it back in her purse at Elizabeth's head shake. Connie held up a butane lighter between her thumb and fingers and waited. After a moment, Dante took the lighter from her. Lipstick stained the end of the cigarette as she put it to her lips, inhaling deeply as he held the flame to the other end. Dante closed the lighter case with a snap and handed it back to her.

"Thanks." Connie picked a piece of tobacco off the tip of her tongue and wiped it on her dress while studying Elizabeth through a haze of smoke. "You'll have to excuse Dante. He's shy, same as when we were kids. Well, most of the time anyway. Huh, Dante?" When he didn't answer she shrugged and continued on. "I'm Constance Santini." The woman extended her hand, the movement stirring up the strong scent of Tabu perfume. The handshake was brief as the woman leaned forward and in a conspiratorial whisper said, "He was sweet on me in school."

Elizabeth glanced at Dante. The scowl on his face seemed to belie the woman's words. "Nice to meet you. I'm Elizabeth Wellman." *Hmm, the two of them together?* Elizabeth couldn't see it, but who was she to judge?

"Yeah, everyone knows who you are." She turned to Dante. "I told my father I'd ask about his suit."

Elizabeth tamped down her irritation at the woman's dismissive manner. "If you two will excuse me, I think I'm going to go sit with your mother for a bit." She leaned toward Dante. "A closer look?"

Dante gave an almost imperceptible shake of his head. She nodded and turned to the other woman. "It was nice to meet you, Miss Santini." Elizabeth smiled and left them.

"Likewise. What's she talking about, a closer look?"

"Nothing."

Elizabeth collected two glasses of lemonade and joined Maria on a bench in the shade.

"Thank you, my dear. I haven't had a chance to tell you. You look very pretty today."

"It's the dress. I've never worn it here."

"The dress is lovely, but I don't think that's it." Maria took a sip of the drink. "Dante came home very late the other night."

"Mrs. Montenari, I'm sorry, that was my fault when I, ahh, fell and hit my head. I can assure you nothing happened."

"Really? That's a pity."

Elizabeth choked on her swallow of lemonade. "What?"

The woman gave her a smile. "Do I shock you? Well, you'll get no apologies from me. Dante is a wonderful man, but he's shut himself off. Except around you. And unless these eyes are failing me, I think you like him too."

"I do. He's the first real friend I've had in a long time."

"Friends, hmm. Well, that's a good start. Couples should be friends and get to know each other first."

"Mrs. Montenari, I think you're reading too much into it. Surely, one of these ladies is better suited for him?" Elizabeth looked back to where she'd left Dante. *Is he arguing with that woman?* "What about the girl he's talking to now?"

"Connie Santini? That woman is a she-wolf. In between boyfriends, she's chased him since grammar school. If Dante wanted her, and he doesn't, he could have had her."

"Well, there are other ladies here."

"He's not interested in any of them. It's only since you arrived that I've noticed a little of the old spark in him. He won't admit it, but I know my son."

Elizabeth shook her head. "I think you're mistaken."

"We shall see." Maria took another sip of her lemonade and said nothing else.

A buffet of assorted salads and cold meats was set up early, leaving most of the afternoon visit for leisure activities. "Do you want to play cards?" Mrs. Moretti asked her sister.

Maria shook her head. "No, I think I need some shade. The band is playing for the first time. I enjoy watching the young people dance." She rose from the table. "Miss Wellman, would you like to accompany me?"

Elizabeth looked up from the conversation she was having with Mr. Moretti via Dante. "Ahh, of course, Mrs. Montenari. Excuse me, gentlemen." She looped a hand around the arm the older woman offered as they walked toward the Rec hall. "What band?"

"It's a band the POWs put together. I hear they've been practicing a lot. Mr. Galenti brought in donated instruments a couple of months ago."

"Mr. Galenti? The portly man who likes your *cannoli* so much?"

Maria smiled. "That's him. He loved my mother's *cannoli* even more."

"Back in the old country?"

"Yes. I've known him most of my life. He's been a good friend to me for many years."

The Rec hall had been converted to an impromptu dance hall. Most of the tables were stacked against the back wall while a large group of POWs sat in chairs lining the room. Every few minutes one of the men would jump up and head toward the numerous couples dancing around the floor to the upbeat music. With a tap on the shoulder, the fellow would cut in and dance until the next man came along. Elizabeth recognized Constance Santini as she whirled by, as well as Nicolina and Alessio. The atmosphere in the room exuded sweat, perfume and fun.

"Maria, good afternoon."

"*Ciao*, Gino. This is Miss Wellman. Miss Wellman, this is Gino Galenti."

"Nice to meet you. So, Maria, what do you think?" He indicated the band set up on the low riser.

Elizabeth recognized several of her students among the men with instruments. Horns, clarinets, violins, a bass, drums. And a piano? Someone had been very generous.

"They sound good. Who donated the instruments?"

Gino shook his head. "I think you know who."

"Vincenzo?"

"*Sì.*"

"Well," Maria paused. "Tell him the boys say thank you."

He smiled and nodded.

"And send my regards to his wife."

The smile disappeared from the man's well fed features. "Maria, you know I won't—"

The woman held up a hand to stop him. "I know. I know." She sighed and then smiled. "Sorry, Gino. Miss Wellman and I are going to sit and watch for a while."

His smile was back. "You won't be sitting long with this crowd."

He was right. Within a few minutes, Roberto dropped into the chair next to Elizabeth.

"Hello, Miss Wellman. Do you like music?"

She nodded as the music changed to a Tommy Dorsey tune. *They're really good.* She tapped her foot to the beat.

"Would you like to dance?"

"Thank you for asking, Roberto, but right now I'm keeping Mrs. Montenari company."

He nodded, but stayed where he was.

Maria leaned in close to Elizabeth's ear. "You should dance with him. It'll be good for Dante to think he has a little competition when he gets here."

"Shame on you." Elizabeth laughed. "What makes you think Dante will come in here?"

"Oh, he'll show up. Trust me."

Elizabeth laughed again and turned her attention back to the music. *Teddy would've loved these guys.* And for the first time, the thought of him didn't bring an instant jab of sadness. With that knowledge, Elizabeth enjoyed the music as she knew he would've, singing the lyrics to the songs in a quiet voice.

"Hi, *Zia* Maria. Miss Wellman. Aren't they swell?" Nicolina and Alessio stood in front of them. "Guess what? Alessio is going to sing with them. He's got a wonderful voice." She gave his arm a squeeze. "I'm going to sing back up. I'm not very good yet, but he's teaching me."

"You will be," Alessio reassured her.

Roberto stood and whispered something in Alessio's ear. The young man gave him a questioning look, and Roberto nodded. Alessio took Roberto's seat next to Elizabeth.

"Miss Wellman, you can sing?"

"What? No. Well, yes, but I don't do it much."

"Well, Nicolina could use some help. Would you sing with her? It will give her more," Alessio hesitated. "What's the word? More *confidenza*."

"Confidence?"

"*Sì*. Confidence." He nodded.

"You sing?" Nicolina formed her hands into a prayer gesture. "Oh, please, Miss Wellman. I won't be so nervous with you there with me. Please?"

Can I do this? One way to find out. Elizabeth sighed. "Fine."

"Thank you. Thank you. This is great." Nicolina grabbed her hand and headed toward the band. "Okay, we're going to stand on the side here with this microphone."

Elizabeth stood next to the girl. *Relax, breathe.* The band started to play another song. *Chattanooga Choo Choo. Okay, I know this one.* Alessio stepped behind the center microphone. He did indeed have a wonderful voice, but that's not what surprised Elizabeth. Alessio spoke with a pronounced accent, but sang with no inflection of an accent in his voice. *He's doing a perfect imitation of Tex Beneke. Amazing.* Elizabeth chimed in on time as did Nicolina, albeit in a faint voice. She reached for the girl's hand, gave it a squeeze and continued to work the harmony. The song ended to loud applause.

"Miss Wellman, I'm supposed to sing the next one, but I can't. I want to, to please Alessio. I promised I would, but I can't. I'm going to embarrass myself," Nicolina said in a rush. "Will you sing it?"

"What? No. You can do this."

"I can't, please. Not in front of all of these people," the girl huffed in panic. "Please?"

Elizabeth recognized the hysteria in the girl's voice. She'd felt it herself once, a long time ago. Now, singing ranked low on the panic list. "What's the song?"

"*It Had To Be You.*"

Alessio spoke into the microphone, his accent back in place. "Thank you. Thank you. We have one more song. Miss—" Nicolina tugged on his sleeve. He leaned away from the microphone. "*Si?* Are you ready?" He gave her an encouraging smile.

"Well, no. I don't want to disappoint you, but I can't do—"

Elizabeth stepped up next to her. "I asked if I could do the song, and Nicolina has graciously agreed."

Nicolina gave Elizabeth a grateful smile. "Yes, Alessio. Miss Wellman would like to sing today. That'll give me more time to practice. Okay?"

His smile for the petite girl spoke volumes. "You are such a kind girl. Of course." He looked to Elizabeth. "Are you ready?"

She nodded.

He stepped back to the microphone. "We have a surprise. Our Miss Wellman is going to sing."

Teddy once told her *It Had To Be You* was the perfect song for her alto voice, so it had become one of her favorites. The band played the intro. She took a breath and started to sing. As she slipped into the intricacies of the familiar vocals, Elizabeth closed her eyes. She was back in her old bedroom singing, with Teddy and Katherine joining in from wherever they were in the house and their father shouting to stop that racket. The pleasure that memory evoked permeated each word she sang. Even after the last chord of the song died away, Elizabeth kept her eyes closed, unwilling to relinquish the memory.

Startled from her reverie by claps and whistles, Elizabeth opened her eyes to meet Dante Montenari's stare. She flushed.

"Miss Wellman, that was great. You should be a professional singer," Nicolina gushed.

Alessio came to stand next to her. "Miss Wellman, the fellas want to know if you'd sing with us again."

"What? I don't know. I'd have to think about it." She turned to the men behind her on the stage. "*Grazie.*" They all nodded. She stepped down from the riser.

"Wow." Dante shook his head. "I don't know what else to say. You have an amazing voice."

Elizabeth shook her head. "Actually, Teddy and Katherine were the real singers in the family. They loved it."

"I find that hard to believe." He studied her a moment. "Any other secrets you haven't told me?"

"No, you know them all."

Mr. Galenti rushed up. "Miss Wellman, you're quite the singer. My employer owns several clubs if you're looking for a job."

"Thank you for the offer, but I have a job. I'm a teacher."

"I can guarantee you'd make a lot more money singing." The man pulled a card from his suit coat pocket and handed it to Elizabeth. "Here's my number. Call me if you change your mind."

"She's not interested." Dante took the card and ripped it in half.

Why'd he do that? "Dante, what's wrong?"

"She wants nothing to do with Don Salucci."

"Dante, be a good boy."

"I'm not ten anymore, Mr. Galenti."

"So, stop acting like it and respect your elders." Maria Montenari joined the group and patted the older man's arm. "I'm sorry, Gino, for Dante's bad manners. Perhaps I can make up for it with a dance? Shall we show these young people how it's done?"

"I'd be honored." They moved off in a waltz.

"What was that all about?" Elizabeth waited.

"Nothing. Just stay away from them."

"Who's Donald Salucci?"

"That's not his first name. Don is a term of respect. His name is Vincenzo Salucci."

Vincenzo? As in the man who bought the instruments? Elizabeth decided to keep it to herself. "So, who is he?"

"No one you want to meet. He controls everything around here."

"Does he control you?"

He shook his head. "Mostly clubs, casinos and brothels. If he doesn't own the business, whoever does pays him to stay in business."

"So, you pay him?"

"No."

"Why not? I'm confused."

"I don't know why. Just stay away from Galenti outside of here. It's bad business. Understand?"

"Fine. I get it. You don't have to shout."

"Sorry. I don't want you to get hurt. Be careful when you're out."

"What? Dante, what are you talking about?"

"Nothing. Forget it."

Elizabeth refused Dante's offer of a ride home and caught the bus. The evening twilight cloaked houses in shadows as she walked down the quiet street. A light burned on the second floor of the Sargent house, the first floor was dark. She sighed in relief and slipped into her house, unaware of the sudden orange glow from a lit cigarette on the porch next door.

Chapter 10

October 1943

Elizabeth glanced up at the clock as she waited for the man across the desk to speak. *I'm not going to have time to go home and check on the house.*

"Thanks for stopping by, Miss Wellman."

"You're welcome, Principal Forrest. What can I help you with?"

The man drove a finger into the knot of his tie to loosen it. Light from the window behind him revealed thinning hair despite his best efforts to hide it. "First of all, I want to say you're doing a tremendous job here. Your students in particular are doing excellent work, and because of that, the school's overall English scores have risen by a significant percentage. That's not an easy task."

"Thank you."

"Not that I expected any less. Education wise, you're more qualified to sit in this chair than I am."

"Principal Forrest, it takes more—"

He put a hand up to stop her and smiled. "Benjamin. Remember?"

Elizabeth nodded. "Benjamin, I know it takes more than degrees to effectively administrate a high school. You're the best person for the job."

He smiled and ducked his head for a moment. "Thank you."

She glanced at the clock again. "Is that all you needed to talk to me about?"

"Actually, no." A frown wrinkled his forehead. "As distasteful as I find this, I've received a letter questioning whether or not you should be allowed to teach here."

"What?"

He held up a hand. "Wait. I just want you to know it's my responsibility to investigate. I'm not saying I believe it."

"What kind of accusation?"

He pulled his desk drawer open and drew out a piece of paper. "Basically, someone is accusing you of fraternizing with the enemy. Because of that, they feel you're poisoning young minds and aren't fit to teach."

"What?" Elizabeth jumped up. "That's preposterous. Who's accusing me?"

"Miss Wellman, I've been holding this several weeks. I knew you'd be upset. Please, sit back down."

She dropped into the chair and immediately slid forward to the edge of the seat. "Who?"

He shrugged. "It's not signed."

"Can I see that?" She scanned the paper. One line stood out. "You've got a traitor in your school." *Traitor? Mrs. Sargent, of course, who else?* Over the last few weeks several strange things had happened at Elizabeth's house. A dead rat in her mailbox. A hole in her window the same size as the golf ball she'd found on the kitchen floor. And yesterday, she'd arrived home from school to find someone had ripped up all the rose bushes in the backyard— her mother's rose bushes. It took every bit of self-control she could muster not to march over and bang on the woman's door. Instead she replanted as many as she could save. The outrage she'd felt upon seeing the damage flared again. *How dare she?* Elizabeth tossed the paper on the desk.

"Do you know who wrote that?"

"I have an idea, but no proof, so I'd rather not say."

"Well, can you at least tell me what this is about?"

Elizabeth nodded. "I think so. For a few months now, I've been going to Port Johnson to teach English. On my own time and with my own supplies."

"Port Johnson? Where the Italian soldiers are housed?"

"Yes. Maybe I should've asked you first, but it never crossed my mind. I admit, it's hard for me to think of them as enemy soldiers, or soldiers at all, for that matter. A good number of them are the same age as our seniors. And they are all desperate for education."

"Be as that may, by teaching POWs, you are technically fraternizing with the enemy. You may have to stop."

"What?" She waved a hand at the paper. "That's not right, just because someone—" she stopped and picked up the letter. "Wait a minute. I don't have to stop."

"I don't see how you're going to be able to continue."

"You do remember that Italy surrendered last month and became an ally?"

"Of course. It was in all the papers."

"And you know the government has formed the Italian Service Units?'

"Yes, I read that too. They're doing road work, dock work, things like that. I read they're even getting paid, $8 a week. Is that true?"

Elizabeth nodded. "So, they're not POWs anymore."

"Yes, but they were when you started teaching them."

"But this allegation didn't exist then. Do you remember the date Italy surrendered?"

He scratched his head a moment. "Not the exact date, sometime at the beginning of September. Why?"

"September 8th, to be exact. Look at the date on this." She handed him the letter.

"September 13th. Okay?"

"So, if we're being technical and I think we should be—when this allegation was made, I wasn't teaching enemies, I was teaching allies."

He thought about it for a minute and then smiled. "You're absolutely right. If anyone ever asks, I can say unequivocally you are not fraternizing with the enemy." He slapped his hands on the desk, palms down. "Case closed. Thank the lord. I thought for a while we might lose you over this."

She shook her head. "I have no plans to leave at this time, Principal Forrest."

"Benjamin."

"Sorry. Benjamin. Was there anything else, sir? If not, I need to be going."

"No, no. That's it."

She was almost to the door when he spoke her name. Elizabeth turned. "Yes?"

"Those Italian boys, they're a good sort, you say?"

"Yes, sir. Very nice. Very respectful."

He nodded "That's good to hear. My daughter has gone to a couple of their music shindigs with some of her friends."

"That's nice. I'll see you Monday." With that she was out the door.

Elizabeth got off the bus. There hadn't been enough time to go home and come back. It was probably just as well. She wasn't sure she'd be able to stop herself from heading right to Doris Sargent's door. That letter was the last straw.

The weather had finally cooled down enough for the promised *lasagne* lesson. It was still early; Elizabeth wasn't due at the Montenari's for another hour. She looked around. None of the buildings looked familiar. She walked back to the corner and checked the sign post. It was the right street. She studied the store front signs. Riley's Meat Market. O'Brien's Mercantile. O'Shaughnessy's Spirits.

I must've gotten off on the wrong end of the street. Maybe I could bring something to dinner? Half an hour later, she stepped back onto the street with her purchase. She'd checked out several shops, sampling cheeses, meats and even chocolate potato cake, but in the end it was Flynn's flower shop that got Elizabeth's money. She inhaled the scent of the mixed flower bouquet and smiled. *Perfect.* She walked several more blocks, trying to ignore the pinch of the low heels she'd bought to go with her outfit, a cream colored dress with orange flowers and matching orange belt, topped off by an orange peplum jacket. Elizabeth relaxed a little when Italian names gradually began to appear on signage. *I must be getting closer.* She'd just hurried across a busy intersection when someone stalked out of the alley in front of her. She almost collided with the man.

"Sorry," she murmured, stepping to the right. The man stepped with her, blocking her way. The odor of perspiration assailed her nose, even in the cool October air. When she stepped the other way, so did he.

"Now, where's a fine lookin' lass like you goin' in such a hurry on a day like this?"

"I said I'm sorry, sir. Now, please excuse me."

He didn't move. "You hear that, boys? She called me sir. We got a real lady here."

Elizabeth craned her neck to see the man's face and wished she hadn't. His grin was wide, exposing missing and decayed teeth.

He bent closer. "Where you goin'?"

She gave an involuntary shiver as his fetid breath washed over her face. "Just up the street. Excuse me." She made it halfway around him before a greasy hand clamped onto her wrist.

"Not so fast. What's the matter? Ain't I good enough for ya?"

"Unhand me."

"Unhand you? La-dee-fuckin'-da! I'll unhand you when I'm done with ya." He yanked her toward the alley.

"Let go of me." Elizabeth slapped at him with the bouquet.

He ripped the flowers out of her hand. "What? Flowers for me? Lass, you shouldn't have." He tossed them on the ground. The other men with him laughed.

"Please, help me," Elizabeth pleaded in a loud voice, but people just hurried by, eyes averted. *No one's going to help me. What do I do?* Without further thought, she lifted her foot and drove the heel of her shoe into his instep.

The man stopped, his yowl interspersed with curses. "Son of a bitch! Ohh, damn. That hurt. You slut! You're going to pay for that. Move."

If you do, you'll never come out of that alley alive. Elizabeth shook her head. "No."

He squeezed her wrist tighter.

"No," Elizabeth hissed through gritted teeth.

"Yes, you will." He grinned, pressed harder and then twisted.

Elizabeth screamed as bone scraped against bone. Tears ran down her face. "Please. Stop."

"Yeah. I will. Eventually." He dragged her to the end of the alley and pinned her against the wall with one hand while he grabbed the hem of her dress with the other hand, yanking up the material. He torpedoed a hand between her thighs.

She struggled in earnest. "Help me." Her scream echoed off the brick walls.

"Shut the hell up, ya banshee!" He backhanded her.

Elizabeth didn't see the slap coming and landed on her back, smacking her head on the pavement. The man yanked on his belt, or she thought he was. She couldn't really tell. It was as if a fog had settled over the whole alley.

"Mr. Flanagan?"

Is that someone else? Please help me.

The man turned to the speaker. "Get the hell out of here. This ain't none of your business."

"I'm afraid, sir, I can't do that."

Do I know that voice?

"And just why not, old man?"

"I need you to send the young lady out."

"What? Like hell."

"I'm afraid I must insist—on behalf of Don Salucci."

"Salucci? What's she to him? One of his whores?"

"Her relationship to the Don is none of your concern."

The man left Elizabeth's line of vision. "Bugger off, you fat wop faggot before I turn you into a punchin' bag. Yeah, I know about you."

"Mr. Romano, could you and the boys please remove Mr. Flanagan? Oh, and feel free to use him as a punching bag."

Elizabeth listened as a scuffle ensued followed by several shouts, then silence.

"Miss Wellman?"

It took a moment for Elizabeth to focus, unsure of what she was seeing. She struggled to sit up.

"Let me help you."

"Mr. Galenti? What are you doing here?"

"My business is nearby. First things first. Let's get you up. Can you walk?"

She nodded. "I think so."

He placed an arm around her and helped her into the back seat of a waiting car before climbing in the front with the driver. "Miss Wellman, what are you doing on this end of town?"

"I, ahh, I'm having dinner with Dante and his mother, but I think I got off at the wrong bus stop."

"I see. Don't worry, we'll have you there in a few minutes."

Dante told me to stay away from him, but I'd still be in that alley if not for him. Elizabeth touched her swollen mouth and flinched. Her fingers came away wet. She stared at her shaking hands slick with blood for the rest of the short ride.

The car door opened. "Miss Wellman, we're here."

She eased out of the car, and the old man guided her toward the side of the building. "No wait. The lights are on in the shop. Please, I want to go there."

The man nodded and helped her into the shop. "Dante?"

"Yeah? Mr. Galenti?" Dante came from a room off to the side. "What are you doing here?" He caught sight of Elizabeth and made it to her in a few strides despite his leg. "What happened?"

"Dante." A tear rolled down her cheek and then another. "Dante." She reached for him.

"Shh, shh. It's okay." He held her and looked over her shoulder at the other man. "What happened?" he mouthed.

"Why don't you take care of Miss Wellman, then we can talk."

Dante nodded. "Elizabeth, we need to clean your face. It has blood on it."

She pulled back. "I think my lip is split. I got blood all over your shirt."

"That doesn't matter. Are you hurt anywhere else?"

"I don't know. Maybe my wrist." She rotated it with a grimace. "Yes, my wrist." Elizabeth dropped her gaze as tears threatened again. Several drops of blood splattered on her shoes. "And my new shoes. The toes are all scuffed up." She tried to smile, but burst into tears instead.

Chapter 11

The doctor stepped out of the room, followed by Maria Montenari.

"How is she?" Dante's patience was at an end after waiting outside the bedroom for almost an hour.

"Shh." Maria closed the door.

"I want to talk to her."

"She's sleeping. Let the girl rest. Come away before you wake her up."

Dante looked at the door one more time, then followed his mother and the physician back to the living room. "Is she going to be all right?"

The doctor nodded. "I had to put a few stitches on the inside of her lip. Her wrist isn't broken, but there's a severe sprain. I've wrapped it, and she should use a sling for a week or so—once she's on her feet. She has a few contusions and abrasions; most will heal in a few weeks. There are two abrasions on her back that are of some concern." He hesitated a moment. "At first, Miss Wellman was reluctant to undress so I could examine her. She has some severe scarring on her back, making the skin there susceptible to infection, so I've dressed those wounds as well. She wouldn't say what caused the scarring. Do you have any idea?"

Dante shook his head. "No."

"Hmm. Well, whatever happened it must have been very painful to leave scars like that. Strange. Anyway, I've given her a sedative." The man handed Maria a small brown bottle. "Give her two teaspoons of this for pain in about four hours, or when she wakes up. She's going to need it. And those dressings on her back will need to be changed tomorrow. If it looks like infection is setting in, give me a call."

"Yes. Thank you, *Dottore.* Would you care for a glass of wine before you go?"

The doctor shook his bald head. "Thank you, Mrs. Montenari, but I never touch the stuff. More of a bourbon man myself. I'll just go on home. My wife will have dinner on the table."

"Thank you for coming so quickly. I appreciate it." Dante shook the man's hand.

"You're welcome."

Maria Montenari closed the door after the physician. "What happened to her?"

Dante shrugged.

"You can lie to the doctor, but you can't lie to me. You never could."

He sighed. "Fine. I'll tell you, but you can't tell Mrs. Tessio or anyone else. *Capisce?*"

"Yes, of course. *Capsco.* I understand."

"She was in Hawaii when the Japanese bombed Pearl Harbor. She was injured. Her parents and brother were killed. Her sister survived the attack too, but she's off somewhere else. Elizabeth is alone."

"Poor lamb." Maria shook her head. "She's not alone. She has us."

It was Dante's turn to shake his head. "Yes, and look at how that's worked out for her."

Before Maria could say anything else, there was a knock at the door. She pulled it open. Gino Galenti stood on the other side. "Come in."

The man took a seat on the sofa as Maria left the room.

"What happened?" Dante came to stand in front of Gino. "I warned her to stay away from you."

"Why? Dante, it's not what you—aww!"

Dante lifted the man by the lapel of his suit. "Why'd Salucci do it? Is this a message for me?"

"What? A message? No." The old man waved his hands. "You misunderstand."

"Let him go. Right this minute."

Dante released the man and stepped away.

Maria came forward and set a tray down on the coffee table. "I'm sorry, Gino." She smoothed his lapel and patted his cheek. "Dante didn't mean it. He's just upset."

"Maria, he'd never harm anyone in your family, especially not—"

The man stopped when she placed a finger on his lips. "Shh. I know that. No need to say more." She smiled. "It's okay. How about a glass of *vino*?" She pressed the goblet into his hand. "It's okay."

She turned to her son. "You need to apologize to Gino. Neither he nor Don Salucci had anything to do with this."

"How can you be so sure?" Dante kept his back to her as he stood at the window.

Galenti took a sip of the wine and set it back on the table. "It was Flanagan."

That had Dante's attention. "Flanagan? How'd she come across him?"

"Miss Wellman got off the bus in Irish Town by mistake. I've been making some inquiries, and as far as I can figure, she bumped into him in the street. Mario Lorenzo recognized her from Port Johnson and came to get me."

"The bastard. I'm going to take care of this once and for all." Dante grabbed his coat and checked the pocket for the reassuring weight of his gun.

"No need." Gino took another sip of the wine. "It's good, Maria. Thank you." He gave his attention back to Dante. "I already took care of it."

Dante stopped. "What's that mean? Did you kill him?"

"Dante, Gino wouldn't kill anyone. Right, Gino?"

The man chose to answer Dante's question. "No, he's not dead, though it wouldn't be any great loss. The man is a pig. Let's just say Mr. Flanagan has been persuaded to move on." He lifted his head toward the bedroom door. "How is she?"

"She's pretty banged up, but it could've been worse. I do owe you an apology. Thank you for helping her."

"No apology necessary, Dante. You were just worried about your lady friend. I understand."

"She's not—"

Maria cut Dante off. "Gino, I'm going to put together a *lasagne*, and I made your favorite for dessert. Would you like to stay for dinner?"

"*Cannoli?*"

She nodded.

"Of course. How about I help you? We'll make the *lasagne* together. Like we did with your grandmother when we were kids." The gray haired man shook his head, causing his ample jowls to swing. "It's hard to believe that was forty years ago. It feels like yesterday. Remember, your *Nonno* Anton would sit outside drinking *vino* and not be able to get up for dinner?"

Maria chuckled. "I do. My *Nonna* Teresa used to get so mad at him. Remember the day she dumped water on him?" They both laughed. She sighed. "I miss those days sometimes, before everything got crazy, don't you?"

"Yes. I do." Gino slipped off his suit jacket and rolled up his sleeves.

"C'mon, I'll get you an apron." They headed to the kitchen. "Dante, would you like to help?"

He shook his head. "I'm going to sit with Elizabeth for a while."

"Dante, she's asleep. She needs to rest."

"I know. I just want to sit with her."

His mother nodded. "All right."

Dante slipped into the room that had once been his and approached the bed. Elizabeth Wellman laid unmoving, thanks to the narcotics the doctor administered. The left side of her mouth and cheek were swollen out of proportion in comparison to the rest of her face. Her injured arm lay across her chest, her wrist swathed in cotton batting and wrapped with an elastic bandage. *The bastard. If he doesn't leave town, I'm going to kill him.*

Elizabeth shifted in her sleep and moaned before settling down again.

Dante moved an armchair closer to the bed. *What am I going to do?* At this point, it'd be safer for Elizabeth if she stopped associating with them. He wasn't sure he'd be able to convince her of that. And he had to admit, if only to himself, letting her go was the last thing he wanted to do, but he would. This place had a way of chewing up the people you cared about and spitting them out in pieces. He'd lost Luciana. He most likely would've lost Elizabeth today if Gino Galenti hadn't been there. *I can't go through that again.* There were two options. They could leave. And go where? He didn't hold much hope for that. He'd never convince his mother to leave the neighborhood. This had been her home since coming to America. And what about Elizabeth? Would she be safe here if they left? *Do I try to convince her to come too? What have I got to offer if I leave here?* Leaving at this point was too complicated. The second option—kill Flanagan if he's still around and Salucci too, if necessary. It was the only way. *If they're gone, maybe we'll be able to live in peace.*

Later, after dinner and a few hands of cards, Gino left and Dante headed toward the bedroom.

"Dante, what are you doing?" His mother followed him to the living room.

"I'm going to go back and sit with her."

"No, you're not. Come out here."

Dante stopped at her loud whisper. "Mama, I'm not going back upstairs."

"Why not?"

He shook his head. "I'm not."

"Fine." Maria moved down the hall and opened the narrow closet door next to the bathroom. "Take these, and make up the couch." She shoved the linen into his hands and went back to the kitchen. Dante heard the clink of glasses as she tidied up the kitchen table.

Maria came back in as he dropped onto the makeshift bed. "You know, she should have been awake by now." The woman yawned. "Oh, I'm getting too old for these late nights."

"Mama, go on to bed. I'll be awake if Elizabeth needs anything."

"Are you sure?"

He nodded. "And if I can't handle it, I'll come get you? *Bene*?"

She smiled. "Okay."

Dante rolled over and got off the couch. Again. He turned on the lamp in the hallway before stepping into the room. A groan sounded. "Elizabeth?" He kept his voice low.

She groaned again. "Where am I?" The words sounded distorted through her swollen lips.

"Elizabeth? It's me, Dante."

"Dante? I hurt."

"I know, *cara mia*. I'm sorry." He sat on the edge of the bed, and reached for the bottle on the nightstand. "I have some medicine to help you sleep right here. You just have to open your mouth a little. That's good. One more spoonful. Good girl."

"Water?"

"Yes, of course." He placed a straw against her lips. She pulled a small amount of liquid up through the straw before giving up.

"More?"

"No. Hurts too much. What happened?"

"You were attacked in the street today. Do you remember?"

Elizabeth closed her eyes for a moment. "Yes." The muted light caught the glisten of a tear as it slipped from the corner of her eye. "Why? I didn't even know that man."

"Remember, I told you about being careful? People like him are what I was talking about." He took a deep breath. "Elizabeth, I've thought about this a lot tonight. I think it would be best if you stopped teaching at Port Johnson and," he hesitated. "And if you stopped your acquaintance with me—with all of us. I can't protect you. There are bad people in our world. There'll always be bad people in our world. It's a way of life for us, but it doesn't have to be for you."

Her tears flowed in earnest now.

"You need to go back to your old life. You'll be safe."

"No."

"Elizabeth, listen to me, it's the only way I can think of to protect you."

"I didn't ask for your protection, and there are bad people in my world too."

"Elizabeth, it's better—"

"No. I'm not giving up Port Johnson or any of you. You're my only friends."

"You'll make more friends."

"I don't want more friends. I want you—all of you." She tried to lift herself to a sitting position only to cry out when she put weight on her damaged wrist.

"Elizabeth, stop. You're going to hurt yourself more. Please don't try to get up. We'll talk about this later. Right now, you need to rest."

She laid on the bed, unable to sniff back her tears. "Please don't leave me alone."

"You're not alone. I'm right here." He got up, went to the other side of the narrow bed and stretched out alongside her, resting on his side. He brushed her hair out of her face with great care. "I'm right here." His touch seemed to calm her. Or maybe it was the morphine, perhaps a combination of both. Within a few minutes the crying stopped. It was so quiet Dante could hear the squeak of the cobbler's metal sign from across the street as the night wind pushed it.

He watched the slow rise and fall of her chest in his mother's borrowed nightgown. She rolled onto her side facing him, her eyes closed, so close he could feel her warm breath on his cheek. "I don't want to be alone. Not again," she murmured before surrendering to the narcotics. Dante savored her nearness, welcoming the heat of her body. He planted a light kiss on her forehead. "We don't always have a choice, *cara mia*."

Chapter 12

"Why don't you stay in bed just a while longer?" Dante paced back and forth at the foot of the bed. "I'll take you home in a couple of days. I promise."

Elizabeth shifted her position and shook her head. "I've made my mind up. I've been in bed almost a week. It's time."

"Are you sure?"

"Yes. Even the doctor says I should be up and around. He said my back is healing well, and after he removes my stitches this morning, I'd like you to drive me home. I've missed a week of school and two lessons at Port Johnson, I need to get back to it."

"About Port Johnson—"

Elizabeth shook her head. "Forget it. I'm not stopping."

"Why do you have to be so stubborn, woman?"

"I'm not. I made a commitment. I need to see it through."

He continued to pace for a few moments. "For how long?"

"For as long as it takes."

He threw his hands up. "I told you it's not safe."

"It's perfectly safe."

"No. It's not. Look at you."

"That had nothing to do with Port Johnson. Dante, listen to me. I've had lots of time to think while lying in this bed, and you know what I figured out? It was a bit of a revelation actually; I just wasn't ready to see it. I've been hiding out for most of my life. Especially since Pearl." She paused as a thought hit her. "What do you know, the press was right."

"What press?"

Elizabeth waved a hand in dismissal. "It doesn't matter. That's all changed now, thanks to teaching at the high school and Port Johnson. I've met so many wonderful people, first and foremost, you—and your mother, of course." She smiled. "For the first time ever, I'm not just watching other people enjoy life, I'm enjoying it too, and I refuse to let a random mauling in the street, or anything else for that matter, put me back into hiding."

"I told you, it may not have been random."

"It was. He didn't know who I was. He saw someone weaker and took advantage of it."

"Fine, but from now on, I'm driving you and taking you home after class. No more taking the bus." Dante stopped pacing and stood with his arms crossed.

"Dante, the bus is safe."

He gave a slow shake of his head from side to side, but otherwise didn't change his stance.

Elizabeth sighed. "All right. You can drive me." She paused for a moment. "But on one condition."

"What's that?"

"I'm not going to hide anymore and neither can you. You need to start living."

Dante shook his head. "I don't know what you're talking about. I live."

"You do? What do you do?"

He shrugged. "What do I do? I go to work. I come home. I drive to Port Johnson twice a week."

"That's it?"

"Yeah. What else is there?"

"Lots. What do you like to do for fun?"

"Fun? I'm a little old for fun, don't you think?"

Elizabeth shook her head. "That's just it. You're never too old for fun. My sister and brother always knew that, I was the only one that didn't get it, but I do now. Teaching, cooking, even singing, it's all fun. There are so many things I've read about and never tried, but I'm going to. You need to have some fun too."

"What do you suggest?"

She ignored his dry tone. "I don't know. When was the last time you went out on a date?"

"Don't start this again."

"When?"

"Okay...ahh..." He snapped his fingers. "We went to the movies, remember?"

"What? That wasn't a date. We didn't even see the movie. Besides that time?"

"I don't know." He pointed a finger at her. "What about you? When was the last time you went on a date? Huh?"

"Well, now that you mention it—never." Elizabeth couldn't miss his surprised countenance. "But, but I'm going to put it on my list, and I'm going to do it." She pointed to her mouth. "As soon as this goes away." The swelling was gone, leaving the bruise on her face an ugly shade of yellow.

"You've never been on a date?"

Elizabeth flushed. "Well, no."

"And you're trying to manage my love life? I don't think so."

"That's my condition, Dante Montenari. Take it or leave it."

He said nothing for a few moments.

"Well?"

"Fine, but you don't get to choose what I do for fun. I do."

"Deal."

"The *dottore* is here," Maria announced as she came through the open door, the physician right behind her.

Dante turned to leave. "If I was you, Doctor, I'd check out her head again. She has some crazy ideas this morning."

Two hours later, Dante pulled into Elizabeth's driveway and came around to help her out of the car. "The back door again?"

Elizabeth shook her head. "The front door will be fine." She was headed to the front porch when she caught a movement out of the corner of her eye. Mrs. Sargent was working in her flower bed near the driveway.

The woman got to her feet and stood gawking at the two of them. "Well, well, I was wonderin' what became of you. I thought maybe you'd gotten yourself fired and left town. I expected a For Sale sign to go up any day now."

Elizabeth handed Dante her purse. "My keys are in there, but I can't hold it and get the keys out with my arm in this sling."

He fished the keys out. "Are you ready?"

"Not quite." She smiled at him. "I'll be right along. I'm going to have a quick chat with my neighbor. Would you mind opening up the house? Maybe open a couple of windows for a few minutes? It must be stuffy in there after being closed up."

"Sure. Be careful coming up the steps."

"I will. Thanks." She turned on her heel. "No more hiding," she whispered before marching around the car and up to Mrs. Sargent, who hadn't moved.

"What the hell happened to you? He beat you up again? He's an I-talian, isn't he? I can tell by his looks." The woman pointed her garden trowel at Elizabeth. "Damn guineas. I told you they were no good, but what do I know?"

Elizabeth looked the woman in the eye. "Not much, I'm afraid."

"I beg your pardon?"

"I doubt you've ever begged for anything in your life. You've been too busy belittling everyone around you. Well, now it's your turn." Elizabeth took a breath. "You're mean and selfish and spiteful. And for some reason, you're not happy in your own life, so it seems you've made it your mission to make everyone else miserable too."

"You've got some nerve." The woman raised the trowel a little higher.

No more hiding. "I know it was you who did those things to my house."

"I don't know what you're talking about." Doris Sargent dropped the trowel to the ground and dug around in her apron pocket, pulling out a crushed pack of cigarettes and a lighter. She lit one, took a deep drag and exhaled the smoke in Elizabeth's face. "Besides, you've got no proof." She took another long pull on the cigarette, this time tipping her head back to expose the wrinkled skin of her neck as she blew the smoke into the air above her head. She brought her gaze back to Elizabeth. "I warned you folks wouldn't like it, you bein' a teacher and runnin' with those kind of people, but I can see by lover-boy, you didn't listen. I'm sure the principal will be gettin' wind of it any day."

"He already has."

A slight smile curved the woman's mouth. "Really? Well, it's too bad you lost your job, but you'll find something else, somewhere else. There's always lots of factory work."

"Oh, I didn't lose my job."

The woman's mouth dropped open in a perfect O.

"In fact, some are saying perhaps it was a put up by Nazi sympathizers, angry at the Italians for surrendering. I hear there's likely to be an investigation. The FBI might even be called in to look at the handwriting on a letter the principal has. This is serious business with the war and all. Can you imagine?" Elizabeth smiled. "Nazis right here, in our little city?"

Doris took several puffs on the cigarette in rapid succession.

"No, I plan on being here for a while. And of course, my friends will be welcome here too, whether they're Italian, Irish or Eskimo. It's true, most of my friends are Italians. Wonderful people, the Italians. I got to meet Dante's uncle the other day, perhaps you know of him, Don Salucci?" Elizabeth paused. "I can tell by your face, you've heard of him. Isn't it strange how they call him Don? I thought it stood for Donald at first."

Mrs. Sargent dropped her cigarette into the dirt of the flower bed, immediately lit another and continued to puff.

"He's a lovely man. I'll be sure to introduce you when he comes to visit. Well, I really do need to get a little rest now. I'm glad we had this chat." Elizabeth turned away. *What a pack of lies. She's never going to believe them.*

But she must have...three days later, there was a For Sale sign on the front lawn and the Sargents were gone.

Chapter 13

Dante came into the kitchen as his mother pulled a baking sheet out of the oven. He grabbed a cookie off the plate on the table. "Mmm. Good."

Maria used a spatula to slide more sugar cookies onto the plate. "They were always your favorite."

He buttoned his coat before taking another cookie. "I'm going now."

"What are you doing? Picking up Elizabeth?"

"Yeah." He took another bite. "I promised her I'd take her shopping today. Then we're going to get her a Christmas tree and put it up. I guess she bought a few decorations, and we're supposed to make the rest. Another one of her fun ideas."

"Good."

A faint sound caught his attention. "Did you hear that?"

His mother shook her head. "No, it's probably just the radio."

"Yeah, probably. Well, I'd better shove off. It's Saturday. Downtown is going to be busy."

"Wait. Wait just a minute." She hurried from the room.

He followed her into the living room, only to find she wasn't there. "Mama, I've got to go."

She came out of the bedroom and handed him a small tissue wrapped package.

"What's this?"

"We have so many ornaments on the tree. I thought I'd give Elizabeth one for her tree. Be careful with it, please. It was from my first Christmas tree here in America."

Dante smiled at his mother. "You're a good woman." He gave her a kiss on the cheek. "I'll be back later."

"Okay. Is Elizabeth going with us to the dance tonight?"

"As far as I know." He headed to the door. "She's supposed to be doing a couple of songs with the band."

"Wonderful. She has a beautiful voice. Please remind her about midnight mass on Christmas Eve. She wanted to come with us."

"Will do." A moment later he pushed open the door to the outside. The sound of breaking glass carried through the brisk morning air from somewhere below.

"What the hell?" Dante hurried down the steps as fast as his leg would allow and around the corner to the front of the building. "Son of a bitch." He scanned the area, but saw no one. "I don't believe it." He slammed a hand against the brick wall. "Son of a bitch." The front windows of the shop were gone, just a few shards of glass clung to the edge of the frames. He reached inside the now empty window of the door and flipped the lock before pushing the door open. Several bricks lay on the floor amongst shattered glass. "What the hell? Who's doing this stuff?"

Last month, someone slashed all four tires on his car, as well as set his dumpster on fire. Dante was doubtful it was Flanagan, nobody had seen him since Salucci's men worked him over. That only left Salucci, though Gino Galenti swore he had nothing to do with it. Dante didn't know what to think, but someone had it in for him. "Damn it, I'm going to be late." He went to his desk in the back to call Elizabeth.

Dante pulled his car to the curb as church bells rang in the noon hour. The sidewalk was busy with pedestrian traffic, everyone out doing holiday shopping on the last weekend before Christmas. He turned to Elizabeth. "Are you ready for this?"

"Yes. I can't wait. Let's go."

They moved with the crowds from shop to shop, Elizabeth examining many things. Among her packages, a lovely lavender shawl for Dante's mother and perfume to send to Katherine. Dante held her purchases. "Okay, which way now?"

"I know it's late, but to tell you the truth, I'm starving. Do you mind if we get some lunch?"

"Not at all. Let's get rid of these packages first."

They made a quick trip to the car and headed back down the street. Elizabeth linked her arm with his and smiled. "This is fun. Thanks for bringing me."

He smiled back. "You're welcome. Where do you want to eat?"

He has such a nice smile.

"Hello? Lunch?"

Elizabeth shook her head to clear it and looked around. "Ahh, I don't know. How about right there?" She pointed to a small two-story structure weathered to an indeterminate shade of gray, tucked in between much taller, more modern office buildings. The sign on the front was barely legible.

"At that place? What's it called? Annabelle's?"

"I think so. Have you ever eaten there?"

He shook his head. "Maybe we should go to Joseph's Steak House. It's only a couple of blocks over."

"What's wrong with this place?"

"Nothing, I guess. It just looks a little run down."

"So? The food could be great. How are you going to know if you don't take a chance?"

"Let me guess. It'll be fun, right?"

Elizabeth grinned and tugged him along.

The booths were full. The hostess, a short woman with snow-white hair, seated them at a table for two in the back room. She laid single sheet menus in front of them. Her hands were gnarled and warped out of shape. "I hope you folks don't mind sitting out here. We don't use this room much nowadays, but with the Christmas shopping and all, we have a few more customers. Your waitress is going to be Nancy." The multitude of wrinkles on the old woman's face deepened as she smiled. "She'll be with you folks in just a couple of minutes. In the meantime, what would you like to drink?"

"We're in no hurry." Elizabeth smiled back. "I'll have a cup of tea. Thank you. "

"I'll have coffee."

The woman nodded and hobbled toward the front room again.

"Maybe we should try another place," Dante said after they'd been waiting almost ten minutes.

"Well, maybe you're right, it's taking longer—"

"Hi. Sorry to keep you waiting." A tall thin girl sat two cups down on the table. She smoothed her blond hair back, glanced at the swinging door on the other side of the room and pulled a small pad of paper from her apron pocket. "I'm Nancy." Her smile was as faded as her yellow uniform. "Today our specials are vegetable soup, chicken and biscuits and fried haddock. We also have a western sandwich with a pickle." She glanced at the door behind her again. "What can I get you?"

Elizabeth smiled at the pale girl. "I'll have the vegetable soup."

"And you?" The girl looked at Dante.

"I'll have the western sandwich with ketchup."

Nancy scribbled on the pad. There was a loud bang somewhere in the back of the restaurant. "I'll put that order right in." She turned to leave.

"Miss?" Elizabeth called after her. "Can you tell me where the powder room is?"

"Right through this door and to the right, or you can go back out in the main room and take a left," the girl answered without turning around as she pushed through the door.

"Still think this was a good idea?"

Elizabeth shrugged. "It's not bad so far. I'm waiting for my food before I pass judgment. Right now, I'd like to wash my hands before we eat. I'll be right back." She headed to the door, letting it swing closed behind her and turned to the right. The bathroom was old and worn, but clean. She was headed back when she heard a noise from the other end of the dim corridor. *Is that a baby crying?* Elizabeth followed the sound until she came to an open door.

"Thomas, did you try giving them a bottle of water?" It was the waitress, Nancy, talking to a man who towered over her.

"Yeah, I tried that, but they didn't want no bottle."

"Okay. Well, maybe they need a diaper change."

The man held up his arms. Two sets of pincher-like hooks replaced his hands.

"I know. I know. I'll have to do it when I come back. I've got customers. Can you keep them entertained until I'm done?"

"I doubt it."

A second cry was added to the mix. Elizabeth glanced around the adults to the other side of the room. A wooden play-pen was set up and held two crying babies, one in pink, and the other in blue.

The man shook his head. "Jesus, they're givin' me a headache!"

"I'm sorry." Nancy picked up the baby in blue. The other one cried harder. "I'll take them out in the big room as soon as we close. Right now, you have to stay here and watch them for me."

"I'm supposed to meet Frank and the boys down at the pub at four o'clock, ya know, so you'd better hurry up. I ain't no babysitter."

"Well, you are today." She sat the baby back in the play-pen and picked up the second child only to have the first child start crying again. "You have to stay here. Do you hear me?" She bounced the baby against her hip for a moment. "Do you?" She turned to the baby left behind in the play-pen. "Shh. Shh."

"Can I help in some way?" Elizabeth stepped forward.

"Oh, ma'am, I'm sorry if we disturbed you."

"No. No. I was just on my way back from the rest room." She stepped closer to the play-pen. "May I pick her up?"

The woman nodded.

Elizabeth reached down and lifted the crying baby. She slid one arm under her legs and the other around her back. She'd never held a baby before. They sized each other up. The baby's blond hair stood up in flyaway wisps all over her head. Her bright blue eyes were fringed with lashes clumped in spikes from her tears. Her cry diminished to an occasional hiccup. "She's beautiful. What's her name?"

"That's Margaret, and this handsome fellow is Matthew. They're twins."

Elizabeth smiled at the baby in her arms. "Hello, Margaret."

"And this is Thomas. My husband. Thomas?"

"How do." It was barely more than a mumble.

"Nice to meet you, Thomas. I didn't mean to interrupt."

"You didn't, ma'am." The baby, Matthew, laid in the crook of Nancy's arm as she rocked him from side to side in a rhythmic motion. He blinked several times before his eyes closed. "At this time of day, they're usually in for a nap, but my sitter had to take her husband to the hospital, it turned out he has appendicitis, so we had to bring them down here today."

"Poor things. Are they going to have to stay through dinner too?"

The man's gaze narrowed on Elizabeth. "What's it to you? They're being looked after."

"Thomas." The one word was a warning. The waitress smiled at Elizabeth. "They'll be fine, we're closing soon. We don't do dinner, we used to, before," she stopped for a moment. "Now, it's just breakfast and lunch." She continued to rock the baby, as if unaware she was doing it.

"What she means is before I came back with these." Thomas manipulated the hooks to open and close. "Can't do much of nothin'. Not very pretty, huh?"

He's trying to scare me. Elizabeth kept her gaze locked with that of the unshaven man. "I've seen worse."

The man snorted, but looked away. "Yeah, right, lady. Where? Your garden club, or maybe the country—"

"I said enough, Thomas. Ma'am, if you go on back to your table, I'll bring your lunch right out." She gently laid Matthew in the play-pen and held her hands out toward Margaret. With a laugh, Margaret fell into her mother's arms. Nancy snuggled her and then set her in the play-pen. The baby's lower lip quivered for just a second before she burst out crying. The noise woke Matthew and he started in too.

"Nancy, I can't stand it!" Thomas dropped onto a pile of several sacks of potatoes.

"You can and you will. These are your babies too." Nancy turned and walked past Elizabeth. "Sorry. I'll check on your meal."

"Wait."

Nancy stopped.

Elizabeth smiled at the young woman. "Why don't you bring them out? There's more room out there for them to move around. It's only the two of us. I know Dante won't mind."

"We couldn't do that. You're paying for a meal. You should be able to enjoy it in peace."

"I insist. May I hold her again?"

Nancy nodded and ignored her husband's glare. She handed Elizabeth the baby girl and then lifted Matthew out of the play-pen. "Are you sure?"

"Absolutely."

"Well, it is almost time to close. So, maybe it's okay, this once." Nancy pulled a folded quilt off a low shelf and handed it to Thomas. "Can you carry this?"

The man lifted his arm and then clamped down on the blanket with his elbow when she put it next to his side. He turned and left the room without another word.

"Thank you. I really appreciate it. We need every cent we can get." Nancy sighed. "I apologize for Thomas. He hasn't been the same since he came home. You know, a faulty detonator took his hands, but the war took a whole lot more." She tapped her temple. "In here. He doesn't talk about it, but he dreams, and no amount of alcohol can stop the dreams." Nancy swiped at her eyes, then shook her head. "Sorry. Here you are, just in for a bite to eat, and I stand here blathering away."

Baby Margaret reached up and touched Elizabeth's cheek. Elizabeth kissed the palm of the tiny hand. "It's fine. I understand."

"You do?" Nancy smiled. "Thank you. I noticed your husband walked with a limp when you came in. Was he hurt in the war?"

"Yes, he was, but we're not married."

"Well, your boyfriend then."

"Not really boyfriend, more like best friend."

"Hmm. Are you sure about that?"

"Of course. Why?"

"Nothin'. Just the way he looks at you, I guess, but I could be wrong. Lord knows I have been before." She glanced to the door her husband had left through. "Maybe best friends is better. Always a date on Saturday night with none of the rest of the stuff that goes with it. When Thomas and I met he managed this place for his mother after his father died, and I was a buyer for Closson's department store. We'd only been dating a couple of months when Pearl happened. He enlisted the next day, and asked me to marry him before he left. I did, of course." Nancy rolled her eyes. "It seemed so romantic at the time. We had three days together, and then he was gone. I found out a few weeks later I was pregnant." She paused and gave Matthew a kiss atop his fuzzy hair. "And here we are."

Thomas came back. "It's all set."

"Lead the way then."

Thomas led the small parade back through the door. While he'd attempted to spread the quilt in the corner; it was still half folded.

Elizabeth grinned at Dante's surprised expression. She strolled to the table. "We're having some company for lunch. This is our waitress Nancy's husband, Thomas."

Thomas gave a curt nod.

Dante nodded in return. "Nice to meet you."

"Nancy just put Matthew on the blanket over there, and this is Margaret. They're twins. Isn't that special?" Elizabeth beamed and leaned in a little closer. "Holding a baby isn't on my list, but it should be. Isn't she beautiful?"

Nancy came through the door with two plates and sat them on the table. "Why don't I take her, and you sit down and eat your lunch before it gets cold?"

"If it's not too much to ask, could we get some lunch? Is this a restaurant or a babysitting service?"

Elizabeth looked up to find two women seated at a table in the opposite corner.

Nancy hurried to set Margaret next to Matthew on the blanket, then rushed over to their table. "I'm sorry. We're actually closing. Did the hostess seat you?"

"Hostess? There was no one out front. We wanted some privacy, so we came back here. Why are there children in here? They're not going to cry, are they? Do you even have menus?"

"We'll remove the babies if they cry, and yes," Nancy reached around the corner, "Here's our menu." She quickly recited the specials.

The woman tossed the menu on the table without even looking at it. "None of it sounds very appetizing. I'll just have a Cobb salad."

"I'm sorry. We don't serve that."

"What?" The woman sighed. "Fine. A martini then. Two olives. Shaken. What about you, Margie? Do any of their specials sound that special to you?"

"I'm sorry. We don't serve alcohol."

"What? What kind of restaurant is this? Forget it, Margie." The well-dressed woman pushed her chair back and stood. "We're going to Joseph's, even if we have to wait." She marched away, leaving the silent Margie to trail along.

"Snooty bitch," Thomas mumbled under his breath.

"Thomas." Nancy hurried to the front after the women left and flipped the sign to Closed. "I'm going to bus these two booths. I'll be right back."

Elizabeth and Dante ate in silence as Thomas stood on the other side of the room, corralling the babies with his feet.

"How's your lunch?" Nancy was back.

"This is excellent soup."

Dante finished chewing a bite and swallowed. "It's a very good sandwich."

"Good. I'm glad you're enjoying it."

"Nancy, is Ma lettin' you knock off a few minutes early?"

The girl's smile disappeared. She didn't turn to her husband. "Yes. Her and Grannie said they'd finish up, so we could take the babies home for a nap."

"You don't need me for that, it's only upstairs. I'm leaving. I'll see ya later tonight. Don't bother waitin' up again." With that, he left the restaurant, the front door banging closed behind him.

"Fine." Nancy closed her eyes and stood still for a moment before finally pulling out her pad. "Are you folks having dessert? We've got apple pie and pumpkin spice cake today."

Both Dante and Elizabeth declined.

"Okay, then, here's your check. You can pay Grannie—I mean the hostess on the way out. Thanks for coming by. Come back again." She lifted two tiny coats off a set of hooks nearby and bent down on her knees to tussle with each baby a few moments to get the buttons done up. She then lifted Margaret and balanced her on one hip as she attempted to work her other arm around a wiggling Matthew and haul him up to her other hip. She took a deep breath and slowly rose as she balanced the babies.

"Here, let me help you." Elizabeth jumped up and lifted Matthew off the girl's hip. "I'll take him for you."

"Thanks. He doesn't like touching them. He's afraid he'll hurt them with his hooks." The girl readjusted her hold on Margaret. "There, that's better. It's really nice of you to offer, but I don't want to put you out. I'm sure you've got other things to do."

"No, that's fine. Lead the way." Elizabeth turned toward the table. "I'll be right back." She followed the girl out to the hall and to the right again, taking the next left after the bathroom door. They were in the kitchen.

"Bye, Annabelle."

A large boned woman stopped scraping the grill. "You takin' the babies up to bed?"

"Yes."

"Good. We had a busy day." She spied Elizabeth. "Where's Thomas?"

"Ahh, he had to meet Frank Porter downtown."

"At the bar you mean? That man. He's got to do somethin' to get himself together, or he ain't gonna last long at this rate." She shook her head. "It ain't right. Forget about this place, but he's got them babies to take care of."

"I know. I'll try talkin' to him again." Nancy's voice sounded tired.

"Good girl. You hang in there. He needs a job, something to make him feel useful again. I'm not sure what it is, but hopefully something will come along soon."

"I'm sure you're right. Probably any day now." Nancy gave her mother-in-law a weak smile. "Well, I've got to get the babies upstairs. I'll see you later." She continued through the kitchen and out the back door. "This way." She climbed a steep narrow flight of stairs and opened a door. Elizabeth followed into a small kitchen.

"You can put him down on the rug in there. I'm going to change Margaret, and I'll be back for him."

Elizabeth walked into the living room, but continued to hold the baby as she looked around. Despite the worn furnishings the place was immaculate.

"Okay, here I am." Nancy laid Matthew on the couch and made quick work of changing his wet diaper and pulled on fresh plastic pants to cover the dry one. "There. All done. Off to bed with you, sir." She disappeared through a doorway off the living room and was back in a moment. "Thanks for your help, and for," she hesitated, "for listening earlier. Thomas is going through a hard time right now. He did try looking for a job when he first got home. There are lots of factory jobs, but they kept telling him a factory was no place for a cripple." She shrugged. "Pretty soon he started believing it. Now, he won't even go out and look for work."

"I'm sorry. I hope things get better soon."

"Me too." The girl forced her features into a smile. "Well, at least it's Christmas. We don't have much in the way of decorations, but we're supposed to go pick out a tree tomorrow."

"That's what Dante and I are doing next, picking out a tree. In fact, I'd better get going or it'll be dark by the time we get it to the house, and we still have to decorate it." Elizabeth extended her hand. "It was nice to meet you, Nancy."

The girl shook her hand. "Likewise." She walked to the door with Elizabeth and pulled it open. "I hope you'll come back for lunch again, real soon."

"I will." Elizabeth stepped through the doorway and turned back. "You know, Nancy, Thomas came home when many didn't. I don't know what it is, but please remember there's a reason for that."

Chapter 14

It was close to twilight when Dante untied the rope holding the tree on the car. "You know, they would've delivered this."

"I know, but it was already so late. I was afraid it wouldn't get delivered today."

"I'm sorry we started out late, Elizabeth."

"No, no. It's not your fault. I know that. Besides, I'm the one that suggested lunch." She shrugged. "I just wanted it here so we could decorate it. That's all. It's going to be fun."

Dante pulled the tree off the roof of the car and stood it up. "Fun like last month when you tried to make fried chicken and set the pan on fire? That kind of fun?"

"Ha. Ha. Ha. I just wanted to try it. I didn't know the grease would boil over so fast. Now I do. C'mon, Dante. Please?"

"Okay, Okay. Lead the way."

Two hours later the tree was set up. Garlands of popcorn and cranberries wound from bottom to top. Foil covered paper cup bells hung from branches, along with the multicolored glass balls Elizabeth had purchased earlier in the week.

"I almost forgot. My mother sent you over a little something for your tree too."

"Really? That was so nice of her."

He reached for his coat, pulled out the small package and placed it into Elizabeth's hand. "She picked it because it was on her first Christmas tree here."

Elizabeth sat on the couch and carefully opened the paper. "Oh, Dante, look." She held up the tiny milky green glass ornament. It was a perfect replica of the Statue of Liberty. "It's beautiful."

"I remember that one. She used to tell me the green lady was to remind us we could be anything we wanted to be here."

She walked to the tree. "I'm nervous about hanging it. What if it gets broken?"

He lifted it from her fingers and hung it on a branch. "It won't. It survived me."

She smiled. "Oh, one more thing." She picked up an angel decoration and pushed a low stool in a little closer. "This will be perfect." She stretched toward the top of the tree, rising on her tiptoes to reach. "Just a little further."

She wobbled for a second, and Dante put his hands on her waist to steady her. "Be careful."

She glanced back at him and smiled. "Thanks. Just a little more."

Dante stared at his hands on her waist.

"There. Is it straight? Dante?"

He dragged his eyes upward. "Yes." He cleared his throat and dropped his hands. "Yes. It is."

"Great." She hopped off the stool and stood near him, her shoulder slightly overlapping his. "It's a beautiful tree. Thank you for helping me."

As natural as breathing, he slid an arm around her shoulders, pulling her a little closer as she leaned back. "You're welcome."

They stood this way for several moments before she turned to him. "You know what? I'm going to put my presents under the tree. It's close enough to Christmas." Elizabeth headed down the hall and was back in a couple of minutes. "Here we go. I have your present here, but no peeking." She grinned, then bent down on her knees and arranged the boxes underneath the tree. "That looks better." She tapped a fingernail on a box wrapped in red paper and tied with a large gold bow. "This is the one the boys at Port Johnson gave me on Wednesday night after class. Remember?"

Dante nodded.

"They said they wanted me to open it today. I wonder what's in it."

"You'll have to open it and find out."

"Okay." This time she threw caution to the wind as she sat on the couch and tore through the red wrapping, lifting the lid off the box to fold back the tissue paper. "What's this? A dress?" She lifted it out of the box. "A beautiful dress. Oh, my word, look at this." She stood up and held the emerald green garment draped against her body. "How could they afford this?"

"I believe they each chipped in some of their wages to buy the materials."

"Still, it must have cost a fortune. Velvet and lace. The workmanship is excellent. It hangs beautifully." She twisted from side to side a couple of times, and the material followed her movements. "Did you see that? Katherine would kill for this dress."

"Yes, and the lace sleeves and insert at the top gives the illusion of it being strapless, while at the same time covering you up."

Elizabeth dropped back onto the couch and sat open mouthed. "What?"

"You made this dress."

"No, I didn't. What are you talking about? No."

"Yes, you did. You're a terrible liar, Dante."

He dragged a hand through his hair a couple of times. "Okay. Fine, I did."

"I knew it. Did you design it too?"

"Yes, but you can't tell anyone."

"Why not? You'd have at least a dozen women lined up for orders."

"Which is exactly why you can't say anything. I admit I enjoy the design work, but not the piecing together. That's why I do men's clothes. Simple, uncomplicated."

"But you'd make a fortune in—"

"No."

"Okay. Okay. But how'd you know my size?"

"I just took a guess."

"A guess? How?"

"Well, I estimated by looking at your waist and your..." He pointed to her chest. "Your...ahh. I just figured it out." He backed toward the door. "I'll be back in a couple of hours."

It was well past dark when Dante returned. Several lights burned in Elizabeth's house, emitting a warm glow as he walked up the porch steps to knock on the front door.

Elizabeth opened the door. "Come in. I'm just about ready. What do you think?" She turned in a slow circle. The velvet material of the full-length gown clung to her body and flared at the knee, the bottom of the dress swirled with each step. The front of her auburn hair was rolled back, while the remainder hung down her back. Earrings embedded with green stones adorned her ears.

"I think I'm going to have to beat the wolves off tonight." His grin was wry.

"I'll get my coat." She stopped in front of a small mirror in the living room, pinched her cheeks a couple of times and applied lipstick. Elizabeth caught him looking at her in the mirror. "What? Is it too much? I thought red lipstick, green dress, Christmas, you know, but I can wipe it off." She headed toward the hall.

"No. No. You look beautiful."

"Really?" She turned and slipped her arms into the coat he held up for her. "Well, maybe someone will ask me out, and I can cross first date off my list after tonight." She tugged on black gloves. "What do you think?"

She'd shown Dante her list of Fun-Firsts several times and added to it daily. It ranged from simple things like growing a vegetable garden to cliff diving in Acapulco, and lots of things in between, including a first date. "About you having a date?" He cleared his throat and stood silent for a moment, then pointed to her earrings. "Are those real?"

She put her hand up to touch an earring. "Yes. They were my mother's. She loved emeralds. And sapphires. And diamonds. Now that I think about it, she loved jewelry of all kinds. And furs. I don't wear jewelry much, so most of it stays in the safety deposit box, but these are my favorite. I thought since it's Christmas, and I have this lovely new dress, I wanted to look as special as I feel. Thank you for making it for me." She leaned forward and gave him a quick kiss on the cheek. "Oops. Sorry. Lipstick." She rubbed a gloved fingertip against his skin.

Dante didn't move during her administrations. Her light perfume floated in the air between them. He balled his hands into fists to keep from touching her.

"There. Handsome as ever."

She bestowed a smile on him, and he fought the urge to groan out loud.

"Are you ready?" She headed toward the front door. "Did you leave the car running? Otherwise, your poor mother is going to be freezing."

He let his breath out in a gust. *This is going to be a long night.* "My mother isn't coming. She got one of her bad headaches late this afternoon and took some of her powders. It knocked her right out."

"That's too bad. If she's not feeling better by tomorrow, maybe you could come and get me. I'll cook her something."

He pulled open the front door for Elizabeth. "Fine, as long as it's not fried chicken."

Twenty minutes later, Dante slowed the car to a stop. "I didn't realize there'd be so many people here." Cars lined both sides of the street outside the parish hall. "Maybe I should drop you off and park the car at home. I can walk back. It's only a few blocks over."

"All right, but I'll walk back with you." Elizabeth paused. "Wait, is someone pulling out down there?"

He pulled the car into the vacated spot and soon they were inside, standing in line to check their coats.

"Look at all the people in there." Elizabeth leaned in close. "Isn't that Constance Santini? She's looking very fetching tonight."

Dante didn't as much as glance that way. He stepped up to the counter. "Good evening, Mrs. Carapetti. How are you tonight?"

"I'm fine, Dante. How are you?"

"Good. I'm good."

The heavy set woman leaned out over the counter. "Where's your mother?"

"She won't be coming; she's got one of her headaches."

"Ohh, that's too bad. Poor Maria." The woman pulled one of two small tickets off a metal hanger. "How about you give me your coats?"

"Sure." Dante handed his coat over and Elizabeth's too, a moment later.

"Here's your check stub. What a lovely dress, miss?" The woman hesitated. "Miss Wellman?"

"Yes."

"Sorry, I almost didn't recognize you. You look so—what's the word? So glamorous. Just like Maureen O'Hara."

Elizabeth blushed.

"Dante, what are you waiting for? A teacher and so beautiful. You'd better marry this girl before someone beats you to it. I've got boys who could use a good wife to help set them straight."

"Mrs. Carapetti, we're not—"

Dante cut Elizabeth off. "I'll take it under advisement. Merry Christmas, Mrs. Carapetti." He offered his arm, and they walked into the large room. White paper snowflakes hung from the ceiling. Red bows adorned each of the large windows. A decorated Christmas tree was set up on the stage behind the band.

People squeezed into every part of the room, some dancing, while others stood talking. Older people, dressed in their finery sat at tables at the far end, watching the dancers or talking to others.

Dante leaned close to her ear to be heard over the jazzy music of horns. "Would you like some punch?"

"Yes."

As they strolled to the refreshment table, Dante noticed people watching them. He glanced at Elizabeth. She seemed unaware of the stares. He handed her a glass of punch.

Within half an hour, Roberto and several other young men had joined them, some were from Port Johnson; but not all. Several guys from around the neighborhood, including one of Mrs. Carapetti's sons, Carmine, rounded out the group. Elizabeth chatted away with her students as if it were a Wednesday night class. Most of the men stood enthralled with rapt smiles, especially after she gave each of them a hug in thanks for the dress.

Carmine Carapetti held out his arms too.

Elizabeth didn't move. "I'm sorry, but I don't think we've been introduced."

The lanky man grinned at her, his Brylcreem saturated black hair shiny in the light cast from the stage. "I'm Carmine Carapetti." He extended his arms again. "Now, how about that hug?"

Dante stepped closer to her side.

"It's nice to meet you, Mr. Carapetti." Elizabeth extended her hand.

Carmine hesitated a moment before reaching out to shake her hand. "Okay, okay. We'll do it this way. Nice to meet you, Miss Wellman." He continued to hold her hand. "I hear you're a singer. I'm a singer too."

Elizabeth's smile was polite, even as she tugged her hand back. "That's wonderful, Mr. Carapetti. Where do you sing?'

Someone snickered. "Yeah, Carmine, tell the lady where."

"Shut up." Carmine glared at the man Dante recognized from around the neighborhood. "Well, right now, me and the guys get together on the corner, but we're gonna be big someday."

"I'm sure you're very talented, Mr. Carapetti."

"I am." Carmine straightened his jacket as the band started a new song. Already couples moved around the floor in a close embrace to the slower music. "Hey, I love this one. Miss Wellman, would you like to dance?"

"Actually, Miss Wellman promised me this dance." Dante held out his hand.

"What? Oh, yes. I'm sorry, Mr. Carapetti." Elizabeth took Dante's hand and let him lead her out on the floor. "Are you sure about this? What about your leg?"

"It'll be okay as long as it's a slow dance. I've been practicing," he admitted in a low voice.

"You've been practicing? Really? Is this a choice on your list?"

"I don't have a list. Would you forget that damn list?" He pulled her into his arms.

After a few minutes, she relaxed in Dante's embrace as they moved in small circles to the music. He relaxed too, enjoying the feel of her body so close to his, her breath warm against his neck as her head rested on his shoulder. The band played another slow song. They kept dancing.

"Psst. Dante. Miss Wellman."

Someone tapped his shoulder. "Go away, Nico."

"Miss Wellman, I wanted to let you know we're on after this song."

Elizabeth raised her head. "Okay, Nicolina. I'll be ready."

Nico giggled. "Hey, Dante. Look up."

Dante did. Straight overhead, hanging from a string was a sprig of mistletoe.

"You know what that means," Elizabeth whispered.

He looked down at her and hesitated, but slowly brought his lips to hers. The moment they made contact, he tightened his hold. Elizabeth's hands slipped to the back of his neck. She interlocked her fingers.

"Miss Wellman?" Alessio's voice echoed over the microphone.

Dante groaned.

Elizabeth pulled back as people in their vicinity chuckled. "Oh dear, I guess I got carried away." She cleared her throat. "Umm, I've got to go sing now."

He nodded, not trusting himself to speak and dropped his hands.

She hurried through a side doorway, a few moments later appearing in the bright lights of the stage. She took her place next to Nicolina and gave the girl a smile.

Dante worked his way toward the stage, Elizabeth's flushed cheeks drawing him as surely as a wayward ship to a beacon.

The band played the beginning notes, and Alessio stepped to the microphone to sing the latest Bing Crosby hit, *I'll Be Home For Christmas.* The time Elizabeth had spent with the girl on the harmony parts showed as the women joined in on the chorus. Elizabeth would look out at the crowd and then back at Nico with a smile, while the girl kept her eyes on her teacher to get her cues. Dante stopped a few feet in front of the stage. Elizabeth glanced down for a moment as she sang and gave him a smile. He smiled back.

"Did you see that? She smiled at me."

Dante looked to his left. One of the butchers from Russo's Market and another guy he didn't recognize stood staring at the stage, big smiles on their faces.

"She is beau-ti-ful. An angel. I wonder if she'd go out with me."

The other guy laughed and shook his head. "I doubt it. She's gorgeous and really smart too, or so my kid sister says. She teaches at the high school. Look at her, what would she want with any of us?"

"Yeah, you're probably right." The meat cutter glanced over and nodded at Dante. "How ya doin'?"

"Okay."

"Good singer. A little too rich for guys like us, huh?"

Dante nodded. The song ended to applause. The band sat down, and Elizabeth walked to the center of the stage, her earrings flashing in the light as she turned her head. Dante stood transfixed.

Alessio lowered the microphone stand, and she stepped up to it with a smile. "Good evening, ladies and gentlemen. I'd like to do a song by the Gershwin brothers, *Someone To Watch Over Me.*" Over the opening bars of piano music, Elizabeth added, "Dante, this is for you." She blew him a kiss.

"Huh? Who's that? Him?"

Dante glanced at the two guys next to him. He shrugged and gave them a sheepish grin.

The simplicity of the piano accompaniment complemented Elizabeth's voice as she played with the notes of the song, taking her time, her eyes never leaving Dante.

He didn't as much as blink. The last piano notes hadn't even died away as Dante headed for the side door to the stage. Applause filled the room.

"Thank you." Elizabeth turned away.

He stepped through the doorway looking for her and stopped. She was halfway down the steps. Without a word, they came together in a collision of bodies. Dante channeled the long months of frustration and longing into the melding of their lips. Wrapping his arms around her, he deepened the kiss as Elizabeth's arms slid around his neck. A few moments later they broke apart, only to come back together as he leaned against the wall and angled her closer to kiss her again.

"Ahem. Excuse us."

Dante stopped kissing her, but didn't move.

Nicolina and Alessio pounded down the stairs and out the door, their laughter echoing in the hallway.

He held Elizabeth's face between his hands, placing light kisses on her forehead, her eyes, her nose and finally her lips again. "What?" Dante whispered when he pulled back and found her smiling. "What?"

"I'm not sure this is on the list."

"The list again? Yes, it is. Kissing. It's like number nine or something."

She shook her head. "No. That's not it."

"Okay, well you add stuff all—"

She cut him off with another kiss. "No. Falling in love," she whispered against his lips.

Dante groaned and pulled her tight against him, reveling in the feel of her. "I love you too. God, help me, I didn't want to, but I do."

They stayed this way, lost in each other, and so at first Dante didn't register the shouting from the main room. "Something's going on." He pulled her along with him.

"Dante. Dante." Mrs. Carapetti hurried up to them, short of breath. "Here, take your coat. Quick," she huffed.

"What's going on?"

"A fire. Your place is on fire."

"Stay here." Dante bolted.

Chapter 15

Cold air ripped at Elizabeth's lungs. *Where is he? Is Maria safe?* She continued to run as best she could in the low heels, trying to ignore the stitch in her side. Her coat flapped open in the wind, but she didn't stop to button it. *God, please let them be okay.* She slipped on the sidewalk and fell to her knees. *Get up. You can't stop. Get up.* She kept going.

Other people rushed in the same direction. It seemed as if everyone in the city had converged on this spot, drawn to the flames like moths. Elizabeth finally managed to get to the corner of the Montenaris' street. Fire reached into the sky, casting the whole area in an eerie orange glow. She elbowed her way through the crowds, fighting to get closer.

The roof of the building was gone, consumed, while the brick remained intact. It looked like a gigantic chimney, belching smoke from every window. Two fire trucks hosed down the adjacent buildings. A fireman dug around in one of the compartments on the side of the truck.

"Excuse me?"

He turned. "I'm kind of busy here. What'd you need?"

"Why aren't you putting water on the fire?"

He shook his head. "No sense in it. We cleared the building, it's a total loss."

"The lady that lives there—she got out?"

"She's out."

His voice got quiet, and he wouldn't meet her gaze. A sense of dread churned in the pit of Elizabeth's stomach. "Where is she?"

"Look, lady. I don't have time to stand here jawin'. We're tryin' to save these other buildings." He slammed the metal door and hurried away.

Desperation drove Elizabeth closer to the fire, searching as she worked her way through the crowd, hoping to spot a familiar face. She turned to look behind her. In the mouth of the alley the firelight flickered on a face before it shifted, putting the area in darkness again. Elizabeth gasped. Was that Flanagan? *You have to find out.* She stood in place, unable to move. A moment later, the light illuminated the alley entrance again. Nothing.

Elizabeth caught the faint sound of sobbing nearby. Afraid of what she might find, she was nonetheless drawn forward. With each footstep, the weeping became clearer. She walked into a parking lot on the right and turned the corner of the building. A small group of people stood clustered together. Elizabeth recognized Gino Galenti and Mrs. Moretti, weeping in her husband's arms.

"Where are they?" Elizabeth wasn't sure if she said it out loud or not, but she must have—Gino stepped up to her.

"Miss Wellman, this is not a good time."

Elizabeth could barely make out his face in the dark, but she heard the hitch in his voice. He was crying. "Mr. Galenti? Where's Dante and Mrs. Montenari?"

"They just took her in the ambulance. My poor Maria." The old man used the wadded handkerchief in his hand to swipe at his eyes. "It don't look too good."

"Oh no." Tears welled in Elizabeth's eyes. She tried to swallow the lump in her throat. "Where's Dante?"

"The police gave him a ride to the hospital. They need to talk to him."

"The police? Why?"

"The fire was set, so it got reported."

"Someone did this on purpose? Why?"

"I don't know. But I mean to find out and when I do," he hesitated. "We'll take care of it."

"Can you tell me which way to the hospital?"

"It's across town. Listen, Miss Wellman, I know you're Dante's friend, but why don't you go on home? I'm sure Dante will come to see you tomorrow. I have a car here." He guided her to the far side of the parking lot, to a dark sedan. He opened the door and Elizabeth got in. "I'll tell Dante you were here."

She sat silent in the back seat as the car glided through the night. *How did this happen?*

The car pulled to the curb. The driver got out, opened her door and waited. Elizabeth stepped out. "Thank you."

The man nodded and shut the door.

Elizabeth climbed the porch steps and fit her key in the lock. *How did he know where I live?* She turned. He was gone. She shook her head. "Strange."

She walked to the hall closet, flipping the light switch up on the way and hung up her coat. The hall light shone on the Christmas tree, drawing Elizabeth's attention. It was hard to believe so much had happened in the few hours the tree had stood in her living room. The tiny glass ornament from Dante's mother glowed in the light. *Please let her be all right.*

She took a quick bath, tears mixing with the water, pulled on a nightgown and crawled into bed, only to toss and turn before drifting into a fitful sleep.

Elizabeth sat waiting for Dante the next day when the phone rang. "Hello?"

"Hello, Elizabeth."

"Dante. Where are you? How's your mother?"

"I'm at the hospital, there's no change yet. I'm not sure when I'll be by."

"That's okay. Do you need me to bring you anything?"

"No." There was a moment of silence. "Elizabeth, I want you to stay away from here. Someone is after me, and I can't be watching out for you and be here too."

"You don't have to watch out for me."

"I do. Look, now is not the time to talk about this. I'll call you again in a few days. I have to go. Good bye, Elizabeth."

"Good bye. I love—," she stopped. He'd already hung up.

Several days passed. She went to school, graded papers and wished the kids a happy holiday when they left for school break. She dreamed of Maria and Don Salucci, though Elizabeth couldn't see his face, followed by a jumbled nightmare about Mrs. Sargent and Dante. The woman called him a dirty I-talian and tried to bury him in her flower garden. Only he wasn't dead. He kept calling her name. "Elizabeth. Elizabeth." He reached out and touched her, his hand cold. She jerked upright.

"Elizabeth." Dante stood next to the bed. "I didn't mean to frighten you. I let myself in."

She rose to her knees and flung her arms around his neck. He wrapped his arms around her.

"I'm sorry, Dante. I'm so sorry," she murmured, stroking his hair.

He squeezed her tighter, and Elizabeth could feel his body shaking as he wept into the material of her nightgown. She just held him. After her family's deaths, it was the one thing she'd longed for on so many lonely nights. The comfort of a loving embrace.

"Sorry," he whispered a few minutes later.

"It's okay. How is she?"

"Still in a coma. She has some burns, but the immediate concern is the smoke in her lungs." Light from the hall fell across his face. The anguish in his voice matched the pain in his eyes. "The doctors think there's been some improvement in her breathing. Now, it's a waiting game. It hurts to watch her struggle." He shook his head. "I feel so helpless. Gino is there now. I'm checking into a hotel, but I had to see you first, to talk to you."

"Okay. I'm glad to see you too. I've been worried these last few days." Elizabeth climbed off the bed. She put a hand along either side of his face and raised up on her toes to lay a tender kiss on his lips. "I love you."

He nodded. "I know. We need to talk. Let's go out into the living room."

"Okay." She pulled on her robe and led the way, sitting on the sofa. "Would you like some coffee or something to eat?"

"No, thanks. I'm not hungry." Dante dropped down next to her and rubbed his hands up and down his face a couple of times.

"Dante, Mr. Galenti said the fire was set. Is that true?"

He nodded. "Someone doused the shop in gasoline."

The face Elizabeth thought she'd seen earlier flashed in her mind. "Maybe it was Flanagan."

"No one's seen him since that day with you in the alley. He's gone. It's Salucci. He's had men following me for months."

"What? How do you know?"

"I know. Trust me. I've lived around this kind of stuff my whole life."

"Why is he after you?"

"Maybe he thinks I'm in cahoots with the Irish 'cause I didn't go to him when Flanagan tried to put the squeeze on me." He ran his hands through his hair. "I don't know, but I'm going to find out."

"Mr. Galenti works for him. What does he say?"

"He still insists it isn't Salucci."

"Don't you believe him?"

"I don't know." Dante shrugged. "Whenever I ask Gino, he just says it isn't the Don, but won't say anything else."

"Well, maybe it isn't him."

"Maybe." He leaned his head back against the sofa.

"Dante, have you thought about what you're going to do?"

"As far as what?"

"The shop. I'm sure insurance will pay to help you rebuild it."

"Nope." He didn't lift his head. "No insurance."

"What?"

"Nobody would insure the business. Not in our neighborhood." He sighed. "How did the insurance agent put it? Oh yeah, he'd be more than willing to insure it, if I relocated out of Little Italy."

"Never mind that. We'll figure something out."

"Thanks, but there's nothing to figure out. I have some money in the bank. That's going to go to Mama's hospital care and finding a place to bring her home to."

She squeezed his hand. "That's fine. We'll worry about the rest of it later."

He was quiet for a few minutes. "Elizabeth, that's why I came here to talk to you."

She didn't like his serious tone. "What do you mean?"

His sigh was deep. "I want you to know I love you, probably from the first day I laid eyes on you at Port Johnson." He turned to look at her. "More than I've ever loved anyone or anything."

She gave him a tentative smile. "I love you too."

Dante's expression remained serious as he studied her face. "We're not going to be able to see each other anymore."

Elizabeth sat upright. "What are you talking about? No. Not this again."

He sighed. "Elizabeth, you've got to see reason here. Someone is after me, what better way to get to me than to use you? I'm not having it."

"You don't have a choice. We're together."

He sat upright and shook his head. "I do have a choice. The women in my life always end up hurt. I can't let that happen to you." Dante stood up. "I wanted to come and say goodbye."

"What?" Elizabeth jumped up off the couch.

"I've arranged for Nico's father to give you a ride on Wednesdays and Sundays."

"No. Please, Dante. You can't do this." Elizabeth could hear the hysteria in her own voice.

"It's done. I have to stay away. It's for the best."

"Please, you can't leave me." It came out as a wail.

"Shh. Shh." He brushed his lips against hers. "I'll always love you, Elizabeth. Always."

"No, no, no." She stared at the door he closed behind him for several moments before collapsing onto the floor. She laid there and sobbed until there were no more tears, and still she didn't move. She'd been left alone again.

Chapter 16

"Okay, gentleman, that's it for tonight's class. Please pick up your new worksheets on your way out."

"*Arrivederci.*"

"*Arrivederci,* Roberto. Good work tonight."

"Miss Wellman?"

"Yes, Alessio?" She gave the young man a faint smile. "What do you need?"

He cleared his throat. "Well, the band has a dance to do Saturday night, and they wanted to know if you'd sing with us?"

"Oh, I'm sorry, Alessio. I have a prior engagement." *Liar.*

"Okay, no that's okay." He tried to mask his look of disappointment. "Maybe another time."

She nodded.

"I talked to Nicolina on the telephone this afternoon, so she will probably ask you in school tomorrow too." He turned to leave, but turned back. "It is good news about Mrs. Montenari, no?"

"I'm sorry. What news?"

"She woke up yesterday afternoon."

"Really? That's the best news I've heard in weeks."

He nodded. "Nicolina says she's in and out, of waking up, you know. I guess she is not speaking much yet and doing a lot of coughing, but she drank some water."

"That's wonderful, Alessio. Thank you for telling me."

"You're welcome. Good night."

Dante must be ecstatic. Dante. It'd been over a month since he'd walked out her front door. For the first few days after, every car had Elizabeth running to the window, and every night she'd double check to make sure the spare key was in its spot. But, true to his word, he'd stayed away. She'd put the velvet dress at the back of the closet, and as the days seeped into weeks Elizabeth reverted to her bun, black oxfords and drab dresses. Slipping them on felt like donning armor. Just what she needed to protect her from anyone ever hurting her this way again.

Two weeks ago, she'd looked up Mr. Galenti's telephone number and called to inquire about Maria. He'd said her burns were healing, but other than that not much change. When Elizabeth mentioned visiting the hospital, the man had told her she wouldn't be allowed in without special permission from Dante, she wasn't family. So, she'd stayed away. *Surely, now that Maria is awake it'll be different.* Just because Dante didn't want her anymore wasn't any reason to shun his mother.

"Mr. Moretti?" Elizabeth nudged the man awake. He often slept through the Wednesday night class. "*Finito.*"

"*Sì? Finito?*"

She nodded. "Would you take me to the hospital?"

He removed his hat and scratched his bald head. *"Non comprendo."*

"You don't understand?" She pantomimed coughing and put her hand to her forehead.

"Oh, *sì. Ospedale.*"

"Yes. Yes. Thank you."

It was late when Mr. Moretti dropped her off. Elizabeth's oxfords squeaked on the tile in the quiet hallway. *218. 220. 222.* That was the last room number in the corridor. She took a left around the corner. A waiting area at the end of the squat hallway housed a couple of chairs and a coffee table. A folded newspaper and several cups sat on the table. *I must have missed it.* She turned to leave and stopped. *224.* Elizabeth stood in front of the closed door, not sure what to do. It was past visiting hours.

The heavy portal pushed open with a quiet swish. Elizabeth stepped inside. The warm air smelled of rubbing alcohol with an underlying odor of disinfectant. There was no one in the room. She approached the bed. Maria Montenari lay on her side facing the door, her eyes closed. The wheeze of labored breathing could be heard through the oxygen mask strapped over her nose and mouth. Thinner, Maria's skin looked translucent, adding to the aura of frailness. A scabbed-over burn marred her cheek, as well as two more burns on her arm.

She's going to get better. The thought brought a sense of relief and tears to Elizabeth's eyes. She fumbled in her bag for a handkerchief.

"'Lo."

The sound was so quiet behind the mask Elizabeth almost missed it. She glanced at the bed. Warm brown eyes returned her gaze. "Oh, Mrs. Montenari, I've missed you so much." She dropped to her knees beside the bed, eye level with Maria.

Maria raised her index finger an inch or so to point at herself and gave an almost imperceptible nod.

"You too?" Elizabeth smiled and in a careful gesture, covered the woman's hand with her own. "I'm not going to stay long. I just wanted to come and see you for a moment and to let you know I'm thinking..." The swish of the door stopped her. She rose and turned, expecting to come face to face with Dante.

Instead, it was an older man Elizabeth had never seen before. He was well dressed in a suit and overcoat. He removed his hat, revealing gray hair with a few remaining streaks of black. His lean, still handsome features registered surprise for just a moment. He nodded. "Miss Wellman."

How does he know my name? I don't know this man. Though he did look vaguely familiar. "Have we met?"

He shook his head. "No."

Is he here to hurt Maria? Elizabeth took a step closer to the bed. "I don't know who you are, but I think you'd better leave. Mrs. Montenari needs her rest. The nurse will be back any minute." She took another step back, bumping into the edge of the bed.

The man shook his head. "No, she won't."

What'd he do to her? Maybe that's why no one had stopped Elizabeth on the way in. Panic churned in the pit of her stomach. *I've got to protect her. Think.* Elizabeth's eyes darted around the immediate vicinity, finding nothing she could use as a weapon. "Get back. I'm warning you."

"That is not necessary."

"I won't let you hurt her. You'll have to get through me first." Elizabeth felt the slightest tug on the back of her coat. "Don't worry, Mrs. Montenari. I won't let him near you, I promise." Another tug, more insistent. "Don't move." She quickly glanced behind her and brought her gaze forward again. The man hadn't moved. Another tug. She turned sideways, keeping the man in sight. "Mrs. Montenari, please. I'm trying to protect you." She glanced down at the woman. Maria Montenari shook her head and tried to say something, only to produce a spasm of coughing.

"Now, look at what you've done."

The man pushed past Elizabeth in a brusque movement to bend over the woman in the bed. "Maria, *cara mia.* Remember what the doctor said. Take a deep breath in through your nose. Relax." He rubbed the woman's back. "There. That's better. Would you like a sip of water?" The man's voice was gentle.

Elizabeth glanced past him to Maria. The woman wore a calm expression as she shook her head.

"Okay, you rest now." He turned to Elizabeth. "Outside." There was no gentleness in the order.

"You get some rest. I'll be back soon." She patted the woman's arm before following the man out to the hallway.

"Miss Wellman, I don't—"

"How do you know my name?"

"I know a great deal about you. Even that you have a passable singing voice."

Is he trying to scare me? "Lots of people know I sing. Were you at the Christmas dance at St. Anthony's parish?"

He shook his head. "Your sister sings also. Where is she now? Still in England?"

No one but Dante knew about Katherine. "How do you know that?"

"I make it my business to know about people."

His penetrating stare and lack of emotion were beginning to make her nervous. "Who are you?"

"Vincenzo Salucci."

"You're the Don?"

His expression hardened. "I am a business man."

"What business do you have with Mrs. Montenari?"

"I'm not in the habit of explaining myself."

Elizabeth swallowed as he stood silent. *Don't back down.* She too remained silent.

"Fine." He held up a gloved finger. "This one time, but never again. It's not good for business. Do you understand?"

She nodded.

"I've known Maria since she was a girl back in the old country. She's a very special woman."

"Yes, she is, but you're not family. In fact, Dante thinks you're the one who set the fire. I can't believe he would allow you to visit her."

The man said nothing.

The silence in the hall was punctuated by the faint clank of the elevator arriving down at the other end of the corridor.

"He doesn't know, does he?"

The man stood with his arms crossed as he shook his head, and Elizabeth was hit with a niggling sense of familiarity again. "I mean no disrespect, sir, but perhaps it would be better if you left."

"I think not. You're right, Dante doesn't know, which explains why I'm here so late. But why are you here at this time of night? Unless of course, for some reason Dante doesn't want you here either."

Elizabeth stiffened at the man's words. It hurt to have the truth stated out loud. "He doesn't, but it's not because he doesn't trust me. It's because we're no longer together."

He nodded. "It's probably just as well you broke it off. It's obvious you're well educated, but you two are from different worlds. He has nothing to offer you. No business. No money."

Without thought, Elizabeth stepped closer to the man. "How dare you? Dante is a wonderful person. It doesn't matter if he has money or not. For all your money, he's a better man than you'll ever be."

"He is a better man." His gaze didn't leave her face.

Elizabeth was close enough to smell his expensive cologne as well as see the tiny mole at the corner of one of his unblinking eyes.

"At first, I didn't know, but he did well to choose you. You should reconsider and take him back, Miss Wellman."

She stepped back and held herself erect. "Not that it's any of your business, but Dante broke it off. He said he was afraid I'd get hurt." She narrowed her eyes. "By you. Does he have anything to worry about? Are you planning on hurting me?" Elizabeth held her breath, unable to believe she was having this conversation.

"If I wanted you hurt, it'd already be done." The man relaxed his posture after a moment and shook his head. "No. Any more than I would hurt Maria." He sighed. "I love her. I've always loved her. Even when I married someone else. Even when she married someone else. And she loves me too." His voice sounded tired, resigned.

"Does Dante know this?"

"No. He isn't to know. Maria's always been insistent about that."

"Why? Mrs. Montenari's husband is dead. She's free now."

"But I am not." He pulled off his overcoat. "Miss Wellman, believe me when I say I would lay down my life to keep Maria and Dante safe. It's not me who brought this misery into his life, but I am going to do whatever it takes to find out who's responsible and end it."

"I hope you do. He doesn't deserve this. He's been through enough."

The Don nodded. "Perhaps if you reassure him it's not me, he'll come back to you. Do you want to know where he is? I can tell you the hotel."

"No. It won't do any good. Someone is doing these things. He'll still stay away thinking he's protecting me." She sighed. "Besides, I wouldn't be able to convince Dante I know it's not you unless I tell him about this conversation."

"*Sì.* That is true."

"And then he'd probably put a stop to these visits."

"No one, not even Dante, will stop me from visiting Maria."

His features tightened, leaving Elizabeth no doubt this statement came from the Don Salucci. "Which is why I'm not going to tell him." Laughter from around the corner pulled her attention away for a moment.

Gino Galenti and an older woman in a white uniform rounded the corner. "Good evening, Mr. Salucci. How are you?"

"Fine, Nurse Raynor. How was the food?"

"Delicious. And Gino—Mr. Galenti is such a good dinner companion. You all are spoiling me, bringing all this food in."

Vincenzo Salucci smiled at the squat woman. "We just want to thank you for taking such good care of Mrs. Montenari."

"Well, thank you." The woman's gaze shifted to Elizabeth and her smile lessened. "Who's this? You know, I haven't said anything about you being here late at night, Mr. Salucci, but I can't have all kinds of people in here. I'll get in trouble."

Gino stepped forward. "Miss Wellman, what are you doing here? I told you over the telephone Dante—"

The Don put a hand up to interrupt him. "It's okay, Gino. Nurse Raynor, my niece just stopped by to check in. She and Mrs. Montenari are very close. You wouldn't mind if she stopped by once in a while to visit, would you?"

"Gee, I don't know."

"Gino, why don't you have Nurse Raynor try one of the pastries we brought from DeLuca's Bakery?"

"Sure, boss. Right this way. I left them down by your station." He led the nurse away.

"Thank you."

"You're welcome, Miss Wellman. Please come back and see Maria soon."

"I will." *Is this right, deceiving Dante?* "Ahh, good night." She turned away.

Chapter 17

"They are not gone whose lives in beauty so unfolding
Have left their own sweet impress everywhere;
Like flowers, while we linger in beholding,
Diffusing fragrance on the summer air.
They are not gone, for grace and goodness can not perish,
But must develop in immortal bloom;
The viewless soul, the real self we love and cherish,
Shall live and flourish still beyond the tomb.

They are not gone though lost to observation,
And dispossessed of those dear forms of clay,
Though dust and ashes speak of desolation;
The spirit-presence - this is ours alway."

Elizabeth closed the book.

"Thank you for reading to me." Maria smiled. "That was beautiful. Who wrote it?"

"A poetess named Hattie Howard. It's one of my favorites. Sometimes it helps me to read it when I'm missing my—when I'm lonely." Elizabeth sat the book on the stand next to Maria's bed. "I'm going to leave it here, in case you'd like to read more later."

"Thank you." Maria coughed and shifted in the bed. "Elizabeth, I made Dante tell me what happened after I saw your scars. You know, sometimes it helps with the hurt to talk about family."

Elizabeth nodded. "Maybe, but I still find it hard to talk about them." She cleared her throat. "So, I don't."

"I understand. But if you ever want to, I'm here to listen." Maria paused for a few moments. "You know, Dante will come to his senses sooner or later."

"I don't know about that, but how is he doing? Really?"

The woman shook her head. "In my opinion, not so good. He took work in the munitions factory. He's been doing double shifts to make extra money. He's also been to several banks about a loan and no one will give him the money to rebuild. He has nothing left to back it up."

"He has talent—that should be back up enough for anyone. Do you know he made my dress for the Christmas dance?"

"I do."

"It's the most beautiful dress I've ever owned, and more importantly, I felt beautiful in it. That hasn't happened in a long time. He needs to find a backer and expand his business. There has to be someone." Tears welled in Elizabeth's eyes. "I miss him so much. He's my closest friend here."

"I think you two were becoming closer than just friends. *Si?*"

Elizabeth blushed. "Yes. I thought so. He thinks he's protecting me, by not seeing me. All he's doing is hurting me. "

Maria gave Elizabeth a sad smile. "That boy, he's always trying to do the right thing for the wrong reasons." She sat silent in the bed for a few moments. "You know, I understand the hurt of losing someone you love."

Elizabeth shifted in the chair. "Your husband?"

"Marco? No." The woman shook her head and raised a hand at Elizabeth's surprised look. "Oh, don't misunderstand. Marco was an excellent father to Dante and a good man, we got along fine." She sighed. "No, I'm talking about most of my family—my parents, grandparents, and except for Rosa, the rest of my sisters and brothers. I never saw them again once I got here."

"You couldn't afford to go back?"

"I couldn't afford to go back for my family's sake. It would—" A coughing spasm cut off her words.

Elizabeth poured some water and helped Maria take a drink. "Maybe I should let you rest now."

"No, No. I'll be okay." The words came out with a bit of a rasp. "Please don't leave. I enjoy your company. I just need a couple more sips of that water." After drinking, Maria laid her head back on the pillow. The tick of the steam radiator sounded across the small room as Maria studied the ceiling for a moment, her gray hair mussed by the pillow behind her head. "Where were we?"

"You were talking about going back home, or not going back actually." Elizabeth sat the glass on the night stand.

"Yes. Yes, that's right." Maria pushed herself up a little higher in the bed.

"I'll get you another pillow." Elizabeth scooped a pillow off the foot of the bed and tucked it behind Maria's back.

Maria settled against the pillow and sighed. "Thank you. I can breathe a little better now." She ran a hand over her hair to smooth it. "You know, back in the old country, just like here, there were families headed by a Don. Only there, the families were much more powerful. To make even stronger alliances, the Dons would arrange marriages between their children, often at a young age."

Elizabeth dropped into the chair next to the bed. "Your father was a Don?"

"No, no. My family was very poor, but Vincenzo's father was." "Don Salucci?"

"Yes. His father betrothed him when he was only four, to the daughter of another Don."

"That's horrible. I couldn't imagine that."

The woman shrugged. "It was the way of things."

"So, how did you meet Don Salucci?"

The woman smiled. "Through Gino. My parents took Gino in when his mother and father died in an influenza epidemic. We grew up together. When I was nineteen, Gino went to work for the old Don. He was young; he wanted money. Anyway, he got to know Vincenzo and brought him home to a Sunday dinner after mass. From the moment I saw Vincenzo, I had to be near him, and he felt it too. Soon, we were spending what time we could together using poor Gino as an excuse. My father would have killed me if he'd known what I did. One thing led to another," she paused and studied her folded hands. "And the next thing I knew, I was with child." She didn't look up. "I have no excuse for this behavior other than to say we were in love. Vincenzo wanted to marry right away and went to his father." Maria attempted to clear her throat. "Could I have another sip of water, please?"

Elizabeth handed her the glass and waited. *The Don and Mrs. Montenari?*

Maria took a sip and coughed, and then took another before handing it back. "The old Don told Vincenzo he would think about it." Maria shook her head. "Instead he had two men take me right off the street outside my house and bring me to him. I can't tell you how scared I was."

It was clear from the woman's face some of that fear still lingered all these years later. "He told me Vincenzo was just passing time with me, he was betrothed. I got so mad at hearing Vincenzo was to marry someone else I forgot who I was talking to. I called him a liar and spit in his face. He punched me so hard, he knocked me out. When I opened my eyes, poor Gino was there looking as scared as I felt. I didn't move. The old Don was ranting that he was going to get rid of me, so nobody would find me or the sin I carried in my belly." She smoothed her hair back again. "I knew if he said it, it was as good as done. I remember tears running down my face as I lay there on the dirty, cold floor, but I didn't make a sound." Maria had a faraway look in her eyes. "To this day, I still can't believe Gino had the nerve to step up to the Don, but he did. I couldn't hear what was being said, but a few minutes later the Don came over and lifted me off the floor by my hair." She shook her head. "He was such a vicious man. I thought he was going to kill me right then. Instead, he told me Gino was putting me on a boat to America that day. I wasn't to take anything or tell anyone. If I did, he would kill my family. He said I was to never come back. If I did, he would kill my family."

"Couldn't you go to the police?"

Maria shook her head. "It didn't work that way. The only chance I had of saving my baby was to get on that boat, or I can assure you, I would have been dead by the next morning. I think the only thing that saved me was the old man had no idea Gino and I knew each other, or he would've never sent him to the docks with me."

"Did you ever ask what he said to the Don?"

"Gino told him he'd recently been in a similar situation with a girl, and his priest advised him it was better to let your blood live than burn in hell for eternity."

Elizabeth couldn't hide her shocked expression. "Mr. Galenti? He got a girl in trouble?"

"No. Gino's never been with a woman in his life. He's, how should I say it, not interested?"

"Ohh?" Maria nodded as realization washed over Elizabeth's features. "Ohh."

"Sì. But the old man didn't know that—nobody did, but me. Gino knew it would only be a matter of time before the Don, or someone else figured it out, and then he'd be dead too, so when I sailed away Gino Galenti was with me."

"Wow, that's quite a story." Elizabeth shook her head and rubbed her arms. "It gives me goose bumps. Do you mind if I ask you another question?"

"Of course not."

Elizabeth hesitated. "How'd you meet your husband?"

"Well, we came to New York through Ellis Island. Gino had enough money left to rent a room for a month, but we often had growling stomachs those first few weeks. Then Gino found a job in a factory. But me, there was nothing for me. Until the day I was out walking to forget my hunger and saw a help wanted sign in the window of a tailor's shop. I was desperate, so I went in. At first, Marco Montenari said no, but when he saw my stitching, he agreed. After a month, he asked me out for coffee. After two months, he asked me to marry him. I said yes. He was a widower and close to forty. I was twenty. But it was okay. The baby and I were safe. Shortly thereafter, we moved here to New Jersey and eventually Gino settled here too."

"Wait. So, you had another child before Dante?"

Maria shook her head.

"Oh, I'm sorry. How insensitive of me. Did you lose the baby?"

Maria shook her head again. "No. You misunderstand." She said nothing for several moments. "I've only ever had one child. Dante."

"What? That would mean..." Elizabeth's eyes widened. "No."

"Yes. Dante is Vincenzo's child. His only child."

"Does Dante know this?"

"No."

"Why not?"

The woman shrugged. "I always planned on telling him someday. It's just never seemed like the right time, you know? He loved Marco. And I guess I still worry he will think less of me for what I did—without the benefit of a marriage bed."

"Dante loves you very much. I think you're underestimating him." Elizabeth sat quiet, letting all these details sink in, and Maria let her. "Do you mind if I ask how Don Salucci came into the picture again?"

Maria hacked into a handkerchief. "This cough is so tiring. If only my lungs would clear up, I could go home."

"Would you like some more water?"

"Not now. Thank you." Maria sighed. "Vincenzo? Well, when he couldn't find me, he confronted the old Don. The Don told him Gino and I ran away together, and even got witnesses to swear to it. Vincenzo didn't believe it for a minute. He'd already figured out about Gino, but he had no idea if we'd really left or if his father had us killed. Either way, he had nowhere to look. Several years passed, and he finally gave in and married the woman his father had chosen. And after five years of marriage and no children, the old Don passed." Maria shook her head. "Isn't it strange how sometimes one little thing can change your whole life? At his father's funeral, someone approached Vincenzo to offer condolences, and to tell him a story about running into Gino Galenti in a restaurant in New York. It didn't take him long to find us. Poor Gino. He told me later when he first saw Vincenzo, he thought he'd come to kill him."

"What happened?"

"Gino brought him to the park where I took Dante every day. At first, I thought I was seeing a ghost. I could hardly believe he was there. We sat and talked about all that had gone on until Dante came over to us. I'll never forget, he introduced himself and stuck his little hand out to Vincenzo like he'd seen Marco do."

"How old was Dante then?"

"Seven. You should have seen Vincenzo, he couldn't take his eyes off him. And after Dante ran off to play with another little boy, Vincenzo wept. It broke my heart and made me angry at the same time."

"Angry about what?"

"Everything. I was angry at the old Don, at Vincenzo for taking a wife, at myself for taking a husband. I just got up and left the park with Dante." Maria shook her head. "For weeks, I was miserable and made sure everyone around me was too. My poor husband. It didn't help Vincenzo kept sending messages through Gino. Those were dark days for me—for all of us."

"What happened?"

The woman shrugged. "I grew up in those few weeks and got through it. I had to. I loved Vincenzo, but he had a wife, and I had a husband and a little boy who loved him. I told Vincenzo all of this when I finally agreed to talk to him. He told me he loved me and Dante too, but admitted he couldn't leave his wife, it would cause a war between the families. So, that was that, and he went back to the old country." Maria leaned her head back against the pillow and closed her eyes.

Elizabeth waited. Just as she concluded Maria had fallen asleep the woman spoke.

"But after seeing Dante, he couldn't stay away. Within two years, as the Don of the Salucci family, he decided to move the business here. There wasn't much I could say about that." She turned toward Elizabeth and gave her a rueful smile. "He's been here ever since, watching out for us. He gave Gino a job. And though he never came himself, I know over the years he's sent his people to my husband's shop for suits, to make sure Marco stayed in business, and we stayed here." The older woman's features softened. "The only thing he's ever asked in return was for me to keep him informed of how Dante was doing. Vincenzo even made sure he went to college through an anonymous scholarship. He's always wanted the best for his boy. You know, I don't much care for his wife. She grew up a spoiled girl and ended up a spoiled woman. I often wished she would've had a child he could claim, but she never conceived."

"I have to tell you, Dante doesn't trust him. He thinks the Don is behind all of this because he's had him followed."

"Would you give me a little more water, Elizabeth?" Maria took another drink. "Vincenzo's had him followed to try and protect him."

"Mrs. Montenari, I need to ask you something else."

The woman nodded.

"Why are you telling me all this? Why don't you just tell Dante?"

The woman sighed and shifted her thin frame in the bed. "Because I trust you. I may not be ready to tell him, but I realized after the fire if something happened to me, neither Vincenzo nor Gino would tell him out of respect for me. When the time is right, Dante deserves the truth. But I must warn you, please don't discuss this matter with others. It would not be good."

She's serious. Elizabeth studied the other woman's solemn features. "I would never do that, but I think you should tell him yourself."

"We'll see."

The door opened. It was Don Salucci. "Good evening, ladies."

"Hello, Vincenzo." Maria's voice was soft with just a hint of hoarseness.

He smiled at the woman in the bed, and it struck Elizabeth why she thought she knew him. *You don't know him, you know his son.* Dante was a younger version of the Don with many of the same mannerisms. It was all too much to comprehend at the moment. "Well, I think I should be going. Mrs. Montenari, I'll be back in a couple of days to visit again." She pulled on her coat.

"Miss Wellman, my driver is downstairs. Please, let him take you home. Just tell him your address."

Elizabeth gave Vincenzo Salucci a sardonic smile. "I bet he already knows it. Good night."

Chapter 18

Elizabeth hung the man's overcoat up on the rack near the door. "Please have a seat. Would you like a cup of tea, or I can perc you some coffee?"

Gino Galenti unbuttoned his suit coat and settled onto the sofa before pulling out a large gold watch. "That's very kind of you, Miss Wellman, but no thank you. I have a dinner meeting in about an hour."

"I'll get right to it then, I don't want to make you late." She took the seat across from him. "First of all, thank you for coming."

He nodded and waited.

"Ahh, the reason I asked you to stop by is I've been thinking about something for a few days and doing some research on the idea, but can go no further."

"Okay. Why is that?"

"Well, the problem is I have no contacts here. I thought being a local business man maybe you could help me, or at least put me in touch with the right person." She gave him a weak smile. "I'm not making much sense, am I?"

"Take your time." Gino was the picture of patience.

"Sorry. It's just I'm not quite sure how to go about this." Elizabeth studied her intertwined fingers. "Or even where to start."

The large man remained relaxed against the sofa. "Well, Miss Wellman, why don't you start at the beginning?"

"Yes. Good idea. The beginning? I'm not sure where that is exactly." Elizabeth took a deep breath and exhaled. "Mr. Galenti, did you know Dante's been to numerous banks looking for a loan to restart his business and has been turned down by every one of them?"

Gino nodded. "Yes. Maria told me. I've offered Dante money to rebuild the business several times over the last few weeks, but he's refused each time. He hasn't come out and said it, but I know he thinks it's the Don's money. It's not; it's mine."

"Dante is a proud man. He would consider any such offer charity." Elizabeth hesitated a moment. "Which is why I have another idea, but some of it depends on whether you can help me with contacts."

"What kind of contacts?"

"Just a moment, I'll get to that. But first, my idea." She took a breath. "I think Dante should design and manufacture clothing."

"What kind of clothing? He's a tailor. He makes suits."

Elizabeth straightened up in the chair. "Any kind of clothing, all kinds of clothing."

"Does Dante want to design clothing?"

"He's told me he doesn't mind the design part, and he has a natural flair for it." Elizabeth slid forward to the edge of her chair.

"As I told you, I've been doing a little research. I've visited all of the downtown stores. Every single store had at least a small section of what the salesgirl called off-the-rack. At Closson's, every department—men's, women's and even children's featured a ready-to-wear section. I think Dante could design and have other people do the actual sewing."

"Other people? Who?"

Elizabeth shrugged. "I'm not sure. But I bet there are women from around the neighborhood who can sew and would like to make some extra money. We might even be able to hire a few men for some of the heavier stuff. We'd have to—he'd have to advertise, to see who applies."

"So you're talking about Dante going from a one-man shop to opening a factory?"

Elizabeth ignored the skepticism in the man's voice. "Yes, I guess I am. Look, Mr. Galenti, I know it sounds like a lot, but I think it would be fine. If we can find the property, he could start out small. And if at all possible, the property should be somewhere near the bus routes, so people could get there easily."

"You're serious?"

Elizabeth nodded. "I think he could handle it."

"Miss Wellman, I can tell you've put some thought into this." Gino cleared his throat. "The thing is, I'm not sure you've thought it all the way through."

"I beg your pardon?"

He held up a hand. "Please don't take this the wrong way, but have you ever been in business for yourself?"

Elizabeth hesitated for a moment. "No, but my father's company was very successful."

"Did you work there?"

"Well, no, but I was there a lot."

"Miss Wellman, there's no question you're a smart woman, but I've been in business for years and no offense, all the book learning in the world won't prepare you for running a business. Only time and experience can do that. Besides, you're forgetting one thing." His tone was gentle.

"What?"

"If Dante can't get a loan, and he won't take money from anyone, how do you propose he pay for this factory?"

Relief washed over Elizabeth. "Oh, I think I have that part figured out. Again, I'll need some help from you. I'll be right back." She stood and disappeared down the hall to return with a mahogany box she put on the coffee table. "Hold on. This will just take a few minutes."

"Do you need help?" The man started to rise.

"No, no. I'm fine." Elizabeth made several more trips. In the end, eight identical boxes, stacked two high, sat on the coffee table. Each box had six thin drawers. She sat on the sofa next to Gino and rested a hand on the top of the box nearest her. "Mr. Galenti, as I told you, my father was a very successful business man. Because of that my family enjoyed many fine things in life." She pulled open the top drawer of the first box. Rings, bracelets, earrings and several large necklaces rested against a cushioned black velvet lining. All were set with diamonds. Elizabeth slid the drawer closed and pulled open the next one. It was just as full, but each piece contained rubies. She rubbed a finger across a large blood red stone in a teardrop setting suspended from a heavy gold chain. "I remember this piece. My mother wore it to our annual Christmas party once when I was young." Moments passed as she studied the necklace. The faintest scent of Chanel No. 5 drifted from the box. Her mother's favorite perfume. Tears welled up as Elizabeth gently pushed the drawer closed. "Please excuse me a moment." She went into the kitchen and swiped at her eyes with a tea towel.

"Miss Wellman?" Gino called from the living room. "I'm going to need to leave soon for my meeting."

You can do this. "Coming." Elizabeth drew in a deep breath and tossed the towel on the counter. "I'm sorry, Mr. Galenti." She settled back on the sofa next to him. "I inherited this from my mother, and though a few of the pieces might remind me of her, I have to be realistic. I never wear it and probably never will. So, I'd like to put it to good use by selling it and putting the proceeds toward the rest of my plan." She picked up a bundle of folded papers off the table and handed it to him. "Here's a copy of the last appraisal done on my part of the collection."

"Your part? This isn't all of it?"

Elizabeth shook her head. "Goodness no. My sister has an equal share too."

Gino's mouth dropped open.

She reached over and gave his hand a gentle squeeze. "I told you my father was successful, and my mother had no qualms about spending his money on expensive jewelry. She used to refer to it as her rainy day fund."

He looked the papers over. "Miss Wellman, are you sure you want to do this? According to this list, there's a sizable fortune in these boxes. Someday you may need what money these jewels will bring for yourself, or at least want to pass some of it on to your own children."

Elizabeth shook her head. "Mr. Galenti, even though I wasn't allowed to run my father's company after his death, I was more than capable of negotiating a substantial settlement with the board of directors for my sister and myself. When it was over, Mr. Whitman, the chairman called me an extortionist." She smiled. "I took that as high praise. Regardless, the point is, I already have more than enough funds for my simple life style. And as far as children, it's not an option at this point, but in the unlikely event it should ever happen, I've saved a few special pieces." She produced another piece of paper. "My mother also had numerous furs. They're in cold storage right now, but I'd like to sell them too. Can you help me with this?"

"I've had some experience with this type of transaction over the years. The Don's wife likes jewelry as well." Gino smoothed down his mustache. "I'd say a collection of this size needs to go to one of the New York auction houses. But are you sure you want to do this? Have you really thought this over?"

Elizabeth nodded. "Yes, to both questions."

"Okay then. I'll get it arranged as soon as possible. You said you wanted to put the proceeds toward the rest of your plan." He pulled out his watch again. "Can you tell me the rest in the next fifteen minutes or so?"

"Yes, of course, since I'm going to need your help. This part isn't as clear cut. First of all, do you have contacts in the banking business?"

"Sì."

"Contacts who'd be willing to stretch the truth a little?"

"Maybe." The man's furrowed brow bunched his beetle-like eyebrows. "What'd you have in mind?"

"Well, my thoughts were if we can find a suitable property, we'll purchase it with the proceeds from the auction. Then, I was thinking your contact in the bank could offer it to Dante as a foreclosure loan for a few thousand dollars."

"Hmm." Gino thought for a moment and then nodded. "That just might work, but I don't think you need to sell all this." He glanced at the lists again. "I think one box, maybe two should get you enough funds for the purchase."

"Maybe, but I want to make sure I have enough money for equipment too."

Gino gave her a quizzical look. "What equipment?"

Elizabeth shrugged. "To be honest, I have no idea of specifics. What do you think? Some sewing machines? Maybe tables for cutting? Or is there some kind of machine that cuts?"

"I don't know, but I can do some checking around." He tucked the lists in the inside pocket of his suit coat. "Do you mind if I ask you another question?"

She smiled. "Not at all, but I'm warning you, I know nothing about sewing."

"It's not about sewing." Gino cleared his throat. "I know Dante has stopped seeing you. So, why would you do this for him?"

"I told you, I think he's really talented." Elizabeth shifted on the sofa.

"Is that the only reason?"

"Yes, of course."

"I'm glad to hear you say that. I was worried you thought this might bring him back to you."

"What?" Elizabeth splayed her hand flat on her chest. "Absolutely not."

"Good, because if Dante ever finds out we did this, he'll never forgive you. Or me." Gino slowly raised himself off the couch.

"He'll never hear it from me. In fact, I don't think we should tell anyone. Not even Mrs. Montenari."

He nodded. "Fine."

Elizabeth rose too. "There is one more reason." She picked at her fingernail for a moment.

"Yes?"

When Elizabeth looked up there were tears in her eyes for the second time in less than twenty minutes. "Because I love him. I'll always love him, whether we're together or not. I can't help it."

"Ahh—that I understand. We love who we love, there is no changing that—for you, for me, for anyone." He gave her shoulder a gentle squeeze. "I'll be in touch."

Almost two weeks had passed when Elizabeth's telephone rang on a Friday evening. "Hello?"

"Miss Wellman, it's Gino Galenti. How are you?"

"Mr. Galenti, I'm fine, thank you. How are you?" She held her breath.

"Good, good. I think I've located a place suitable for purchase. Would you like to come and see it?"

Excitement coursed through Elizabeth. "Yes, of course. When? Now?"

"No, no. I'm going to visit Maria at the hospital tonight and bring her some dinner."

Elizabeth tamped down her disappointment. "Oh, that's wonderful."

"Hopefully soon, we can bring her home. Her breathing isn't strong yet, but she'll get there. My Maria's a fighter. Hold on a second, Miss Wellman."

Elizabeth heard him talking to someone before he continued.

"Miss Wellman, if you're available, I'll be by your house tomorrow morning at nine o'clock."

"Tomorrow. Nine o'clock. Yes, of course."

"Good. I think you're going to be pleased. I'll see you then."

Elizabeth found it hard to sleep and waited on her porch as Gino Galenti's car pulled up to the curb the next morning. She flew down the steps and climbed in next to Gino as soon as the driver opened the back door.

"Ready?" Even though it was a Saturday, Mr. Galenti looked very natty in an impeccable black suit.

"Yes, I can't wait." Elizabeth's smile lit up her face.

"Good. It won't take too long to get there."

They rode along in silence, heading west. Soon, the closely built neighborhoods fell away to houses with large lawns. They kept going. Elizabeth studied everything out of her window. She'd never been this far out of town before.

"Here we are. Adolfo, please pull up to the glass door in the front."

The car came to a stop, and Elizabeth had the door open before the driver could do it for her. A large stockade fence stretched around the perimeter of the parking lot and continued on behind the large brick building before her, its many windows gleamed in the morning sun. "How far does that fence go?"

"All the way around this part of the property. Shall we?" Mr. Galenti unlocked the front door. "The realtor handling this property is a close friend of mine." He led the way into the building. "In the front there's a lobby and several offices. Pretty standard. This way." He pushed through a door at the end of the lobby into a large room. Several rows of tables were arranged down the length of the room to create a center aisle. "This is a large work room. Perhaps for cutting material?"

She nodded. "Maybe, I'm not sure, but I bet Dante would know."

"True." He headed to the right. "Over here," he opened one of a set of double doors, "we have what looks like a dining room and kitchen, though I doubt it was ever used." Elizabeth glanced inside. The room was filled with boxes and smelled musty. She stepped back and he closed the door before heading to the main room again. "Now you have two choices to get to the floors above. Stairs, or there's a freight elevator at the other end of the floor."

"Stairs." She slowed her pace to match Gino's as they climbed. "This place is huge."

"It is. There are several out-buildings too." They finally reached the second floor, and Elizabeth could hardly believe her eyes. The room was filled with small tables aligned in numerous rows, and each table held a sewing machine. She walked between the tables, stopping to check out a machine. It looked old. "Do these still work?"

Mr. Galenti nodded. "Yes, according to the realtor. They may need some maintenance."

"How many are there?"

"110."

"My goodness. That's a lot. What's on the third floor?"

"A few spare rooms, but mainly that's where the garments were pressed and packed for shipment."

Elizabeth glanced around the room again. "So, this really was a sewing factory?"

"Of a sort. From what I understand, it was more of a sweat shop and had been since the mid-30s." Gino walked to one of the windows. "The workers were all immigrant women with no families and no place to go. The owner let them stay in those buildings out back and then collected their wages as rent."

Elizabeth came to stand beside him. Several rows of tiny identical cottages stood behind the factory. "How awful. That's little more than a slave. What happened? Did he get arrested?"

Gino shook his head. "No. It seems one of his workers killed him with a pair of scissors after he got drunk and raped her, or so the story goes."

"What happened to the workers?"

"They left that night, none of them wanted to deal with the police. Most people think they're working in the garment district in New York now."

"Unbelievable. Well, at least they got away." Elizabeth studied the landscape. "Can we look at some of the other buildings?"

"Of course."

Elizabeth walked around in one of the cottages. A kitchen-living room area comprised the front of the cottage. The back half held two bedrooms with a minuscule bath in between. Broken furniture and dirty mattresses littered the floor of every room. "How many people lived in here?"

Gino shrugged. "There's really no way of knowing for sure, but probably at least twenty."

"In this tiny place? Unbelievable. And why is there a mattress in the bathtub? Is there running water?"

"I believe so." He walked to the kitchen sink and turned the faucet handle. Nothing came out. Gino pulled a handkerchief from his pocket and wiped his hands. "It hasn't been turned back on yet. The owner didn't turn it on to save money. There's an old horse trough out in the back he'd fill two or three times a week. The women used buckets to haul water into the houses."

Elizabeth shook her head. "That's horrible." She looked around the cottage again. "You know, these could be fixed up. Do you think maybe Dante and his mother could live here?"

"I agree they could eventually be renovated, but not for Dante and his mother. Come with me." Gino led the way back to the front of the building and headed toward the tall stockade fence at the edge of the property. He swung open a gate and stepped through, waiting for Elizabeth. "This is where Dante and Maria can live."

She stepped through the gate and stopped, looking at Gino in disbelief. "Oh my." A two story federal style house much like the one Elizabeth had grown up in stood in the middle of several huge elm trees. A large porch stretched across the front. "Oh my. This comes with the factory?"

He nodded. "The fence was to keep the owner's wife from seeing the truth of his business, and it worked right up until she got cancer and died. He never stayed in the house again. From what I understand he slept on the third floor of the factory."

Elizabeth shook her head. "What a crazy story. But with all of this property, it must be out of our price range."

"Not really. All of the jewelry sold and for a considerable amount more than what you had it appraised for." He reached in his coat pocket. "Here are the proceeds minus the auction house's commission."

Elizabeth was stunned. The amount on the check was for twice as much as she'd expected. "So, there's enough to buy this whole place?"

Gino nodded. "Yes, and even with that, there's a sizable chunk left over. There's a war bond drive going on, if you're interested in some long term investment."

Elizabeth shook her head. "No. I don't mean to sound unpatriotic, but my family's already given a lot to the war effort. So has Dante. Financing the war is not what I'm looking for in long term investments."

"I understand. Perhaps you could do as your mother suggested and put the rest of it away for a rainy day?"

She smiled. "Perhaps I will. But for now, what do I need to do next?"

"Don't you want to know any of the details, like the price of the property?"

"Not if I don't have to. I just want it all taken care of so Dante can have a place to start his business and bring his mother home to."

"Miss Wellman, this is a lot of money. I can't believe you don't want some type of accounting for what your money is being invested in."

"Mr. Galenti, when it concerns Dante, I trust you. I know you love him like a son. And as I told you before, I have enough money for my needs. Personal experience has shown me you can have all the money in the world, and it won't keep you happy, or safe—or even alive. Besides, I know what my money is being invested in. I'm investing in Dante's business, of course, but," she indicated the brick building behind her. "I'm also investing in his workers, who'll in turn invest in the community—by shopping here, buying houses here, living here. That sounds like a much better long term investment than letting it sit in a bank or purchasing war bonds."

"Maybe you're right. Let's hope so. Okay. If you sign the back of the check, I'll take it to my contact at the bank and get the paperwork started."

"Do you have a pen?" She laid the check on the rail of the porch steps and signed her name. "There you go." Elizabeth handed him the check and the pen.

"What are you going to do if Dante doesn't want to buy this place?"

"He'll want it. Who wouldn't? The house alone is worth it. If he doesn't want it, I guess I'll have to live here." She smiled. "But he's going to take it. Have faith, Mr. Galenti."

"You know, I hope Dante comes to his senses soon and marries you. You are a rare woman."

Elizabeth shrugged. "Not really. It's just the right thing to do, and I feel good about this." She glanced up the steps. "Do you think we can take a quick tour of the house before you take me home?"

"For you, my dear, anything."

Chapter 19

Dante mopped sweat from his forehead with the sleeve of his shirt. Early morning sunlight flooded the high-ceilinged room, heated by the glass of the large windows. A bit of a cool breeze washed across his skin from one of the two windows he'd managed to lever open. He tipped his head back and enjoyed the relief the air afforded him, noticing for the first time other sounds drifting in the windows. *Birds.* Several different trills echoed from the nearby trees. He never remembered hearing any birds at their old place. Too many city sounds. He smiled. *Mama's going to love that. Maybe I should make her a couple of feeders. She can watch the birds from the front porch.*

Dante looked around the huge room, still unable to believe his luck. The same banker who'd turned him down for a loan a few weeks ago thought of him when the bank had a foreclosure. Apprehensive at the size of the property, Dante felt better about the purchase after discussing it with his mother and Gino Galenti.

Both had advised him to take the offer and use as much of the property as he needed. He'd signed papers a little over a week ago now. In that time, he'd managed to get the telephone, electricity and water back on and hired some of the men from Port Johnson to help him clean the place out in the evenings after their regular work day. As they hauled refuse from the buildings, Dante had worked on the sewing machines, pleased a lot were still functional, despite being old.

Both his mother and Gino had also encouraged him to run a help wanted ad in the newspaper. Dante wasn't sure he was ready for employees yet, even one or two, but didn't expect much, so he wasn't too worried about it—until the first day the ad ran. The phone started ringing and hadn't stopped yet. The main telephone line was in the office on the first floor of the factory, so unless he happened to be down there he'd have to hurry downstairs in an attempt to answer it. By the end of each day, his leg hurt worse than ever. But Dante now had at least a partial solution to that problem. Late yesterday afternoon, *Zia* Rosa, *Zio* Basili and Nico had shown up to look the place over and share their dinner. Nico volunteered to answer phones after school and on the weekend. Dante knew some of her impetus was the fact Alessio would be around. It didn't matter. He was thankful for the help.

He'd given them a quick tour of the factory and then the house. The furniture in the house was of good quality though dusty. He'd apologized to *Zia* Rosa about the condition of the house and explained he hadn't found the time to do the cleaning yet, but Dante assured his aunt he would, as soon as they told him he could bring Mama home. *Zia* Rosa had brushed off his apology, and they'd all sat on the big front porch to enjoy the food. It'd been a pleasant respite, and Dante looked forward to the day when they could have family meals all together again.

The one person missing from all of this was Elizabeth. So many times over the last month he'd wanted to share with her all that was happening, good and bad. *You need to stay away from her, so she can get on with her life.* But no matter how many times he reminded himself, it didn't stop the ache in his gut from missing her.

Nico told him lately Miss Wellman was more like she'd been when she first came to the school to teach. Quiet. Unsmiling. And though she still was teaching at Port Johnson, she hadn't sung with the band since the Christmas dance. Dante sighed. It did no good to dwell on Elizabeth Wellman.

Several car doors slamming sounded outside. *Who could that be?* The boys from Port Johnson were already hard at work. Interviews weren't scheduled for another two weeks. Dante wiped his hands on a rag as he headed downstairs in the freight elevator. Nico was just coming through the large glass front door as he entered the lobby area. "Hi, Nico. I thought I heard somebody."

"You did, but it isn't just me." The girl stepped around the desk to sit in the chair by the phone.

"Who else is with you?"

She smiled. "Take a look."

Dante gave her a confused look.

"Just go look."

Dante shouldered his way out the door as he finished wiping his hands only to be brought up short by several female voices, all speaking at once.

"Yoo hoo."

"Morning, Dante."

"Where's the house?"

Zia Rosa, Mrs. Carapetti, Mrs. Cammareri, Mrs. Tessio, Connie Santini and her mother, along with several more women stood in the parking lot.

Dante tucked the rag in his pocket. "Good morning, ladies. I'm sorry, but the place isn't ready for a tour."

"A tour? Maybe another day." Mrs. Carapetti stepped forward. "We're gonna tidy up the house for Maria. It's the least we can do. Your mama's helped every one of us at one time or another. It'll feel good to help her out for a change." She turned to the car parked behind her and smacked her palm flat on the hood. "Carmine, you'd better be getting out of that car and comin' to help, if you want any money this week." The plump woman shook her head and then picked up a bucket filled with rags and cleaning supplies. "Which way?"

"This way." Zia Rosa answered for Dante. The women marched off without another word, as organized as any army. Connie Santini, a turban over her hair, gave him a smile and stopped. "Hi, Dante. How are you?"

"Fine."

"Ma's still waiting for you to come over for dinner." She pouted. "How come you haven't?"

"I've been busy."

"That's okay." Connie smiled and glanced around. "I can see why. This is quite the place. You're going to really make something out of yourself." She glanced at Carmine Carapetti, who'd just climbed out of his car to light a cigarette. "Not like some of the lazy bums around here. I should've paid more attention to you when we were kids, but who knew?" She studied the brick factory for another moment. "Are you still spending time with the teacher?"

Dante shook his head.

Connie turned to look at him, and for just a second a smile widened her mouth before she donned a more solemn look. "Oh, that's too bad. I'm real sorry about that." She laid a hand on his arm. "It's her loss, and maybe it's for the best, ya know? She ain't like us." The touch of Connie's fingers became a squeeze as she moved nearer, her breast touching his arm. "Maybe you should look a little closer to home?" Her thinly plucked eyebrows gave a slight lift in unison with the questioning intonation of her words.

Dante took an involuntary step back, his nose assailed by the odor of cigarette smoke and her cloying perfume carried on the morning breeze. "Actually, Connie, it's my loss. Elizabeth Wellman is a smart and very kind woman." He lifted her fingers from his arm and retreated another step. "And everything a man could want."

She followed him. "What? I think she's a little uppity myself. Besides, how smart can she be, if she couldn't hang onto you?" Connie licked her lips. "You know, maybe we should give it a try? They say look out for the quiet ones. I'll bet once you loosened up, you wouldn't be half bad. We started something once, remember that time?"

Dante snorted. "That time? When we were in eighth grade, you mean, and I was stupid enough to think you liked me?"

"Really? You thought I liked you just because I told you to put your hands on my boobs?" She gave a loud laugh. "You were such a rube. I was just trying to make Ernesto Grimaldi jealous."

"I know." Ernesto and his friends had caught up with Dante after school. When the beating was over, Dante was bloody with two broken ribs. He'd banged up his bike with a rock and told his mother he'd had an accident riding it to cover up the beating from the bigger boys.

Connie gave him a sultry look. "So, you took a couple of smacks. It was worth it, right?" She tried to rub up against him again.

"No. It wasn't. It still isn't." Dante took another step back. "It never will be."

The woman narrowed her eyes, her expression hard. "Well now, don't you think you're something special? You always did. Just because you went to college, and now you got this big factory and that fancy house? Well, you ain't. You're still the same boring mama's boy you've always been. And I ain't hanging around and cleanin' your house like some maid. I got better things to do." Connie pulled the turban from her head and patted her stiff, bleached hair to fluff it. "Your loss." She smoothed down her dress and presented her back to Dante. "Hey, Carmine. What ya doin'?"

The man leaned against the hood of his car and watched the exaggerated sway of her hips as she strode toward him. He exhaled a cloud of smoke. "Nothin' really. I'm supposed to be helpin' Ma. Why? What'd you have in mind?"

"I feel like goin' for a ride." She stopped in front of him and reached up to drag a long red fingernail down Carmine's chest to his mid-section. "You wanna give me a ride?"

Carmine grinned. "Yeah, sure. Hop in." He opened the door for her and then closed it, leaning against the window frame.

The man kept his voice low as he spoke to Connie, but Dante heard the words nonetheless.

"Ahh, you got any money on ya? I'm a little short of cash right now, and I gotta stop by the drug store to get some rubbers."

"Jesus, you're always short on cash. Get in the damn car."

"Sure. Sure." Carmine hurried around the front of the car. "Dante, tell my Ma I'll be back later to pick her up." He climbed in the car, revved the engine and tore out of the parking lot. Dante shook his head and went to check on his mother's friends.

Hours later, all was finally quiet. The men had returned to Port Johnson. The ladies from the neighborhood had left with their rides, except for Mrs. Carapetti. Carmine never showed up. Dante offered to drive her home, but instead she squeezed into the front seat of Mr. Moretti's truck, which left Nicolina to ride in the back.

Dante helped Nico into the truck bed. She settled against the back of the cab. "You may need to start your interviews sooner than you planned." She handed him a stack of messages. "There were almost thirty calls today from people interested in applying. How many does that make?"

Dante shrugged. "I've lost count. With this batch, over a hundred, if not more."

"Well, I'll be back to help you sort them out tomorrow."

"Thanks, Nico, but don't you go to Port Johnson tomorrow?" Dante no longer attended the Sunday gatherings.

"Yes, but I'm still coming over here. I like doing this. I'm taking a business and typing course this year and really enjoying it. If you're still looking for help when I graduate in June, I may just come and apply for that job you keep threatening me with." She smiled and reached up to tap a knuckle against the back window. The truck engine started.

Dante smiled back. "I'm going to hold you to that." He stepped to the open window of the truck. "Thank you, *Zia* Rosa, Mrs. Carapetti, for all your hard work today. The house looks great, it was a big help. I'm going to see Mama at the hospital first thing tomorrow morning. She'll be very happy and thankful too, I'm sure."

"You're welcome, nephew." *Zia* Rosa gave him a tired smile. "Tell your mama I'll be by to visit her on Monday afternoon."

"Okay."

"And Dante," Mrs. Carapetti leaned forward. "We put stuff to throw away in a big pile on the back porch. Carmine was supposed to carry it to the dumpster, but who knows where he is? Probably off singing somewhere."

If you only knew. "That's fine, Mrs. Carapetti. I'll take care of it tomorrow."

"Don't hold it against Carmine, okay? He just gets distracted easy sometimes. He's going to be applying for a job here. If you give him a chance, he'll do good. I'll make sure of that. Okay?"

Dante smiled to alleviate the worried look on the woman's lined face. "Sure, Mrs. Carapetti." *Carmine?* He'd never held a job for more than a few weeks. "Thanks again, ladies, for all your help.

I really appreciate it." He stepped back from the truck as *Zio* Basili shoved it into gear. "Bye." The truck rolled forward. He raised a hand in farewell to Nico's wave. When the truck was out of sight, he turned and climbed the front steps and let himself in the house.

The transformation inside was no less than amazing. The whole place smelled of lemon oil and beeswax. Dante walked from room to room. Much of the furniture was still there, just arranged in a more pleasing manner. The rugs had been taken outside and beaten clean. The faded heavy drapes were gone, replaced by lace panels that not only framed the windows, but allowed the light from the setting sun to flood the rooms. The floors had been mopped and the walls washed down. Every surface shone, whether it was wood, glass, porcelain or metal.

This would be his first night in the house. He'd packed what few clothes he owned and checked out of the hotel this morning. Tonight he'd planned on setting up the new mattresses and box springs he'd purchased for two of the four bedrooms upstairs, but the ladies had beat him to it. Both rooms had been scrubbed and the beds made up with the new linens he'd bought.

Dante washed up and had just pulled some of *Zia* Rosa's leftover casserole out of the Frigidaire to reheat when he heard a timid knock at the front door. *Who could that be?* He opened the door to find a tall blonde standing on the other side. "Can I help you?"

She nodded. "I don't know if you remember me, Mr. Montenari." She extended her hand. "I'm Nancy Tillson."

He shook her hand. "I'm sorry, I don't."

She smoothed her hair back. "You came into the restaurant where I work just before Christmas. I was your waitress."

Dante shook his head.

"With your friend, Elizabeth, remember? My husband and I have twins, Margaret and Matthew?" She waited in expectation.

Dante flashed back to that day just before the fire. "Of course. That's right. Your husband is Thomas, right?'

The young woman sighed in relief. "Yes, yes. You do remember. Thank goodness."

"What can I help you with, Mrs. Tillson?"

She gave him a nervous smile. "Well, I understand you bought the factory next door and are advertising for help. So, we came over. I'd like to apply for work."

"We?"

"Thomas and me. He's in the car with the babies."

"Oh, I see." Dante cleared his throat. "Mrs. Tillson, I'll be starting interviews in a couple of weeks, if you'd like to leave your name and telephone number."

"Not for two weeks?" Her smile faded. "Gracious, that long? Okay, thank you." She turned to leave.

"Don't you want to leave your name and number?"

She raised a hand without turning back. "Ahh, thank you, no. Two weeks will be too late. Thank you though."

Is she crying? Dante came out onto the porch as she headed down the steps. "Mrs. Tillson? Too late for what?"

She continued walking.

Dante came down the steps. "Mrs. Tillson? Please stop."

She turned to face him. "I'm sorry, Mr. Montenari, but I didn't come here to burden you with our problems. I just need to find work now."

"Why? I thought you had a job at the restaurant. What happened?"

She sighed. "A lot has happened in the last few months."

Dante waited.

Nancy wiped her eyes with the back of her hand. "Grannie passed away right after Christmas. That was hard, but Annabelle, my mother-in-law, and I did the best we could. Then a few weeks ago, Annabelle had a stroke in the middle of the night. We didn't know it until morning when she didn't get up to start the coffee. She's completely paralyzed and needs around the clock medical care now. I tried to do it at first, but I can't. There's things she needs I have no idea how to do. I'm not a nurse." Nancy blew her breath out in a gust. "We had to close the restaurant, and it's been sold to pay for her care. Thank goodness a big company snapped it up, so we have enough to pay for the nursing home, but that's about it. And we just found out we have to be out by next week. They're going to start demolition to put up a new office building."

"I'm sorry."

Nancy gave him a sad smile and backed away. "Me too. Anyway, I've got to go. The babies are probably awake by now."

Dante took a step forward. "Mrs. Tillson, wait. Do you have sewing experience?"

She stopped. "No. I'm afraid not. I was a buyer for Closson's Department Store."

"A buyer? So, do you know about ready-to-wear clothing?"

"Well, yes. I convinced Mr. Closson to put some in his store. I had to leave six months later, because of the babies, but it was really starting to catch on."

Should I? Dante ran his hands through his hair a couple of times at the thought that popped into his head. "Mrs. Tillson, would you like to come to work for me?"

"What? Mr. Montenari, I told you I can't sew."

"Not sewing. Instead of buying, do you think you could work the other side and sell clothing to the department stores?"

"Ahh, I don't know." She thought about it for a moment. "I think so. Probably, given some time."

"Well, time shouldn't be a problem." He shrugged. "I don't have any product yet."

"I'm sorry, Mr. Montenari, I do appreciate the offer, but—"

Dante cut her off. "What does your husband do?"

"What does he do? For a living? He's unemployed. He hasn't been able to find work, because of his hands."

"I remember, but what'd he do for work before," Dante paused, "before the accident?"

"Well, before the war he managed the restaurant and then in the army, he was in charge of supplying the troops."

"With what?"

"I'm not sure. Everything from socks to munitions, I guess."

Could he manage shipping? Dante knew he was taking a risk with this couple. But more than that, it'd be the first time he'd made a verbal commitment to make this business more than just himself, with employees who'd rely on him for a pay check. "Mrs. Tillson, I have an idea. Why don't we go and talk to your husband?"

"Mr. Montenari, as I said, I appreciate the offer, but we're going to be homeless after next week. I have two babies to take care of. I have to find a job and a place to live now."

"I know." Dante looked around. "Where are you parked?"

"Over in the factory lot." She led the way back.

Thomas Tillson stepped out of the car when he spotted them, easing the door closed with his upper arm. "They're still asleep." He came to where they stood, his arms behind his back.

"Good." Nancy smiled at her husband. "Thomas, you remember Mr. Montenari?"

"Yeah, sure. How ya doin'?"

"Fine, thanks. How have you been?"

"Not so good. My grandma passed, and my ma just had a stroke." Thomas kept his eyes down as he scuffed his shoe on the pavement. "If you could give my wife some work, I'd really appreciate it. She's a hard worker, my Nancy is."

"Well, actually, Mr. Tillson, I'd like to offer you both jobs."

"What?" Both the Tillsons spoke at once.

"Mr. Montenari, I don't know if you remember, but I got these." The man held up his hooks. "How am I supposed to work?"

Dante looked him right in the eye. "Just like everyone else. I understand from your wife, you have some management experience and also ran a supply depot in the war. Is that correct?"

"Yessir." Despite his affirmative answer, the man looked perplexed.

"Well, I'm going to need someone to manage my shipping department, once we have product to ship. For that, I need brain power more than I need brawn. Can you use your prosthetics to write?"

"Yeah, some. I do better the more I practice."

"Good." Dante smiled. "I suggest you practice."

"Ahh." The man shifted from foot to foot for a moment. "I hate to mess up my chance at a job, but I gotta say something."

Dante nodded.

"I recognized this place when Nan pulled in. When I first got home from the war, I came here lookin' for a job. The owner was a real jerk." The large man was quiet for a moment. "It was a sweat shop. I can't work in no sweat shop. It ain't right."

"I agree. I'm hoping to employ locals here at a fair wage. You got anything against Italians? There'll probably be quite a few Italians."

The man shook his head.

Dante grinned. "Good. Glad to have you here then." He stuck his hand out to shake.

For a moment, Thomas Tillson stared at the offered hand. Then he straightened up to his full height and extended his hook, laying it flat against Dante's palm.

Dante closed his fingers around the hook and the two men exchanged a handshake. "I've also offered your wife a job. It'll be a while before this all gets going, but in the meantime there's plenty to do around here."

Thomas glanced at his wife. "That might be a problem too. We need time to find some place to live. I had to sell the restaurant and we live above it—until next week."

"I know, your wife told me. I think I have an answer, at least a temporary one, if you follow me." Dante turned to leave.

"Wait. Where are we going? We can't leave the babies."

"The babies. I'm sorry, Mrs. Tillson. I forgot." An unbidden image of Elizabeth holding one of those babies flashed in Dante's mind. What would she think of him offering this family jobs? *She'd be happy, no doubt.* That thought had him smiling to himself. "Listen, if you drive around the building toward the loading dock, there's a dirt road to the left. Follow it to the end, a little ways past a group of buildings and then bear left again. You'll be able to park, right next to where I'll be waiting."

The couple eased into their car, and Dante headed around the building the other way, ignoring the pain in his leg as he slowly worked his way across the overgrown lawn. *I'll have to get this cut soon.*

The Tillsons actually arrived before Dante. They stood in front of the building. "What is this place?"

"Well, Mrs. Tillson, this and those cottages you just passed are where the workers your husband mentioned earlier were housed."

"Really? From the sweat shop?"

"Yes, and to tell the truth, these places were a mess, but most have been cleaned out." Dante used the railing to climb the steps. He stood on the small porch. "This cottage is a bit larger than the others. I think somewhere along the line it might have been the plant manager's place before the house next door was purchased. It has a front and back porch and more privacy because of the trees around it. It may not look it now, but other than a good cleaning and a coat of paint, I think it's in good shape. Come take a look." He opened the door, and they stepped inside. Dante flipped a switch on the wall, and a bare light bulb illuminated the empty room in harsh light. "I know it doesn't look like much right now, but I think it has potential. This is a combination kitchen and living room." He limped toward the back. "Back here, there are three bedrooms and," he pulled open a door, "a full bath with a tub." He closed the door. "What do you think?"

The couple looked around, but said nothing.

"I know it's hard to see it now, but I think once you get furniture in here, it'll look a lot better." The Tillsons continued to look around. "I understand if it's not suitable. It was just a thought."

"No. No. It's perfect." Nancy glanced at her husband. "Can you believe it, our own house to live in?"

Her husband shook his head. "No, I can't. No offense, Mr. Montenari, but what's the catch? Most company housing ends up costing your whole pay. How much are you going to charge us?"

Dante shook his head. "I don't know. I hadn't gotten that far." He thought for a moment. "How about this? If you two help me do some fixing up around here—whatever you can manage, painting, lawn care, general maintenance and keep an eye on the place for me when I can't be here, I'll consider that rent enough. Does that work for you?"

Both Tillsons nodded in agreement.

"Are you going to be traveling, Mr. Montenari, that you won't be here?" Nancy asked.

Dante shook his head. "No, not really. My mother's been sick. I'm hoping they'll let me bring her home from the hospital soon. When she does come home, she'll need a little extra care at first."

"I see. Well, I'm sorry she's sick. I hope she gets better soon."

"Thank you, Mrs. Tillson."

"Will we be seeing Elizabeth soon?"

Elizabeth? Of course, how would Mrs. Tillson know? Dante shook his head and then turned to Thomas. "If you only have a week to move, you'd better get started right away. I believe Sanderson's Hardware is still open for another hour or so. Two streets down, take a left and it's the third building on the right. Pick out paint, brushes, cleaning supplies, whatever you need to get this place in shape. Put it on my account. I'll call them when I get back to the house to let them know you're coming." He could feel Nancy's eyes on him. "You'd better get going before they close. And Mr. Tillson," Dante paused and cleared his throat. "I just need to say there won't be time for afternoon meetings at the pub."

Dante's words hung in the air between the three of them for a few moments before Thomas Tillson spoke up. "No, sir, Mr. Montenari. Those days have been over ever since my Ma had her stroke. Ya know, I'd been feeling sorry for myself ever since I came home. But then, to look at my mother laying in the bed, and the most she can do is blink—it made me realize there are people a lot worse off than me." The man shook his head. "And I know the way I was actin' may have helped to put her there."

Dante heard a catch in the other man's voice.

"No, sir. Those days are over. Thank you. You won't regret it." Thomas exchanged another handshake with him and then Nancy gave Dante a hug before pulling back to study his face. "Yes, thank you. And I hope we get to see Elizabeth soon. I really like her."

"Me too." Dante stepped back and headed out. "I'll go make that call. Good night, folks. I'll see you tomorrow." He turned when he reached the bottom of the steps. The open door framed the Tillsons locked in an embrace, oblivious to his presence. Dante suddenly felt old, alone, but most of all lonely as he limped away in the growing dusk.

Chapter 20

Dante slipped into the hospital room. His mother lay sleeping in the bed. Her normal routine would've had her awake before dawn, but these last few weeks she'd been asleep every time he'd visited. She seemed more tired with each day that passed. Her body convulsed with coughing before she rolled onto her side, and settled again, her breathing a loud wheeze behind the oxygen mask she still wore to sleep. *Will it ever go away?*

He dropped into the chair by the bed to wait for his mother to awaken, a large yawn stretching his features. Dante hadn't slept well and couldn't blame his new surroundings. *Elizabeth.* After seeing the Tillsons together last night, he realized how much he wanted her to share this new experience and just how much he wanted her. Period. *Forget it. At least until you can figure out who's after you.* That could take years, or maybe never. *By then, she'll have found someone else.* He felt a pang of jealousy. *Better you live with that than how you'd feel if someone hurt her.*

The steam radiator hissed, sending waves of moist heat into the room. He yawned again and removed his coat before rearranging his frame in the hard chair in an attempt to get comfortable. Dante rested his elbow on the bed and supported his head in his hand. *This room is too hot.* He unbuttoned the collar of his shirt and yawned again.

It seemed impossible their life had changed in so short of a time. Both good and bad. A new business and home, but Mama was sick and no Elizabeth. Many times over the last few weeks, Dante had come close to giving in and seeing her. He'd even driven by her house a couple of times. *Leave it alone. It's for the best, and you know it.* The radiator continued to gurgle, its noise and warmth lulling him.

The clank of metal in the hallway startled Dante awake. He'd fallen asleep on the edge of the bed.

"Good morning."

Dante yawned and then scrubbed his hands up and down his face a couple of times. "Good morning, Mama." He yawned again. "It sounds like your breakfast is here." He got up and walked around the room, stretching as he moved. "How are you feeling this morning?"

She shook her head. "Not so good. Tired and my chest hurts, probably because I coughed all night." She yawned. "Is it warm in here? I feel warm."

He nodded. "Yeah, it's real warm in here. It's not too cold out today either, considering it's the end of April."

"Good. Maybe we'll have an early summer. Wouldn't that be nice? I'm tired of winter. I'm just tired."

"Mama, maybe we need to go back to restricting visitors. If you have too many people coming in you won't be able to rest. The doctors said you need to rest to build up your strength. Remember?"

"Yes, yes. I remember." Maria studied her folded hands. "I don't really have a lot of visitors during the day. Really."

"Really?" Dante picked up a small book on the nightstand. "Where'd you get this then?"

"A friend."

He flipped through the book, taking a moment or two to glance at pages. "What friend? Mrs. Carapetti doesn't look like the poetry type."

"It's not Mrs. Carapetti. It's—" she stopped as the door swung open, almost banging against the wall, to admit a pudgy man dressed in white and carrying a tray. "Oh, Albert, good morning. Look Dante, it's Albert."

"Mama, too many visitors isn't—"

"How are you, Albert?" Maria cut off her son's lecture. "Feeling better today?"

The man sat the meal down on her bedside table. He turned aside and gave a sharp bark of a cough into his hand before lifting the cover off the meal, then pulled out a handkerchief and swabbed his forehead before tucking it away again. "Worse today, I'm afraid, Mrs. Montenari." He buttered her a piece of bread and sat it back on her plate. "I still got a fever. Not much I can do about it. I gotta come to work with four kids to feed. You know how that is." He hacked into his fist again. "You want me to pour your coffee?"

"No, that's fine, Albert. I'll do it."

"Okay then." He glanced at the clock on the wall. "I got just enough time to finish deliverin' my trays and get a cigarette break before we start cookin' for lunch." Albert yanked open the door in his hurry. "Oh sorry, Miss." He stepped back. "Please, you first."

Elizabeth Wellman walked into the room, but stopped as soon as she realized Maria wasn't alone. "Dante."

"Elizabeth." *Am I dreaming?* Dante had thought of her so many times since walking out of her house, and here she was in front of him.

"Yes, of course it's Elizabeth. You broke up with her. I didn't." Maria picked up a piece of bread off her plate to nibble on. The muffled sound of a deep hacking cough echoed in the hallway. "Poor Albert. He's been coming to work for almost a week sick like that. He's been coughing almost as much as me." She dropped the bread back on her plate. "I'm really not that hungry today. Do you want this?"

Dante shook his head without taking his eyes off Elizabeth.

"Fine." Maria pushed the plate away. "How are you today, Elizabeth?"

Elizabeth pulled her gaze away from Dante. "I'm fine, Mrs. Montenari. How are you?" She gave Dante another nervous glance.

"Old. Tired." The frail woman pushed herself up a little higher in the bed. "There, that's better." Neither Dante nor Elizabeth answered her. "Oh, for goodness sake, will you two sit down? Please get another chair for Elizabeth from the hall." She waited until both were seated before speaking again. "Dante, what day is it?"

"Sunday, Mama."

Maria nodded. "I thought so. Elizabeth, I'm glad to see you, but why aren't you headed to Port Johnson?"

"Someone arranged a field trip to the Statue of Liberty today, so class was canceled."

"I see." Maria looked at her son, who watched Elizabeth with sidelong glances. "I'm sure Elizabeth would like to hear your news."

Dante shook his head.

Elizabeth turned his way. "What news?"

"It's nothing."

Maria waved a hand at him. "What do you mean nothing? Tell her."

"Fine." Dante ran a hand through his hair. "I found a place to buy and restart the business."

Elizabeth smiled. "That's wonderful, Dante. Where?"

"On the west side of town."

"Do you think your clients will be willing to come there to have their suits made?"

He shrugged. "I have no idea. Maybe, maybe not."

"Dante, what are you saying, maybe, maybe not? Tell her the rest."

"Mama, please." He let out a gust of breath. "Okay, fine. It's a factory. I'm thinking of making clothes there. My designs."

"What? You're serious? Like the dress you made me at Christmas?" A smile played across Elizabeth's features.

He shook his head. "No. At least not at first. I've been thinking about it, with all the war restrictions, I think it'd be a better idea to make more utilitarian clothing. Men's trousers. Cotton dresses.

Shirts. Maybe even some children's clothing. I'm not really sure yet."

"That's a smart idea. Do you have any designs made up?"

"No, not really. Other than here." He tapped his temple. "There's been so much to do around the place, I haven't had time to sketch anything out, but I will. Soon."

"I'm sure you will. How about employees? Have you run advertisements for help?"

Is she really interested? He nodded. "I've actually gotten more applicants than I have space for right now. We'll see how good I am, if I ever get this place up and running. Some days I have my doubts, there's so much to do."

"I'm sure if anyone can do it, it's you." Elizabeth cleared her throat. "Umm, do you have to purchase equipment?"

"Some, yes. There's already sewing machines in place, but they're old. I've managed to get about half of them working, but I don't know when I'm going to be able to get to the rest."

"Why don't you hire a mechanic?"

Dante's smile was wry. "My car is fine."

"Very funny." Elizabeth smiled. "No, I mean someone to work on equipment, sewing machines, boilers, whatever you have around. Anything mechanical. In my father's factory there was a man named Bruce who took care of all the equipment. Everything from the machines on the line to the plumbing in the rest rooms. He was one of my father's first employees. People complained he was crotchety and odd, and maybe he was—just a little, but he was always kind to me."

"Hmm, a full time position, that's a good idea." *She knows more about running a factory than I do.* "What kind of business did your father own?"

"Tools. The company made all different kinds of tools. Wrenches, screwdrivers, that kind of thing."

"Tools?" *It can't be.* "Tools? You father made tools as in Wellman Tools?"

Elizabeth hesitated. "Yes."

"Seriously? That's one of the largest tool companies in the country." Dante was shocked. "What are you doing in Bayonne, New Jersey teaching high school? You're an heiress."

"Please don't call me that." Elizabeth's voice was tight. "I like teaching; I don't care about the money."

"It's easy to say you don't care when you have money."

Elizabeth stiffened at his mother's quiet observation and dropped her gaze, but not before Dante glimpsed the hurt look in her eyes. "I'm sorry, Elizabeth. We've known you long enough to know money doesn't matter."

"Yes, I'm sorry too, my dear. I was just surprised." Maria held out her hand to Elizabeth. "Please forgive me."

Elizabeth clasped the other woman's hand for a moment. "Of course. And I should've trusted you enough to tell you, but experience has taught me most times it's best to keep the past to myself. People can be unkind."

"Do you mind if I ask you a few more questions about your father's factory?"

"Of course not, Dante. I'm not sure I'll have an answer though."

"Did you work there?"

"No. I wanted to, and learned as much as I could about it, but my father wouldn't hear of it, despite my mother's haranguing him to let me work. It irritated him to no end when I'd go there for lunch sometimes and sit with the workers in the cafeteria."

"Cafeteria? They served meals?"

"They did. It was one of the benefits my father implemented for the workers soon after he started the company." A slight smile touched Elizabeth's lips. "Wednesday was my favorite lunch day. Mrs. Edgars, the head cook, made baked ham glazed with maple syrup and served it with mounds of mashed potato. She made great pumpkin pie too."

"It sounds like a nice place to work."

Elizabeth smiled at Maria. "Yes, it was. At one time."

"You said it was one of the benefits for the workers. Do you know of any others?" Dante waited.

She nodded. "My father never talked business around us at home, but I sometimes eavesdropped when he thought I wasn't listening, and his workers talked around the lunch table all the time. The cafeteria was one benefit, of course. For twenty-five cents a week, you could eat whatever meals happened during your shift. He felt a well-fed worker was a more productive one. Let's see, what else? My father gave two paid sick days a year and one paid vacation day for every year you worked there, up to five days. Also, he paid by the hour, not by the piece."

Dante knew some about manufacturing, but he'd never heard of such a thing. "No offense, but how did he make any money? Vacation and sick time? That amounts to paying people for not being there. And hourly pay? Paying by the piece is the incentive for more production."

"The board of directors thought that too, but my father proved them wrong. Year after year. The cost of those few benefits to the company was minimal, but it showed the employees my father valued them. The workers thought the world of him and showed their appreciation by consistently exceeding job quotas."

"And no one ever abused these benefits?"

Elizabeth shook her head. "No, not really. Vermont is very rural, but there was always a long list of people waiting for the chance to be hired. Even if they had to drive from a distance."

Maria coughed. "Listen to her, Dante. She's a smart woman, our Elizabeth."

Our Elizabeth? Dante wished. "That's very interesting. Considering the size of Wellman Tool, he must've been on to something." He pondered her words for a moment. "No other company I know of does that. Why'd he?"

"I'm pretty sure it was the result of an incident during his youth."

"I don't understand."

"One night I overheard him arguing with Mr. Whitman, the chairman of the board, after a dinner party my parents put on. Actually, I think everyone heard them. He wanted my father to stop paying employee benefits to save money, and my father refused. He said he'd never treat his workers like a plentiful commodity."

A plentiful commodity? "What'd he mean by that?"

"I asked my mother that very question the next day. She didn't know, but she did give me a lecture on listening in when I shouldn't have been."

"Did you ever find out?"

Elizabeth nodded

"He told you?"

"No. He told my mother, but only because he was well in his cups as my mother called it. He'd been drinking most of the evening. He was upset because one of the workers was injured that afternoon. A man got his hand caught between two pallets of wrenches. Thank goodness, it was only some broken fingers."

"Doesn't that kind of thing happen occasionally in factory work?"

Elizabeth shook her head. "Not in my father's plant. Not once. Up until that day. I was on my way to get a book when I heard my parents in the library. Not wanting to disturb them, I was headed back to my room when I heard my mother ask what his plentiful commodities comment to Whitman meant." Elizabeth gave Maria a sheepish look. "I know it was wrong, but I had to listen. At first, my father said nothing. I'd just about given up when he started talking. I knew he grew up in a well-to-do family and like other young men in his social set, he attended prep school in Boston. What I didn't know was he became friends with a classmate named Anson Baxter. It seemed Anson liked to spend money. A lot of money. This time, he'd spent all his allowance wooing a young woman and needed more as he'd promised her dinner and a concert. Young Anson decided to pay his father a visit. The Baxter family owned a big textile factory right there in Boston, so my father went along."

"While Anson argued his case in Mr. Baxter's office, my father waited outside at the edge of the production floor. He'd never been inside a textile factory, or any factory. It was noisy, hot and cotton lint floated everywhere, like snow, sticking to anything it landed on. My father was the least poetic person I know, but that's how he described it to my mother." Elizabeth's smile was sad. "He said there were young children everywhere, working right alongside adults."

"That's true," Maria added. "Years ago, when Gino worked in the factory, he told me the same thing about the children." She shivered. "From the stories he told me, it was a miserable place to work for everyone."

Elizabeth nodded. "My father heard a raised voice, even over the racket of the machinery. A man in a heavy leather apron and a small boy stood about twenty feet away. The boy was crying, and the man was shouting at him. Without warning, the man slapped the boy to the floor and then gave him a kick that sent him close to one of the huge machines. My father was shocked, but before he could do anything the boy crawled on his belly under the machine. My father assumed the boy must've been desperate to get away since there was barely ten inches clearance underneath the whirring machine. Father said the soles of the boy's dirty little feet were sticking out from under the frame and a second later they were gone, just that fast. The man in the apron started yelling and waving his hands. The machine stopped, and the man leaned down to look between the huge spindles holding cotton thread. He straightened and turned his head in my father's direction, a grimace evident on his face. Then he hurried past my father into Mr. Baxter's office. Both men came back a few minutes later, followed by Anson. My father heard Mr. Baxter ask which one it was. The foreman said something like, Pulaski number 2...or maybe number 3. He couldn't tell the difference. Mr. Baxter told him to get the mess cleaned up before it ruined any more cotton.

On his way back to his office, Mr. Baxter shoved a wad of bills into Anson's hand and told him not to mention this to his mother."

Dante noticed his mother's eyes close and open again as she fought to stay awake and listen as Elizabeth continued to talk.

"My father asked what a Pulaski number two was as they walked away. Anson told him it wasn't a what, but a who. One of the Pulaski kids got caught in the spinning mule while cleaning under it. It happened sometimes, but as his father said, kids were a plentiful commodity. Can you imagine?"

Elizabeth shifted in the chair. "My father turned back to look just as they were removing the little boy's body from under the machine. His arm and most of his shoulder up to his neck had been torn away. As they dragged him clear, a wide streak of blood smeared the dirty floor. My father made it as far as the alley before he threw up. After that, he no longer associated with Anson Baxter, but he never forgot the incident, or the deplorable conditions."

"I don't think Gino ever forgot either." Maria yawned and closed her eyes. "Please, keep talking. I'm just going to rest my eyes."

Elizabeth lowered her voice. "You know, on the outside, my father often seemed harsh, but on the inside, I think he cared a lot about people; he just didn't know how to show it. As it turned out, the man who'd hurt himself at my father's company was worried about his family—his daughters really. His wife was in the hospital, and the sitter never showed up, so he'd kept his eight-year-old home from school to watch the three-year-old." Elizabeth paused for a moment. "After my father died, I was cleaning out his study, and came across a folder in one of his desk drawers. Inside there were notes he'd made on opening a service to take care of the workers' children, if need be. I have no doubt he would've implemented it had he lived. Do you know what he'd written across the top of the page?"

Dante shook his head.

"The Pulaski Project. After the little boy from the factory. He never forgot."

"How could he? Would you be able to?" Dante sat back in his chair and sighed. "Wow. I hope I'm doing the right thing by opening this factory. I never thought about putting people at risk."

"Accidents can happen, but chances are your workers won't be at risk if they follow protocol. Just make sure your safety signs are displayed in a prominent place to remind the workers."

"Signs? What signs?"

Elizabeth frowned. "Isn't there signage there now?"

"No. From what I understand it was a sweat shop for years. I'm pretty sure signs were the least of their problems."

"Well, you can have someone hand paint some until you can get some printed. My father placed them out on the floor, of course. In the cafeteria. Anywhere."

"There's a lot I don't know. Maybe this isn't the best plan."

Elizabeth reached over to give Dante's hand a quick squeeze. "But you can learn. May I make a suggestion?"

"Of course."

"Call two or three other companies. See if you could do a tour of their plant. Ask questions. Take notes."

"That's a good idea. I will." Dante cleared his throat. "Can I ask you another question?" At her nod, he continued. "It's obvious you could run your father's factory, why don't you?"

"Well, for one thing, our family doesn't own it anymore, and while most of my father's company policies were forward thinking, he didn't believe women should work. Even the clerks in the office were men. The only women he begrudgingly let in the factory were Mrs. Edgars and her helpers in the kitchen. The board of directors felt the same way. When I approached them about running the company after my father's death, the chairman informed me they'd already met. The board felt the pressure would be too much for a woman's delicate constitution, so the vote was a unanimous no." Elizabeth shook her head. "I can't tell you how angry I was at first. If my brother Teddy had made it back, they would've handed him the reins without question. But instead of staying mad, I got even. It cost them a lot of money to get rid of me. And by the time I left that negotiating table, I'd be willing to bet some of those men thought my constitution was anything but delicate."

Elizabeth and Dante continued to talk quietly until the loud wheeze of Maria's labored breathing signaled she'd fallen asleep. Dante got up and lifted the oxygen mask off the hook at the head of the bed and slipped it over his mother's nose and mouth. He rested a hand along her cheek for a moment.

"Her breathing's not getting better. And she's tired all the time." Dante dropped back in the chair next to Elizabeth. "It's frustrating. I can't take her home until her lungs clear, but I think her lungs would heal up faster at home, away from here."

"I'm not sure which would be better, but you're right, her breathing does seem much worse today."

Dante nodded. "I thought so too. She's probably better off here, for now at least. Thank you for coming to visit her. My mother thinks the world of you."

"I think she's very special too. I enjoy our visits."

"Thanks for all the information today too. You've given me a lot of good ideas." Dante's smile was warm and carried to his dark eyes.

"You're welcome."

They talked more about the factory. About Nico. About Port Johnson. They talked about everything, but themselves. A couple of hours passed before Maria opened her eyes and struggled to remove the oxygen mask.

"Hold on, Mama. I'll help you. Lean forward a little, please."

"That's better." Maria huffed as she laid her head back against the pillow. "It's so hot in here, I feel like I can't breathe." Her voice sounded hoarse. "Would you pour me a glass of water?"

"Sure." Dante brought the glass to the bed as Maria struggled with the covers. "Mama, what are you trying to do?"

"Take the blankets off. I'm too hot. Besides, I gotta help Marco today. He's got a big order."

"What? Mama, Papa's no longer here, remember?"

"Oh, oh. *Sì*. Of course." She continued to fuss with the bedding.

"Can I help?" Elizabeth stood up.

"Luciana? What are you doing here? Shouldn't you be at the restaurant?"

Dante and Elizabeth exchanged worried glances.

"No, Mama, this is Elizabeth. You know Elizabeth, she teaches the men at Port Johnson. Here, take your water. I'll fix the blankets."

Maria's hand shook as she held the glass.

"Mama?" Dante laid his hand on her forehead. Heat radiated from her skin. "Mama, you've got a fever. Hold on, I'm going to get the nurse."

Maria's hand trembled, and water spilled unchecked down the front of her gown. "I'm fine."

But she wasn't fine. The doctor arrived within an hour. He examined her, listening to Maria's chest with his stethoscope and ordered the nurse to prepare an injection. After administering it, he turned to Dante. "Let's step into the hall a moment, and let your mother rest."

"I'll keep your mother company."

"Thank you." Dante gave Elizabeth a grateful smile. "Thank you for being here."

Once outside the room the doctor took off his spectacles, rubbing them clean with a handkerchief. He settled them back on the bridge of his nose and hooked the wire bows over the tops of his ears. "Mr. Montenari, your mother has pneumonia. I've given her sulfathiazole, but I'm not sure it will be of any use at this stage. I can hear a very pronounced crackle from the infection in both of her lungs. And with her lungs already so compromised from the smoke inhalation, the fluid is building up at a rapid rate. Although sedatives slow down the breathing, I've given her some to help with the discomfort." He sighed. "I have to be honest with you, at this point, there's not much we can do except keep her comfortable. Her pain will increase as her lungs fill and breathing becomes more difficult. I've ordered sedatives to be given every three hours and more frequently if needed. I'm sorry."

"This can't be happening." Dante shook his head. "It can't be. Isn't there anything you can do?"

"The normal procedure would be to aspirate each lung to drain the fluid, but in this case it will fill back up faster than we can drain it. Mr. Montenari, your mother's lungs are severely damaged. Each time we attempted the procedure not only would it cause her intense pain, it'd only be delaying the inevitable." The doctor gave Dante's shoulder a gentle squeeze. "Do you understand what I'm saying here?"

"Yeah, you're telling me I'm losing my mother again, when I just got her back." Dante's eyes moistened. He looked away for a moment to get himself under control. *This is not about you.* He blew his breath out in a gust and ran his hand through his hair. "How long?"

The doctor shook his head. "There's no way of telling. It could be a few hours, but probably no longer than a day or so."

"Okay. Thank you." Dante went back into the room. The head of his mother's bed was elevated with two pillows propping her up. She slowly opened her eyes at his approach and smiled. "*Ciao.*" Her voice was breathy.

"*Ciao*, Mama. How do you feel?"

Maria rolled her eyes. "Like I'm floating. Really tired."

"Why don't you get some rest?"

"*Sì.*" Her eyes closed.

He moved closer to the bed.

"Dante?"

"*Sì?*"

"I want to tell you something."

"Okay." He waited. "Mama?"

She fought to open her eyes. "Yes?"

"You wanted to tell me something?" He reached for her hand.

"*Sì*. Ahh...it's important. Let me think a moment."

"It's okay, Mama. Get some rest."

"No, wait." She lay still for a few moments. "I can't remember." She shook her head as if to clear it. "Be with the one you love. Find a way. Promise me." She squeezed his fingers with surprising strength. "Promise me." The words were little more than a whisper.

Dante's eyes met Elizabeth's gaze from the other side of the bed. "Okay, I promise, Mama. Just like you and Papa."

"No. Like me and..." Maria's words trailed off. The sedative had taken her.

Dante signaled Elizabeth to follow him to the other side of the room near the door. "She has pneumonia." He paused and swallowed. "She's dying."

"Oh, Dante. I'm so sorry. Isn't there anything they can do?"

"No."

Elizabeth blinked back tears. "What can I do for you? Can I get you something?"

Dante shook his head. "I don't want to impose, but would you mind sitting with me—with us a while longer?"

"Of course, as long as you need me."

By two o'clock Maria's fever was 104 degrees. By five o'clock her breathing was labored. Each time the nurses repositioned her, she cried out in pain, but spoke no words.

"I've given her another injection. It should help. Is there anything I can get you, Mr. Montenari? A cup of coffee?"

"No, thank you, Nurse Raynor."

"How about you? Some coffee?"

Elizabeth shook her head.

"Okay. Please pass my regards on to your uncle, miss." The nurse gave Dante a gentle pat on the shoulder. "Just call me if you need me." The woman hefted her considerable bulk out the door.

"Your uncle? What's she talking about?"

Elizabeth shrugged. "She must have me confused with someone else."

Hours passed as Dante held his mother's hand. Neither Dante nor Elizabeth spoke much, just sat close together, near the bed. At some point, he reached for Elizabeth's hand too. They sat this way as Maria's breathing grew louder in the quiet room, the space between each inhale and exhale lengthening as time clicked by on the large wall clock.

At 2:17 AM his mother took a deep breath and after several seconds didn't exhale. Dante let go of Elizabeth's hand and leaned forward. "Mama?" He touched her. "Mama?" No response. Maria Montenari was gone.

Chapter 21

Elizabeth added several more hair pins to the bun resting at the nape of her neck before settling a small black pill box hat on her head. She reached for a hat pin and bent her head forward to anchor the hat in place. Her gaze landed on the tiny green glass Statue of Liberty figurine Maria Montenari had given her for the Christmas tree. Elizabeth hadn't been able to pack it away with the rest of the ornaments. Tears sprang to her eyes. *I can't believe she's gone.* Images of the small, energetic woman flashed in Elizabeth's mind. Sundays at Port Johnson. The week she'd cared for Elizabeth. And lastly, in the hospital. But by far, Elizabeth's favorite memories were of Dante and Mrs. Montenari together, their mutual love and respect evident in their every interaction.

Unabated tears slipped down Elizabeth's cheeks to soak into the wool of her plain black dress. *This will never do.* She opened one of the small top drawers of the dresser and pushed her jewelry box aside to gather several small white handkerchiefs. *I'm going to need these.* Elizabeth dabbed at her eyes, then fetched a black clutch from the closet and tucked the hankies inside. She glanced at the clock on her nightstand. Mr. Galenti was sending a car for her, but it wasn't due to arrive for another twenty minutes. She headed to the living room. *Sit and read for a few minutes. Reading always calms you.* Not today. She started the same page over for the third time.

Elizabeth hadn't talked to Dante since sitting with him in the hospital. Ever since then, she'd been at war with her own feelings. Despite the sad occasion, it'd been so good to see him and listen to him talk about his plans for the factory. *Why hasn't he called me? It's the least he could do after I—after you what? Bought the factory for him?* Was Mr. Galenti right? Was she trying to buy her way back into Dante's life?

"No." The one word sounded loud in the quiet of the house. Elizabeth slapped the book closed and unable to sit with her thoughts any longer, got up to pace around the room. She slid the book back in the bookcase. *He could've at least called me. I know he still loves me. I saw it in his eyes that day at the hospital. Stop.* Elizabeth picked up two more books off the side table and shoved them into the bookcase. *He doesn't owe you anything. He doesn't even know it was your money. Stop thinking about him. He's not coming back to you!* Elizabeth spent the next ten minutes jamming more books into the case, heedless of their placement. She whirled to grab another book off the coffee table, only to find it empty except for a worn piece of folded paper. Elizabeth unfolded it. *The fun list.* She'd forgotten all about it. How childish it seemed now, in light of all that had happened in the last months. A knock sounded on the front door. She dropped the list on the table and grabbed her coat.

The sun stood directly overhead. Its bright rays warmed the earth, beaming nourishment and life onto the many blossoms and singing birds in the area. That same warmth was felt by the throngs of mourners assembled, their somber black dress soaking up the heat from the sun despite the strong wind.

The priest sprinkled holy water on the casket. "May Maria Montenari's soul, and the souls of all the faithful departed, through the mercy of God rest in peace. Amen."

"Amen," the mourners intoned and turned to leave, several people plucking a flower from the numerous floral arrangements as a remembrance.

Elizabeth glanced across the way at Dante, but he didn't move or even take his eyes off the coffin. Behind him, on the distant side of the cemetery sat a car she now recognized as belonging to the Don. Gino Galenti stood next to Dante and leaned in to whisper something. Dante nodded, stepped forward and laid a single red rose on the mahogany before touching his fingers to his lips and placing them on the wood for a brief moment. Gino did the same and then led the way out of the graveyard. The rising winds literally pushed the rest of the mourners out of the cemetery and down the street to the parish hall. Elizabeth held a hand to her hat and picked her way across the spongy ground behind the rest. When she reached the gate, she turned to look back. Two men waited at a distance, shovels in hand. Don Salucci stood on the backside of the casket, his eyes closed, and his gloveless hand resting on the dark wood.

Elizabeth worked her way through the crowd of people standing outside the hall and up the steps to the door.

"Here, let me get that door for ya." The man pulled on the heavy wrought iron handle and swung the door open. "There ya go."

"Thank you, Mr. Carapetti." Elizabeth stepped over the threshold.

"No problem. Call me Carmine."

It took a moment for Elizabeth's eyes to adjust to the darker interior of the building after the brightness of the sun. Maria Montenari had accumulated many friends over the years with her warmth and kindness, and it showed here with the number of people packed into the parish hall on a weekday. People crowded around the food tables set up at one end of the room. Those that had acquired refreshment sat at tables at the other end of the room, talking amongst themselves. Elizabeth spotted Mrs. Carapetti and Mrs. Cammareri sitting at a table. A large crowd congregated in the open space between the two sets of tables, milling around, talking and drinking coffee. Connie Santini was among this group. Elizabeth felt lost in the large crowd.

"Hi, Miss Wellman. Nice of you to come. How are you doing?"

Elizabeth smiled at the familiar faces. Nicolina stood with her parents. "Hello, Nicolina. Mr. and Mrs. Moretti. I'm sorry for your loss." She gave her student a quick hug and shook Mr. Moretti's hand. When she extended her hand to Mrs. Moretti, the woman pulled her in a tight embrace.

"Thank you for being a good friend to my sister. She thought so much of you, and hoped someday you and Dante." The little woman patted Elizabeth's back. "Dante's a good boy, you know. A real good boy. And he might not admit to it, but he needs you more than ever with Maria gone."

I want him, but he doesn't want me. Elizabeth kept the thought to herself.

"You should talk to him."

Elizabeth nodded at the woman's encouraging words. "I will." But so many people surrounded Dante, she couldn't get near him. She finally slipped away to board the bus she hadn't used in months. Dusk descended as Elizabeth walked down the quiet street to her house. A light shone in the first floor window of Mrs. Sargent's house for a moment, then it was gone. *Hmm, maybe someone finally bought it. I hope it's someone nice. Maybe with children. That would be fun.*

Elizabeth let herself in and went to the bedroom to change her clothes. She removed her earrings and pulled open the top dresser drawer to get her jewelry box. It wasn't there. *That doesn't make sense.* She looked up. The small box was sitting on top of the dresser. *I didn't leave that out. Did I?* It wasn't like her, but anything was possible, she'd had a lot on her mind lately. She put the earrings inside and tucked the box into the drawer.

Ten minutes later, Elizabeth poured boiling water in a cup for tea and turned to make a sandwich. She reached for the hunk of canned meat on a small plate in the refrigerator as well as the mustard. Somehow the jar slipped from her fingers and shattered on the floor. "Darn it." She wiped the yellow splatters off the cabinet doors and opened the back door for her mop.

The kitchen light from behind Elizabeth revealed the form of a man standing just outside the door. She let out a screech of surprise as he reached for her. She tried to shut the door, but he shoved against the portal before she could get it closed. The motion sent Elizabeth backward to slam into the edge of the counter.

"Well, well. Hello, lass. It's been a while."

She hadn't seen the man's face, but she knew that voice. *Flanagan.* Elizabeth scrambled to her feet, but barely managed two steps before he grabbed her by the hair and snaked her back, wrapping a dirty, muscular arm around her neck. Flanagan lifted his arm, forcing her chin up. She clawed at his arm. He slapped her aside the head. Flaying wildly, Elizabeth's hand touched something hot. *The tea.* She latched onto the cup, ignoring the heat and tossed it over her shoulder.

"Bitch," Flanagan howled, but didn't let go. Instead, he increased the pressure across her neck as he lifted her.

Elizabeth's feet left the floor as she struggled to breathe. *Oh, my God, he's strangling me.* It was her last thought as the ceiling light narrowed to a pin point and she lost consciousness.

Elizabeth shivered. *Cold. I'm cold.* Dampness seeped through her pants causing her to shiver again. She opened her eyes. *Where am*

I? A cement floor. She glanced around. She was in a basement, but not her basement.

"It's about time you come to. Can't take much of a punch, can you?"

Flanagan. His voice came from the shadows in the corner. Elizabeth tried to get to her feet, only to find she'd been tied to a metal support column. "Let me go this instant."

"Well, lass, I'm afraid I won't be doin' that any time soon. You and me got some unfinished business."

Just the reminder made Elizabeth sick to her stomach. *Think. I've got to get out of this.* There was little chance of Gino Galenti, or anyone else, rescuing her this time. "It's not very bright of you to accost me again, especially since you know my connections."

"Yeah, I know your connections all right." There was shuffling in the corner, and he stepped forward into the dim light.

Elizabeth gasped.

A huge jagged scar ran the width of his forehead, cutting across one of his eyelids, causing it to droop over his eye. His nose was almost flat against his face as if all the cartilage had been smashed. His cheeks sunk into hollows. Flanagan moved to position himself in front of her, dragging one foot. "Ain't too pretty, huh? This is what your connections did to me. Those bastards left me for dead. But I took worse beatings from my own Da. After I'm done havin' fun with you, I gonna treat you to the same thing. Let's see how you like it when I knock all those pretty teeth of yours out. If you last that long."

She strained against the ropes to no avail. "You won't get away with it. The Don will come after you."

He shrugged. "He ain't caught me so far. They're all thinkin' I'm gone, they are." He touched a crooked finger to the side of his head. "I'm smart. They ain't even gonna connect it to me when they find you and your boyfriend's rotting carcasses in this basement."

"Boyfriend? I don't know who you're talking about."

"What? Now you're goin' to play dumb? I don't think so, lassie." He pulled back his hand and laid a resounding slap across Elizabeth's cheek.

She saw it coming, but couldn't avoid it. The force spun her half way around the post, the back of her head banging against the metal.

"Do you remember him now?"

Elizabeth's head hung like a rag doll as she watched blood drip from her mouth onto the floor. "I don't have a boyfriend." Her words left a fine spray of red on the leg of her pants.

He grabbed her by the hair and yanked her head up. "Ya know, there's lots of things I can do that'll make you say his name. All of them will hurt you, a lot, but I'll probably enjoy 'em." He bent within a couple of inches of her face. "If you remember, I like it rough."

The smell of his revolting breath was reminder enough of his treatment that day in the alley. *Never again.* She spit in his face.

Flanagan jumped back and wiped the blood tinged spittle off his face. "You slut." He hauled off and kicked her in the side.

His heavy boots drove the breath from Elizabeth's lungs in an unexpected whoosh, leaving her no air to scream. She slumped over to the side, unable to catch her breath.

"That's just a taste of what you'll be gettin' and Montenari too, when I get him here."

"He doesn't have anything to do with this," Elizabeth huffed out.

"Yes, he does. The bastard didn't wanna play the game like he was supposed ta. Nobody makes Burt Flanagan look like a fool and gets away with it. Tellin' me the Don had his suits made there, so I'd leave him alone. I believed it too, until the boys down at the pub got wind of it. Called me a stupid mick and laughed me right out of the place. The Don's personal tailor got off the boat with him. I started watchin' Montenari. Then I started watchin' you too—after that day in Irish Town." He limped back to the corner for a moment. "Sometimes even when you're sleepin'. You should hide your key better." He unfolded a piece of paper. "This your list?"

Elizabeth groaned.

"First date? First kiss?" He smirked. "In that case, I'm goin' to make all your dreams come true. But right now, I'm using this for somethin' else. I'll be back soon with your boyfriend. Don't go anywhere, lass." He laughed as he clomped up the stairs.

Heavy, uneven footsteps sounded overhead, then the slight vibration of a closing door. Elizabeth struggled to sit up. The movement caused pain in her side. *Broken ribs?* Probably bruised she decided after taking a couple of deep breaths. *I've got to get out of here.* She twisted and turned her hands behind her back until the ropes chafed enough to draw blood. Flanagan tied her too well.

Chapter 22

"How are you holding up?"

Dante nodded. "I'm fine, Gino. Have you seen Elizabeth?"

The older man shook his head. "I saw her in the cemetery. She's probably here somewhere. There are still lots of people wanting to pay their respects."

One of those people stepped up. *Connie Santini. I don't need this today.*

"Hello, Dante. I'm sorry for your loss. Your mother was a real nice lady."

"Thank you."

Connie extended her hand. "I'm sorry for what I said to you the other day at the factory."

He eyed her hand with trepidation.

"I guess I just got mad."

Dante nodded and placed his hand in hers. She tightened her grip and pulled his hand forward to tuck against her sternum. "I know it must be lonely with your mother gone. If there's anything you need, anything, you call me." Connie's words were solicitous, but her eyes told another story.

Dante snapped his hand back and resisted the urge to wipe it off on his pants leg. "Thank you for coming. I still need to speak to a few other people."

"Ahh, yeah. Sure." A pout shaped her over reddened lips. "I'll talk to you later."

Dante reached his hand out to the person behind her. "Mrs. Cammareri. It was so good of you to come." He talked to her and several others before a boy he didn't recognize cut in line and stood in front of him.

"You Montenari?"

The boy's coat was little more than a rag. His pants were so short Dante could see he wore no socks, as if the boy's pinkie toe sticking out through a hole in the worn boots wasn't clue enough.

"Yes, who are you?"

The boy shrugged. "Don't matter. I gotta give this to you, or he'll beat on Fiona."

"Who will?"

"I can't say." The kid rubbed a dirty hand against his nose. "But I can't have my sister hurtin'. She works in his crib, and iffen she don't get customers the rest of us kids don't eat." He shoved a piece of paper at Dante.

Dante reached in his pocket and handed the boy a couple of bills.

"Thanks, mister."

"Why don't you get yourself something to eat over at those tables? One of the ladies will help you."

"You get out of here. What are you doin' in here?" It was Gino Galenti. "This is a private function. Out."

Dante laid a hand on the man's arm. "It's okay. I just told him to get something to eat."

The boy grinned. "It don't matter. This will buy some bread and eggs for tonight." He tucked the money in his pocket and ran, weaving through the crowd.

"What'd he want?"

"He brought me this." Dante unfolded the paper. "Elizabeth's list. What the hell?" Number 1 was crossed out. Above it someone had written, *#1. Die. If yu dont git hear.* The handwriting was a childlike scrawl, but Dante knew better. "Christ."

"What's the matter?"

Dante refolded the paper. "Gino, are you sure Elizabeth's here?"

The man shook his head. "No. Why?"

"We need to look now." With the help of a couple of Gino's men it only took them a few minutes to figure out she wasn't in the building anywhere.

"I've got to go."

"Go? Dante, where are you going?"

"I have to take care of something."

"Wait. Take care of what? This is your mother's funeral."

"She'd understand, Gino. I've got to go." Dante backed away and worked his way out of the crowded room much as the urchin had done a few minutes before him.

The back door of Elizabeth's house stood ajar. Dante slid through the opening. It was dark. His nose was assaulted by a vinegary smell. *Mustard?* He turned to flip on the light switch.

Nothing happened. He waited a moment for his eyes to adjust to the darkness before heading toward the living room. "Elizabeth?" He listened and heard nothing. Dante headed down the hall to the bedroom. "Elizabeth?" Nothing. *Where is she?* Just as he was about to step back into the hall, he heard the creak of a floor board. "Elizabeth?" He turned in time to see a shadowy figure behind him, arm raised. "What?" The arm dropped, and Dante hit the floor.

Dante groaned. *What the hell? Where am I?* He was in a standing position, his arms stretched over his head and tethered to something.

"Dante?"

It took a moment for the whisper to register. He lifted his head. It was pitch black. "Elizabeth?"

"Yes. Are you all right?"

"I think so." He tipped his head from side to side for a moment. "Except for a headache from where he hit me over the head. I didn't get a chance to see him. Who the hell was it?"

"Flanagan."

"Flanagan? Are you sure? He left a long time ago."

"Trust me. He didn't."

Dante heard the nervous quiver in her voice. "Are you okay? Has he hurt you?"

"He's knocked me around some, but I'm still in one piece."

"The bastard." Dante struggled against his restraints. "If I can just get loose."

"You can't. If he'd left us tied to the post maybe, but we're handcuffed to the beams overhead. He's been planning this for a while, I think."

"Where are we?"

"I think we're in the empty house next door to mine."

"Where's Flanagan?"

"I don't know. He left a while ago." She was quiet for a few moments. "He means to kill us."

"Well, we're not dead yet. Let me think a minute." He lifted his feet off the floor to put extra strain on the handcuffs. After several minutes all he succeeded in doing was scraping his hands raw. "That's not going to work. Dammit!"

"I'm sorry, Dante."

"For what?"

"For getting you mixed up in this. He wants revenge for the beating he took on my account."

"Elizabeth, Flanagan's been after me for a while. I'm the one who's at fault here. I should've realized just because I stopped seeing you didn't mean you'd be safe. I'm sorry."

"It's no one's fault. Flanagan is an evil man." It was quiet in the basement for a moment. "Dante, I want you to know, even if it brought me right back here, I wouldn't trade one moment of the time I've spent with you. Before that, maybe I really was Loonie Lizzie."

"What are you talking about?"

She sighed. "It's the name the press gave me. Loonie Lizzie. And they dubbed Katherine, Carousing Kate."

"Why? What are you talking about?"

"After Pearl, the Northam News did an article on our family as a tribute. Somehow the bigger newspapers got a hold of it. When Kat and I said no to the reporters who flocked to town looking for a story, they interviewed anyone they could get their hands on. While people meant well, their words ended up twisted to fit the sensationalized image needed to sell newspapers. The headlines read: Prominent family killed at Pearl Harbor. Daughters inherit massive fortune. The press painted me as a reclusive eccentric and Katherine as a party girl. After that, the flood gates opened. People wouldn't leave us alone. Friends and relatives we never knew we had, business proposals, marriage proposals, you name it—it was crazy. Most of the time, except for doctor visits, I locked myself in my room or father's study and left Katherine to deal with them all. Finally, she'd had enough. She packed her bags and left for California to pursue her singing career. I just refused to answer the door, though that didn't stop people from coming to the house. When the board turned down my request to take over the company, I knew it was time to go if I ever wanted any peace." She paused. "You asked me how I ended up in Bayonne, New Jersey teaching English. That's the answer, I wanted some peace in my life."

"Instead you got us and even worse crazies. I'm sorry, Elizabeth."

"Don't be. I'm not." Elizabeth hesitated for a moment. "No matter what happens here."

She means if Flanagan kills us. Please don't let that happen. "Elizabeth, remember Mama made me promise to be with the one I loved. To find a way."

"Yes, of course, but I don't think—"

Dante interrupted her. "Well, I love you, and I promise I'm going to try and find a way out of this."

"Dante, it's no use. Flanagan—"

"No. Shh, you listen now. We're going to get out of this, and when we do, we're getting married. I'm not letting another day go by without you with me."

"Either way, whatever happens, I'll be with you."

Her quiet words gnawed at Dante's gut.

"Besides, you haven't asked me."

"Asked you what?"

"To marry you."

The sound of a door closing echoed overhead.

"I'll ask you later, after we're out of here."

"No, ask me now." Silence for a moment. "In case there isn't a later."

"There will be. Try to believe that."

"Ask me."

He could hear the panic in her voice. *Stay calm.* "Okay." Dante swallowed, his throat suddenly dry. "Elizabeth, will you marry me?"

"Yes, Dante, I will." Her words took on a serene note.

The basement door opened and the dim glow of a bare light bulb came on.

Flanagan busied himself in the corner before coming to stand between them, just out of reach. "Well, how are my little love birds? Both awake, I hope."

"Let her go. She has nothing to do with this."

Flanagan moved in close, and Dante could smell alcohol coming off the man in waves. "She has everything to do with this. Do you think I'd look like this if her guinea friends hadn't gotten a hold of me? Your guinea friends too, right?"

"No."

Flanagan drove a fist into Dante's midsection. "Still no?"

Dante groaned. "No."

"You're a fuckin' liar." The Irishman reached into his back pocket and pulled out a small bottle. He took a long pull of the liquid and wiped the back of his hand across his mouth. His eyes narrowed. "Well, let's see if you still say no after I've had a couple of goes at the lady here."

"Leave her alone, you bastard." Dante surged forward, only to be stopped by his restraints.

Flanagan grinned at Dante's futile efforts and stepped up to Elizabeth. "Hello again, lass. Shall we give your boyfriend a little show?" He ran a dirty finger along the base of her throat and down her chest to the opening of her blouse.

Though she remained silent, Dante could see Elizabeth's involuntary shudder, even in the dim light. "Stop," he roared, straining even more. "Leave her alone."

Flanagan tucked the bottle into his pocket and grinned at Dante before turning back. "Let's get rid of this, shall we?" The gentle tone of his question belied the man's actions as he grabbed the lapels of her blouse. Buttons popped as he ripped it in one motion, the two pieces left hanging from the waistband of her slacks. Elizabeth let out an involuntary shriek, and the Irishman slapped her. "Shut up. You'll have the whole neighborhood down here."

Her head hung down, her chin touching her chest. *Maybe he knocked her out.* Dante hoped so, for her sake.

"You're a real man, aren't you? Beating on people who can't fight back?" Elizabeth lifted her head, blood running from the corner of her mouth.

"I'm a real man all right, and before we're done here, I'm goin' to show you." Flanagan grinned and ran a finger up her abdomen. Elizabeth sucked in her breath, the motion caving in her stomach muscles and bringing her ribcage into relief. He paused a moment at the point of her cleavage in the brassiere before continuing up her chest to her shoulder and then up her arm. "What's this?" He laid his palm flat against Elizabeth's upper arm and rubbed. "What the hell is wrong with ya?" He grabbed her arm and twisted her body toward the light. The movement put pressure on her manacled wrists, but he paid Elizabeth's cry no mind, twisting her even further around to get a look at her back. "What the hell happened here?"

For the first time, Dante got a good look at her back also. Numerous scars, some round, some jagged, covered the skin. Even in this light he could see some of them were quite deep.

Flanagan let go of her arm, and she flipped back around.

"What happened?"

She didn't answer, just flexed her hands in the cuffs.

He grabbed her hair and yanked her head back. "What happened?"

She returned his glare and said nothing.

"Let's see how tough you really are." Flanagan released one of her hands from the cuffs. Before she could bring her arm to her side, he grabbed her wrist, twisting it in a slow motion. Elizabeth's face registered the pain, but she didn't look away as she dangled there. As he continued to twist, a small whimper escaped her lips, but other than that, she refused to speak.

"Stop. Stop." Dante's shout came too late as he heard the snap of bone. Elizabeth screamed.

Flanagan dropped her wrist and she swung like a limp puppet. "Well?"

Dante hesitated, and Flanagan reached to uncuff Elizabeth's other arm.

"No. Stop. I'll tell you. She was hurt in the attack on Pearl Harbor."

He moved closer to Dante. "What? You're shittin' me! Pearl Harbor? With the Japs?"

Dante nodded.

"Well, well, I believe we got two fuckin' war heroes here." Flanagan paced to the wall and back. "Am I right?" When no one answered, Flanagan scooped up a piece of scrap wood laying on the floor and brought it across Dante's thigh.

The white hot pain caused Dante's knees to buckle; a loud hum sounded in his ears and nausea swelled in his gut as he fought to remain conscious.

"Am I right?"

"Yes," Dante answered through gritted teeth.

"I thought so." Elizabeth hung from the beam by one arm, her head lolled forward as Flanagan circled her before coming back to stand in front of Dante. "Tell me, boy-o, how do you cuddle up next to that? Leave the lights out? I may have to be doin' that before I'm done with her." He gave an exaggerated shiver and then laughed.

"You know, I'm thinkin' I'll make you a matched set." Flanagan went to the corner of the basement, his back to them.

Dante looked over at Elizabeth, she hadn't moved. *She's out. Try to keep it that way.* He heard a match strike and the distinct smell of gasoline, followed by a low hiss. When Flanagan turned around, he had a lit blow torch in one hand and a knife in the other. *God, help me. Help us.*

"Now, let's see. I could just light you on fire, like I did your building, but that'd be too quick. Sorry about your Ma, by the way. I didn't know she was in there."

"You bastard. You'd better kill me, or I swear I'll find a way to kill you."

Flanagan laughed. "Big words from a man trussed up like a turkey. Oh, I plan on killin' you all right. I'm thinkin' I'll roast you, a piece at a time." He rested the knife blade in the flame as he walked toward Dante. "Where shall we start? An arm? Maybe the face?" He placed the knife within an inch of Dante's cheek.

Dante didn't move.

Instead, Flanagan laid it along the length of his exposed forearm. Dante felt the pain of the burn all the way to the bone. The smell of burnt hair and flesh permeated the air. He groaned, knowing it was just the beginning. And it was. Flanagan cut away Dante's shirt and several times reheated the knife to lay on his chest and back, each time burning an impression of the knife blade wherever it touched his skin.

"You're tougher than you look. I thought you'd be screaming like a lass by now." Flanagan stood heating the knife blade again. "Let's see if we can do somethin' about that." He touched the hot knife point to Dante's abdomen and shoved.

Unprepared, a strangled cry escaped Dante's lips.

"That's more like it, but I'm afraid I'm going to have to end our game." Flanagan leered in Dante's face. "I'm feelin' the urge to move on to your girlfriend, or maybe I should say on top of your girlfriend, if you know what I mean, and I don't need an audience." He jerked the knife out and put it back in the flame, the blood on the blade sizzling in the heat. "Yeah, that looks good and hot. One more, right to the heart and it'll be over for you, boy-o." Flanagan raised the knife.

Dante steeled himself for the blow.

"Stop. You can't. You'll regret it." The words were barely above a whisper.

Flanagan turned. "What'd you say? I'm goin' to regret it? I seriously doubt that, lass. You'll be the only one regrettin' it." He turned back to Dante.

"No, you will. The Don will hunt you down."

Elizabeth, what are you doing?

"The Don's gonna hunt me down 'cause I kilt a tailor—a tailor that don't even make his suits. That's a good one." Flanagan stuck the blade back in the flame to heat.

"No." Elizabeth lifted her head and met Dante's gaze. "Forgive me, please, for telling you like this."

What is she talking about? Is she in shock?

"The Don will surely kill you, and in a way more painful than anything you can do to us, if you kill his son."

Both Dante and Flanagan stared at her.

Flanagan began to laugh. "That's rich. He's the Don's—" The man froze as what sounded like a firecracker went off. First, a small round hole appeared in his forehead and then a thin line of blood ran down between his eyebrows. Flanagan crumpled to the floor.

Dante looked past him before slumping in relief. One of Gino Galenti's men stood on the stairs, a smoking gun in hand.

"Are they there?" Gino's step down the stairs was fast, belying his bulk and age. "Dante? Boy, are you okay?"

"I'm okay."

"You don't look so okay." Gino came to a stop in front of him. "The bastard burnt you? And you're bleeding?" The old man turned and kicked the corpse on the floor with the point of his polished shoe. "*Bastardo*! Get him down," he ordered the men behind him. After a few minutes of searching, the men located the key and unlocked Dante's cuffs. He would have collapsed if Gino hadn't been there to support his weight.

Dante straightened up at Elizabeth's cry and then the abrupt silence. She laid in the arms of one of the men, her head lolled back. "Be careful. I think her arm is broken."

"Put her in my car. Rocco," Gino lifted his head toward Flanagan's body. "Get rid of that piece of garbage and clean this place up." He turned back to Dante. "It's better we not go to the hospital. Best to keep the cops out of this." He reached into his pocket and pulled out a snowy white handkerchief to press against Dante's abdomen. "Can you walk?"

Dante held the cloth in place. "Yes. Thanks, Gino." The two men worked their way to the stairs. Dante grabbed the railing and pulled himself up the stairs first. "You know, I would've already been dead by the time you got here if Elizabeth hadn't stalled him." He gave a bark of a laugh. "She told him I was Salucci's son."

"Really?"

"Yeah, can you imagine? There's a whopper."

Gino said nothing, and soon they were outside. Elizabeth was in the back seat of Gino's car, and Dante could tell by the position of her head, she was still unconscious.

A man moved up the sidewalk toward them, stopping a few feet short of Gino and Dante. "You're all right?"

The Don himself is here? Dante nodded, his eyes not leaving the other man's face.

"Gino, I've contacted Dr. Ciccone. He is expecting them." The Don kept his gaze on Dante.

"*Sì.*" At the wave of Gino's hand, a man standing by opened the back door of the car. "Dante?"

Neither man looked Gino's way. Dante broke the silence. "Thanks for your help."

The man nodded.

"I blamed you for our misfortune."

The Don said nothing.

"Flanagan admitted to setting the fire."

The Don closed his eyes for a moment, inhaling a deep breath. "Then it is a good thing for him that he is already dead."

His words were so close to what Elizabeth said earlier in the basement it gave Dante pause. It was his turn to nod.

"Your mother was a very special woman."

Both men were silent for a few moments until the Don indicated the still form of Elizabeth in the car. "What about her?"

Dante stepped to the side, blocking Salucci's view of Elizabeth. "What about her? She has nothing to do with this."

His gesture did not go unmissed. "You know, for such small creatures, women wield so much power, sometimes without ever knowing it." The Don paused. "I believe Miss Wellman is also a special woman. Don't make the same mistake I did so long ago and let her get away."

"I won't."

The Don nodded. "Have a good life with your woman." He held out his hand.

Dante hesitated and then clasped the other man's hand. "I will."

The older man stepped forward, and for a moment Dante thought the Don was going to hug him. Instead in an abrupt move the man stepped back. "Dante, I..." He stopped and cleared his throat a couple of times. "Good bye, Dante." With that, the Don turned on his heel and walked away without a backward glance.

Dante stood on the sidewalk, feeling as if he'd just lost something, but unable to figure out what. He climbed into the car next to Elizabeth. The dark sedan pulled away from the curb, into the night.

Chapter 23

July 1944

Elizabeth sat in front of the vanity in the brides' dressing room. She worked to nestle the combs of the veil behind the rolled hair at the front of her head. It wasn't sitting quite right. "Oh, why can't I do this?" She'd practiced the hair style several times over the last few weeks, and it came out fine, even with a cast on her arm. The cast had been gone for a few days now. *Probably just nerves.* But Elizabeth knew that wasn't it. She was marrying Dante today and couldn't be happier about it. *Katherine.* She'd hoped Katherine would make it here. Elizabeth wrote to her last address, but hadn't heard anything. Her sister could be anywhere on tour.

Elizabeth tugged off the veil. Several strands of hair pulled out of the rolled part to stand askew. She sighed and removed all the pins to start again, her hair cascading around her shoulders. She stared at her reflection in the mirror as a soft knock sounded at the door. "Come in."

Dante slipped into the room and closed the door behind him. "Hello." He smiled.

"Hello." She smiled back. "You know, they say it's bad luck to see the bride before the wedding. I'm sure Father Rosini would frown on you being in here."

"Bad luck? The bishop gave us permission to wed." He walked to where Elizabeth sat and pulled her into his arms. "Besides, right now, the bishop's and Father Rosini's heads are full of plans for the new parish building."

"It's wonderful they're naming it after your mother."

"It is, and I wanted to thank the donors, but Father Rosini said they wished to remain anonymous." Dante smiled. "Anyway, I wanted to see you." He touched his lips to hers, tender at first, then in a more urgent fashion. She returned the kiss with just as much fervor. It was several moments before they broke apart, both breathing heavy.

"I love you so much. I am glad our wedding day is finally here." He kissed her again and nuzzled her neck for a moment. "You smell good."

"Thank you. I love you too." She cleared her throat and stepped back. "We've got to remember we're in church." She dropped down on the bench again, turning to the mirror.

Dante studied her reflection in the mirror for a few moments. "What's really bothering you?"

Elizabeth shook her head as she pulled the brush through her hair. "Nothing."

"Elizabeth, are you having second thoughts?"

She met his gaze in the mirror. "No, I love you, more than ever. It's just..."

Dante turned her around on the bench and lifted her chin with a finger. "It's just what?" He leaned in and gave her a light kiss. "Tell me." He gave her another kiss. "I want to make you happy."

"I know you do. And I am happy. Honestly. It's just—I was hoping my sister, Katherine, would be able to attend. You made her a beautiful dress, and I've always thought we'd be together on a special day like this." She shrugged. "I know it sounds silly."

"Not at all. I wish Mama was here too. She'd be in her glory. It seems neither of us have much family left."

Gino had told Elizabeth Dante didn't believe her about the Don being his father. Through Gino, the Don had requested she not bring it up again. It would be safer for them both if no one ever knew. She had agreed. "Well, you have Nicolina and your uncle and aunt. It was very kind of your Aunt Rosa to arrange the reception food."

They were marrying in St. Anthony's and the reception would be at Port Johnson. It seemed fitting since so many people in their world were connected to that spot and it was where they met.

"Elizabeth, once we get established, we'll start our own family." He brushed a finger along her cheek. "*Sì?*"

She blushed. "Yes."

He smiled. "I don't think you could look more beautiful than you do at this moment, but I believe our guests are expecting something a little different. Should I send Nicolina in to help you?"

Elizabeth nodded.

"I'm sorry, *cara mia*, about your sister. I hoped she would be here for your sake."

"It's all right, Dante. The important part is we're getting to start our life together." She gave him a quick kiss and turned back to the mirror. "If you could find Nicolina, that'd be wonderful." Elizabeth arranged her features into a smile. "Please."

He nodded and headed out.

"Dante?"

He turned back, his hand on the door knob.

"I love you."

"I love you too. I'll see you at the altar."

Dante went in search of Nicolina. Fifteen minutes later, he located her in the parking lot with several other young girls. He tapped her on the shoulder. "Nico, I think Elizabeth could use your help. She's having trouble fixing her hair."

Nicolina gave him a perplexed look. "What are you talking about? I just saw her a minute ago. Her hair looks gorgeous. In fact, she looks stunning. Marrying you must really agree with her."

"What are you talking about? I left Elizabeth in the dressing room."

"Are you sure?" She pointed over his shoulder. "I think you'd better look again."

Dante turned around. Elizabeth stood on the walkway in front of the church, but not the Elizabeth he'd left earlier. Her hair was arranged in a flawless style and her outfit the height of fashion. She chatted with several men, smiling up at each in turn.

He walked to her side. "Excuse me, gentlemen. Elizabeth, shouldn't you be getting dressed?"

"Elizabeth?" She smiled, exposing white teeth next to her brilliant red lipstick. "Elizabeth?"

He nodded. "Are you feeling all right? If you're not well, we can get married another day."

"Married? Another day?" She paused and her grin got even wider. "Dante? You're Dante."

"Of course I'm Dante. Elizabeth, I think maybe this has all been too much. I can talk to Father Rosini and—"

She cut him off. "Nonsense. I wouldn't miss this for the world."

He gave her a strange look.

"I'm sorry. It has been a bit stressful. You understand?" She smiled again and tucked an arm through his. "Would you escort me back to get dressed?"

He nodded and led her through the side door of the church, his limp accented by the uneven click of their heels on the marble floor as the sound echoed around the hallway. He glanced at her, but said nothing until his hand was on the knob of the dressing room door. "Are you sure you're ready to go through with this?" He swung the door open. "I'm sure everyone will understand if we don't have the wedding today."

"Why wouldn't we have the wedding today? What's wrong?"

The voice came from behind him. Dante swung around. Elizabeth stood in the center of the room, still in her dressing gown.

"Dante, what's wrong?"

He looked from her to the woman in the hallway, who stood grinning, and back to Elizabeth again. He shook his head. "Two."

"Dante, whatever is wrong with you?" Elizabeth rushed to his side. "Tell me."

"I suspect it may have something to do with me."

Elizabeth turned her head at the voice, unable to believe her own ears.

"Hello, Lizzie."

Katherine stepped into the room and Elizabeth flew into her sister's arms. "Kat, you're here. You're really here. I can't believe it." Tears welled.

"Of course I am. I wasn't going to miss my sister's wedding." Katherine loosened Elizabeth's arms. "You can let up. I'm not going anywhere for a few minutes. Your boyfriend looks like he might need a hug though."

Elizabeth glanced at Dante. He still hung onto the door knob, watching the two of them. She slid an arm around Katherine's waist. "Dante, this is my sister, Katherine." He didn't move. "Isn't it wonderful? She made it in time for the wedding. Dante?"

"I take it you didn't tell him we were twins."

Dante found his voice. "I thought you said you didn't have any more secrets."

"Oh, Dante. I don't, honest." Elizabeth shrugged. "It just never came up in conversation." At his bewildered expression, she pulled him into the room. "Dante." She put a hand on either side of his face and stared into his eyes. "I love you, and want to be your wife more than I've ever wanted anything." She stretched up on tip toe and brushed his lips with her own. "Will you marry me?" Her question was little more than a whisper.

"Yes." He kissed her back.

"Are you ready?" It was Gino. The man looked resplendent in his black tux as he stepped into the room, ready to escort Elizabeth down the aisle. "Dante, what are you doing in here? You're not supposed to be here. You're not even dressed. Go get dressed." He turned. "*Santo Christo!*" He crossed himself and looked skyward for a moment. "Sorry, Lord. What's going on here?"

Elizabeth smiled. "Mr. Galenti, this is my sister, Katherine Wellman. My twin sister."

The man's head seemed to be on a swivel as his jowls tried to keep up. "Twins? What do you know? Huh. Amazing." In a gallant gesture, he took Katherine's hand and kissed it. "It's a pleasure to meet you, Miss Wellman. I expect you to save me a dance at the reception. But for now, Dante, you come with me." He patted Kat's hand. "Miss Wellman, we'll leave you and Elizabeth to get ready. I'll be back shortly to escort you ladies."

After they left, the two women stood in silence for a few moments.

Katherine pulled off her hat and gloves. "Well, I think we have a wedding to get ready for. Would you like me to do your hair?"

"Yes, please." Elizabeth slid back onto the bench and watched her sister in the mirror as Katherine brushed her hair.

"Elizabeth, what are you staring at?"

"I can't believe you're here and as always, you look so beautiful. Are you happy doing what you're doing?"

"The touring? It's the best. Sometimes it's tough, and once or twice it's been a little scary." Katherine held the brush up at Elizabeth's alarmed look. "I'm fine. It's nothing like Pearl. Nothing will ever be like Pearl." She was quiet for a moment as she continued to brush Elizabeth's hair. "Thank you, Lizzie."

She sounds so serious. "For what?"

"You saved my life that day, more than once. I know you were hurt protecting me."

"My injuries weren't your fault. It just happened."

"We both know that's not true. I'd probably be dead if it weren't for you."

"Kat, that's not true."

"Yes, it is. You were always one to keep to yourself with your books and such, but after Pearl, you withdrew even more. I know how painful all those operations were, and I felt so guilty. Then those stupid articles came out and all those crazy people showed up. So, what'd I do? Instead of staying to help you, I ran away. I'm sorry, Lizzie."

"There's nothing for you to be sorry about. I did withdraw. I missed our old life so much. To be honest, sometimes I wished I'd died with Mother and Father. I decided no one would get close to me again, not that I thought anyone would want to—with my scars and all."

Katherine dug in her purse for a handkerchief. She dabbed at her eyes and sniffed back tears. "I'm so sorry I left you all alone to deal with everything. I just couldn't take it—"

Elizabeth put her hand up to stop her sister. "Let me finish. Once you left and I found out I wasn't going to be able to run the company, I realized I couldn't stay in Northam any longer either. There was nothing there for me—except memories and people who wanted our money. So, I came here and took a teaching job. No one knew me. I could hide in plain sight. I didn't have to get involved, but thank goodness I did. That's when I met Dante. And Katherine, as painful as life has been at times, everything that's happened to me—to us, had to happen to bring us to this moment. I'm happy and about to get married to the man I love and who loves me. Please don't be sorry, Kat."

Katherine nodded. "I won't say I'm sorry then, but I do thank you, Elizabeth, for saving me that day."

Elizabeth reached up to wrap her arms around her sister and give her a squeeze. "You're welcome. Always." The two stayed this way for several moments.

"I love you, Elizabeth."

"I love you too."

Katherine sniffed again and pulled back. "How about we finish your hair?"

"Please." Elizabeth watched as Katherine worked her hair into several intricate rolls before attaching the veil. "There. All done. This veil is gorgeous." Katherine smoothed it down to rest on Elizabeth's shoulders. "Can I do your makeup?"

"Thank you. I'd appreciate that."

"Your Dante is a very handsome man."

"Yes, he is." Elizabeth smiled. "But better than that, he's kind."

Elizabeth sat for Katherine's administrations until the woman stepped back "There. What do you think?"

The image reflected back from the mirror startled Elizabeth. She looked as beautiful as Katherine. "Thank you."

"You're welcome. I think I could use a little repair myself." A few minutes later, Katherine closed her compact. "There, that's better. I wasn't sure what I was supposed to wear, so I brought several gowns. My luggage is in the vestibule of the church. Maybe we can have someone bring it over?"

"I will, but don't worry about a dress. Dante made you one."

"What? Your Dante? Made me a dress? This I've got to see."

Half an hour later, the sisters stood in front of the mirror for a final look. Katherine twisted right and left. "This is spectacular. I would've never thought of a man creating something like this, but he's incredibly talented. Look at how this fits. It's amazing." The dress was a very pale pastel green satin and close fitting, its off-the-shoulder style and fitted sleeves further accentuating Katherine's small waist. "He couldn't have done a better job if I'd been here for fittings. I want him to make all my clothes. And look at you—you look like a princess in a fairy tale. That has to be the most beautiful wedding dress I've ever seen."

Elizabeth smiled. Katherine was right. It was exquisite. The under dress was white satin, the skirt full, but fitted at the waist and fashioned into a bustier top. A layer of delicate lace formed sleeves and covered the dress from necklace to hem. The clean lines and lack of other embellishments further enhanced the beauty of the simplistic style. "He's very talented."

A knock sounded.

"Come in."

Gino entered and smiled upon seeing the two women. "You two are going to outshine any other women here today." He came to stand in front of Elizabeth. "And you, my dear, are the most beautiful bride I've ever seen. Dante is a lucky man."

"I'm a lucky woman."

He nodded. "That you are. Dante is a good boy. I wish my Maria could have been here for this." He pulled a handkerchief from his coat pocket and wiped at his eyes before clearing his throat. "But I know she's looking down on us and smiling. Are you ready, Elizabeth?"

"Yes."

"Good." He gave her a kiss on the cheek and then reached up to lower her veil. He extended his arm. "Shall we?"

Like so many other times when they had appeared together, people gasped at the sight of Katherine followed by Elizabeth. But for the first time in Elizabeth's life, it didn't bother her. *I'm my own person now, and I have a man that loves me for me.* The thought brought a smile to her lips and her eyes up to search for Dante. And there he was, standing at the front of the church with the priest. *He's so handsome.* Their eyes locked.

Soon, the ceremony was over, formal pictures taken, and they were entering the gates of Port Johnson, chauffeured in one of Gino's car with the rest of the wedding party and guests in assorted vehicles behind them. The driver parked in front of the Rec hall.

Elizabeth gathered her gown close to move when someone tapped on the window.

Dante rolled his eyes. "Our audience awaits. Are you ready, Mrs. Montenari?"

Elizabeth nodded.

He gave her a quick kiss before opening the door.

People milled around outside. Everyone clapped as Dante assisted Elizabeth from the car. Gino and Katherine joined them before heading into the Rec hall.

"What is this place?" Katherine whispered.

"Believe it or not, a former POW camp."

"And you're having your wedding reception here because?" Katherine looked around. "I'll be the first to admit finances aren't my strong point—except for the spending money part, but surely we have enough to afford a more conventional reception hall?" She hesitated. "We do...don't we?"

Elizabeth smiled at her sister. "Of course. I've invested some of my share, but there's plenty left."

"Oh, whew. I was concerned for a moment. So, why are we here?"

"Lots of reasons. I volunteer teach here. Lots of our friends are here...and most importantly, I met Dante here."

"He was a POW?"

"No, silly. He was my interpreter."

"Of course he was. And exactly what did he interpret?"

Elizabeth laughed outright at her sister's dry tone. "Italian. I wrote to you about teaching here."

"Yeah, but I didn't realize your interpreter looked like him. Maybe I should've finished college."

Gino opened the door. Elizabeth and Dante stepped through. Mrs. Moretti waited and gave each of them a kiss on the cheek and then held up a finger. "*Un momento.*"

The band was set up on a low riser at the other end of the hall. Alessio stood at the microphone looking dapper in a white dinner jacket, black tie and black pants. "Ladies and gentlemen, may I present Mr. and Mrs. Dante Montenari?"

Loud applause filled the building as Nicolina escorted them to a table.

"And now, the best man and maid of honor. Mr. Gino Galenti and Miss Katherine Wellman." More applause and murmurs of surprise as some people got their first look at Elizabeth's sister. Gino escorted Katherine to the seat next to Elizabeth and then took his own seat on the other side of Dante.

The hours that followed were filled with laughter, food and dancing as the band accompanied Alessio.

Nicolina bent down between Dante and Elizabeth. "Congratulations."

They both smiled.

"Ah, Miss Wellman, the boys—" Nico stopped at Dante's frown. "Oh sorry, force of habit. Mrs. Montenari, the boys would like to know if you'd consider singing with them, just one time. You can say no, it's your wedding day, but they were wondering."

Katherine leaned forward. "Since when did you start singing of your own free will? That's a switch."

Elizabeth shrugged. "Not often, but once in a while. It's fun."

"You're darn tootin' it's fun. It's the best."

Nicolina studied the woman a moment. "Do you sing too?"

Katherine nodded.

"Nicolina, I'm sorry. You haven't been introduced. This is my sister Katherine. Katherine, this is Nicolina Moretti, Dante's cousin. My sister is a professional singer. She's been touring with Bob Hope's USO show."

"Wow. I had no idea." Nicolina grinned. "Would you like to sing too?"

"Sure." Katherine looked at Elizabeth. "It's your wedding. I guess the least I could do is let you pick."

"Hmm, how about *The Very Thought of You?*"

Katherine grinned. "Good choice. You're taking lead."

Elizabeth nodded. "Fine." She turned to Dante. "Do you mind?"

"No. I love to listen to you sing."

Nicolina straightened. "Let me just check with the band to make sure they know it." She was back a couple of minutes later. "You're all set. The next song, okay?"

Nicolina spoke with Alessio off to the side of the stage as the band finished up a Glenn Miller instrumental. He nodded and stepped behind the microphone when the song ended. "Ladies and gentleman, we have a special treat for you. Miss—Mrs. Montenari and her sister, Miss Wellman have agreed to sing for us. I'd like you to give Miss Wellman an especially large round of applause. She's been entertaining the troops overseas."

Elizabeth gave Dante a kiss. "I'll be right back. This is for you."

More clapping and a few whistles accompanied the womens' arrival on the stage. They stood side by side behind the microphone. The horn section started out. As Elizabeth stepped closer to the microphone Katherine reached over and gave her hand a squeeze.

Our lives have changed so much since the last time we stood on a stage together. Elizabeth squeezed her sister's hand back, but directed her gaze toward her new husband as she began to sing. Her love for Dante resonated with every word she sang. He sat at the table and watched her, a serious expression on his face.

Katherine's harmonies were perfect. They were on the last verse when Dante rose. By the time Elizabeth finished the song, he'd reached the riser, but didn't stop until he stood next to her behind the microphone.

"I love you." He took Elizabeth in his arms seemingly oblivious to the people around them or the fact that his words had been picked up on the microphone. Lost in the kiss, it was several moments before Dante and Elizabeth registered the deafening applause, shouts and whistles. They stepped apart. Though Dante's smile was self-conscious, he kept an arm around Elizabeth's waist, holding her close.

Alessio stepped up to Elizabeth. "Would you be willing to do another one? Everyone loved it."

Elizabeth looked over at Katherine. Her sister's wide smile reflected her own. "Can you sing a few? I'd really like to dance with my husband."

"Sure." Katherine stepped forward to hug her sister, then Dante. "It's plain to see you love my sister, and she loves you. You're a lucky man, there's nobody like her." She laughed and added with a wink, "Except me." Katherine hugged them both at once. "It feels good to be a family again. It's been too long." After a moment, she sniffed and stepped back. "Okay, you two. Go dance. I've got work to do here."

The newly married couple moved to the dance floor as the band played a ballad in accompaniment to Katherine's sultry vocals. Dante took Elizabeth in his arms. She leaned her head against his shoulder and hummed along with the music.

"We're going to have to think about leaving soon," Dante whispered near her ear.

Elizabeth raised her head and glanced at her sister on stage. As usual, Katherine was at ease with her surroundings and enjoying herself.

"Unless you'd rather not go." He hesitated. "We could cancel it."

Their honeymoon was going to be a short trip to Niagara Falls. It was about all they had time for, with the factory opening soon. School was out for the summer, and other than teaching at Port Johnson, Elizabeth had spent from sun up 'til long after sun down working with Dante to get things ready, often falling asleep in the car on the ride back to her house. They'd both been looking forward to a few days away.

Elizabeth glanced at her sister once more before shaking her head. "No. Mr. Galenti sent his driver to book Katherine a room at the Belvedere Hotel until we get back. She's been out on tour for a while, so she's looking forward to being waited on." Elizabeth smiled. "By tomorrow afternoon, she'll be sitting by the pool, and men will be falling all over themselves for her attention."

"You two are so different."

Elizabeth laid her head back on his shoulder as they continued to move to the music. "Most people think we're alike, because we look alike."

Dante shook his head.

"Thank you."

"For what?"

"For loving me." She hesitated. "For me."

Dante stopped dancing and turned Elizabeth's face up to meet his gaze.

"Not for my money, or in spite of my scars, or—"

He laid a finger against Elizabeth's lips to stop her words. "I'll always love you. When you burn fried chicken." Dante smiled at her scowl. "When we argue. When you sing to our babies." Dante's kiss was gentle. "Always," he whispered against her lips.

Elizabeth knew he spoke the truth. She felt the same way. "Are you ready to go?" she asked Dante between kisses.

"Yes."

Hand in hand, the couple left the dance floor to say goodbye to their guests and hello to the new life that awaited.

Chapter 24

August 1945

Elizabeth rolled over and stretched, the movement relaxing her tight back muscles as a yawn escaped her lips. *Another day.* She glanced at the spot in the bed next to her. Empty. The pillow lay atop undisturbed bedding. She'd discovered early on in her marriage, while she barely moved in her sleep Dante had a tendency to sprawl, dislodging bedding on a nightly basis. She touched the cool pillow. *I miss you so much.* She felt tears well in her eyes. *Stop. There's no time for this.* Elizabeth glanced at the alarm clock and pushed herself into an upright position. *You can't just lolly gag around.* There was too much to do, now that Elizabeth worked full time as the plant manager. She stretched again before heading to the bathroom.

Forty minutes later, Elizabeth closed the front door of the house, picked up the newspaper off the porch floor and with tea in hand, headed to the factory. She glanced at the headline. It was yet another story about the two bombs President Truman had ordered dropped on Japan. The picture under the headline showed an aerial view of land scrubbed clean of any life. Elizabeth shook her head. *Is this war ever going to end?* So many casualties on all sides. Then the discovery of Hitler's death camps a few months ago and now this—thousands of Japanese lives taken in a matter of minutes— men, women and children. She'd read an article about the relentless Japanese military and that this show of force was the only way to let them know the U.S. meant business. *But all those lives lost?* Hadn't the world's people already suffered enough? Just about everyone she knew had made sacrifices to this war.

Elizabeth worked her way across the full parking lot. Heat was already coming off the pavement in waves. *It's going to be another scorcher.* She'd chosen to wear a loose fitting cotton dress with short sleeves, just in case the large overhead fans went on the fritz again today. She pulled open the front door to the lobby.

"Good morning, Mrs. Montenari." Emmeline Teagartner, Elizabeth's assistant, stood behind her desk, a stack of papers in hand.

"Hello, Emmeline. How are you today?"

"I'm good." The young woman smiled, showing the gap between her front teeth. "How are you feeling today?"

"I'm fine." Elizabeth headed toward her office, but stopped at the empty desk in front of the office next to hers. "Where's Nicolina?"

"Oh, she called in sick." The young woman pushed black cat-eye glasses back up the bridge of her nose.

"Really? That's unlike her. Did she say what's wrong?"

Emmeline shrugged, but dropped her eyes to the papers in her hands. "I have no idea."

"Hmm." Nicolina had been moping around lately. *She probably misses Dante too.* Elizabeth ignored the feeling of sadness that washed over her at the thought of him. *Shake it off.* "Well, hopefully she's better by tomorrow. Can you bring me the Rochester Company file? Also, could you get Larry Wheeler on the phone?" Elizabeth laid the newspaper on the small table in her office before sitting at her desk.

A few minutes later, Emmeline set the file on her desk. "Here you go. Would you like more tea?"

Elizabeth shook her head. "No, thanks. It's not sitting too well." She opened a desk drawer and pulled out a tin of saltine crackers. "A few of these should help. I didn't get a chance to eat breakfast."

Emmeline gave her a sympathetic look. "That's not good. Do you want me to get you some toast or something from the kitchen?"

"No, that's fine. These will hold me until lunch. Did you reach Larry Wheeler?"

"He's not in yet. His secretary said she'd give him the message as soon as he got there." The phone on Emmeline's desk rang. "That's probably him." She rushed out to answer it and was back in a minute. "No. It's Flora upstairs in sewing. She's asking if you could come up."

Elizabeth rose from her desk. "Yes. Tell her I'm on my way." Pushing through the double doors to the first floor workroom she was met with a chorus of greetings from the workers on the floor. "Good morning, everyone." She worked her way up the flight of stairs to the second floor. The industrial fans hanging from the ceiling on every floor were running at full speed, forcing cooled air down into the large rooms. By this afternoon, despite the fans, the sunshine through the large windows would heat the whole area, making it feel like one of those Swedish saunas. If the fans stopped working again today, Elizabeth would have to call a halt to production. She couldn't have people passing out on the line.

"Morning, Mrs. Montenari."

At the top of the stairs, the resident mechanic stood at a cart with a sewing machine resting on it.

"Good morning, Luca." Elizabeth stopped. "Is the machine broken?"

He shook his head. "Naw. I'm just showing Carmine how to oil it. Again. We gotta do it more often in the summer. This heat makes moisture. You mix that with the lint from the material and it gums up the works."

"I see. That makes sense." She smiled at the squat little man. "Are you doing all the machines now?"

Luca shook his head. "It's best to do it before the girls start sewing and the machines get warm. This is the last one for today. Carmine, you do this one."

The lanky man nodded and stepped up to the machine.

"Good morning, Mr. Carapetti. How's the transfer working out?"

"Mornin'. Pretty good. It's better than shipping. It's too damn hot up there." Carmine worked several screws out and lifted the metal plate off the machine. "How are you doin'?" He hesitated and then gave her a slight smile. "You look good—considerin'."

She stiffened. "Considering what?"

"Well, you know," Carmine stammered.

Luca cuffed the taller man on the shoulder. "Shut up, Carmine, and pay attention to what you're doin'. You're gettin' oil all over the place."

"Sorry. Sorry." The man ducked his head. "I didn't mean nothin' by it."

Elizabeth turned away, but not before she heard Luca whisper, "*Idiota.* Don't you know anything? You shouldn't say something like that to a woman in her state."

Flora O'Hearn hurried up to her. "Good morning, ma'am. I hate to bother you, but we've got a wee bit of a problem."

"Yes?"

"Well, you know the boys shirts we're putting together? Some blue and some red?"

Elizabeth nodded.

The Irish woman held up two sleeves, one red, and one blue. "Well, the problem is we got twice as many navy blue sleeves as we need, and only half the red sleeves we need."

"Okay. Well, that's fixable. Just have the cutters cut some more red sleeves and we'll use the blue ones in another production run."

Flora shook her head. "We can't. We're all out of red material until the next shipment. In two weeks."

Elizabeth took the sleeves from the woman and thought for a moment. "Use the extra blue sleeves on the red shirts."

"What?"

Elizabeth went to the table that held bundles of cut pieces. She arranged the front of a red shirt on the table and then laid the blue sleeve next to it, before tugging out another blue sleeve. "See?

We'll have Nancy Tillson market them as a two-tone shirt that'll go with both red and blue. What do you think?"

The woman nodded and grinned. "Who knows? It may be the next big hit, and all the boys will want them. Thank you, ma'am."

Elizabeth smiled back. "You're welcome. And Flora, they shouldn't, but if for some reason the fans quit again, let me know. It's going to be hotter than yesterday." She turned to leave. "Okay, I'm expecting a call, so I have to get back to my office."

"Yes, ma'am." The woman's face creased into a frown. "Maybe you should take the elevator, it's, ahh...faster."

"No. I'm fine. Thanks."

Elizabeth worked her way back to the office and tried to concentrate on the financial reports laid out on her desk, even as one person after another asked to see her. The dilemmas ranged from the new cutter not being able to do simple math, which explained the extra blue sleeves, to Herbert Wilson asking if there was a policy about employees dating. He wanted to ask Betty Sue, one of the kitchen assistants, to the movies. Elizabeth fielded all of these questions and more before Emmeline called in, "Mr. Wheeler is on the line."

Elizabeth glanced at the clock. Two hours had passed since she came back to the office. *No wonder my back hurts.* "Thank you, Emmeline." She lifted the receiver and pushed a button on the telephone. "Hello, Larry? Elizabeth Montenari here. How are you?" She paused to listen a moment. "No, I'm fine, Larry. Yes, honestly. It's been a bit of an adjustment, but I'm not the first woman to have to deal with it." She cleared her throat. "Ahh, listen, the reason I'm calling is the sewing machines you sold us last month. Four of them have needed to be repaired several times already. My mechanic says it looks to be defective bobbin casings." She listened again. "You know? When were you going to tell your customers?" Elizabeth leaned back in her chair. "Well, Larry, it may not be cost effective for you to notify every customer, but it's not cost effective for my workers to have to keep untangling thread and to re-sew pieces. I'd like new machines here by Thursday, please. Otherwise, I may just have to look elsewhere when we expand again in the spring." She waited a moment. "Thank you, Larry. Talk to you soon. Yes, good bye." She dropped the receiver back in the cradle and stood up. The back of her dress was damp from leaning against her leather office chair. "I think I'm going to take a short walk. I've been sitting in that chair too long."

Emmeline appeared in the doorway. "Oh. Well, I'm sorry, Mrs. Montenari, but Mrs. Stiles is waiting to speak to you."

The cook? Now what? Elizabeth dropped back in the chair with a sigh. "Have her come in." She waited as the buxom woman in a white uniform dress and hairnet settled into the chair on the other side of the desk. "Good morning, Mrs. Stiles. What can I help you with?"

"It's the heat."

"I'm sorry. What about the heat?"

"It's just too hot to light the ovens."

Elizabeth glanced at the clock again. "Mrs. Stiles, lunch breaks start in fifteen minutes. Today is," Elizabeth turned her chair to look at the menu tacked to a cork board on the wall. "Roast pork with mashed potatoes and gravy. Have you prepared any of it?"

The woman shook her head. "It's too hot."

Patience. "Yes, it is hot, and I'm sure we're going to have a few more hot days ahead of us before cooler weather sets in."

Mrs. Stiles nodded in agreement, but remained silent.

"Nonetheless, we have to feed the employees," Elizabeth spoke in a calm voice. "Mrs. Stiles, why didn't you come to me earlier?"

"I don't know." The woman shrugged and wouldn't meet Elizabeth's gaze. "I, ahh, I guess I thought I'd have more time before it started to heat up. I don't know."

She doesn't know? Mrs. Stiles knew everything that went on in her kitchen, and a good deal about what went on in the rest of the factory too. *What's going on today? Dante, I wish you were here.* Elizabeth sniffed and ran a finger along the underside of each eye.

"Are you okay, Mrs. Montenari?"

"Yes, yes. I haven't been sleeping well."

"Well, it's no wonder. What with this heat and everything else that's going on."

"I'm sorry—what else is going on?"

"Nothing. I don't know." Bertha Stiles shifted in her seat. "What do you want to do about lunch?"

Elizabeth ignored the woman's unusual brusqueness and turned to look at the menu again. "Okay. Let's see. You cooked ham yesterday. Do you have leftovers?"

"Of course. I was going to use it to make ham and eggs on Friday for breakfast."

"Why don't you make that into ham salad? Do you have some boiled eggs? Maybe egg salad? Some pickles. We'll have a cold buffet lunch. How does that sound?"

The woman sighed in relief and lifted her bulk out of the chair. "Perfect. Okay, I'd better get started."

"Mrs. Stiles?"

The woman was halfway out the door. "Yes?"

"Can you tell me how long it'll take to prepare? I'll have to let people know."

"Hmm, yes." The woman still kept her eyes averted. "About half an hour, I'd say."

"Good. Thank..." The woman was already gone.

Elizabeth got up and picked at her damp dress. "Emmeline? We need to let people know lunch is going to be late."

"Okay. I don't know why, but the intercom isn't working. Luca's going to check it out. Do you need me to go with you? "

Me? "No, I guess I could do it myself."

"Oh good. I need to get these invoices typed." The girl turned back to her typewriter.

"All right. I'll be back shortly." Elizabeth started at the first floor. "I need to make an announcement." Everyone left their tables to stand as a group in front of the dining room doors. "Unfortunately, lunch is going to be about half an hour late and we've decided to have cold food." Instead of the grumbling she'd expected, everyone just nodded. "Okay, that's it. You can go back to work now." She was half way up the flight of stairs before people disbursed. *This heat is slowing everyone down. Myself included.* Elizabeth continued her second trip of the day up the stairs to the next floor. *I'm going to need to drink some water.* The reaction to her announcement on the sewing floor was much the same as the first floor. Acquiescence.

She headed to the stairs again. *One more flight.* It was with relief Elizabeth stepped onto the landing of the third floor a few minutes later. *Carmine's right. It's definitely hotter up here than the rest of the building.* She spotted Thomas Tillson and crossed the floor to where he stood. "Hi, Thomas."

"Mrs. Montenari. How are you? Are you getting along?"

Without Dante, you mean? "I'm fine." She went on to tell him the altered lunch plans.

He nodded. "No problem. Are you sure you're okay? You look a little flushed."

"It's the heat." Her smile was wan. "And the stair climbing."

"Please take the elevator back. It'll get you to the first floor in a couple of minutes."

"Today, I think I will."

Thomas tapped the call button with one of his hooks. "It should be here in just a moment or two. If you'll excuse me, I need to go downstairs and talk to Mrs. O'Hearn."

"Would you like to ride down with me?"

Thomas shook his head. "No. No. I'll be gone just a second." He patted his flat mid-section. "Plus, Nancy says I'm getting chunky, so I could use the exercise. I'll talk to you soon." With that, he hustled down the stairs out of sight.

What's taking the elevator so long? Elizabeth tapped the button several times and glanced at the stairs as she waited. *Should I?* She had her foot on the top step when the elevator doors slid open. Elizabeth stepped in. *I'm going to have to talk to Luca about this thing. It's way too slow.* It felt like forever before the doors finally slid closed. Her stomach growled. *Well, it has to be lunch time now. I'm starved.*

When Elizabeth stepped out on the first floor all was quiet, except for the whir of the large fans. Everyone was gone. Her stomach rumbled again. "Yes, yes. I hear you. Let me get my tea cup first." She pushed through the doors to the lobby area. "Emmeline, are you ready for lunch?"

The girl wasn't at her desk. *That's strange. She usually waits for me.* Elizabeth retrieved her mug. The usual hubbub of lunch conversation heard through the walls was missing as she approached the dining hall. *They must not be happy with the meal. Or maybe they found a shady spot outside.* That thought appealed to Elizabeth. *Maybe I'll grab a sandwich and go sit on the porch at home for a few minutes...just to get away.* She pulled open the door.

"Surprise!"

Elizabeth jumped and let out a startled shriek. "What?" She laid a hand flat on her chest and glanced around the huge room crowded with people. A large banner hung on the wall with the word Congratulations painted on it, surrounded by numerous painted renditions of rattles, baby booties and blocks. "What's this?"

Nicolina stepped forward. "It's your baby shower. You didn't think we'd forget, did you?"

"I thought you were sick."

The girl shrugged and gave her an impish grin. "I lied."

Elizabeth looked around the room. Not only were all the employees there, but lots of others too. Mrs. Moretti, Mrs. Tessio, Mrs. Cammareri, Gino Galenti. Everyone. It brought tears to her eyes. "Thank you all so much. This is so unexpected." She sniffed loudly, unable to stem the tears that spilled forth and slid down her cheeks.

"Aww." Several people spoke at once.

"Here you go." Nico handed her a handkerchief and addressed the crowd. "I knew she'd need one. Pregnant women are always crying."

Everyone chuckled, even Elizabeth as she mopped at her eyes. "This is so wonderful. Thank you all."

Nico grinned again. "Well, I didn't think we were going to pull it off. We were running out of dilemmas and people to send into your office while we got ready for the party."

"What? No!" Elizabeth glanced at the short redhead standing a few feet away. "So, the sleeves aren't wrong?"

Flora shook her head.

"Herbert, did you really want to ask Betty Sue out on a date?" The young man's face glowed red as he nodded.

Betty Sue giggled and said, "Okay."

Everyone laughed again.

"Mrs. Stiles, where are you?" Elizabeth searched the sea of faces until she located the woman standing in the kitchen doorway. "Did you really make lunch?"

The woman smiled. "Of course I did. It's Tuesday. Roast pork, peas and mashed potato with lots of gravy. One of Mr. Montenari's favorites."

Dante. Fresh tears sprang to her eyes. Elizabeth dashed them away with the small square of cotton. "Sorry. I just miss him and wish he were here for this."

Nicolina nodded. "I understand." A smile spread across her face. In fact, several people were smiling.

"What's so funny? Pregnant women cry. A lot. Trust me, I know." Elizabeth sniffled again and attempted to smile too. "I'm probably a real mess now. A splotchy face to go along with my swollen feet and this." She rested a hand on her distended mid-section as she continued to dab at her eyes.

"You're the most beautiful woman I've ever seen."

Elizabeth froze for a split second before wheeling around. "Dante?"

He smiled and stepped forward, pulling her into his arms to the delight of their employees if the applause and whistles were any indication.

"What are you doing here? You're supposed to be at the trade show in California for another week." Her words were muffled against his chest.

"I was there long enough to take care of what I needed to."

Elizabeth squeezed him tighter. "I've missed you so much."

"Shh, shh, *cara mia*." He murmured against her hair. "Everything's fine. I missed you too." He pulled back to rest a hand on her abdomen. "And how is our little one?"

She laid a hand over his. "Fine. Fine. Wreaking havoc with my emotions, but all the books say that's to be expected." Elizabeth smiled up at him. "I can't believe you're back. Did you take a taxi here?"

Dante shook his head. "No, Nico came and picked me up at the train station early this morning."

"She did?" Elizabeth turned her gaze on Dante's younger cousin. "It looks like you've been a very busy young woman."

Nico shrugged. "Everyone has. Your husband included. We wouldn't have been able to pull it off without his help."

Dante smiled. "Well, let's not let all this work go to waste. How about we eat?"

"Okay. And after," Nico pointed to a table under the banner. "There's cake and ice cream and presents to open."

More than an hour later, people were still in attendance as Elizabeth opened the last of the gifts. There were miniature quilts, tiny sweaters, and many other beautiful things given to welcome the new baby into this world. Dante sat with his arm around her shoulders, admiring the gifts with Elizabeth.

"We should probably get back to work," Elizabeth said, but made no move to get up. "A nap sounds much more appealing. I think I ate too much ice cream." She rested a hand on her stomach.

"Good idea." Dante stood.

"What?"

"Listen up, everyone." He waited until people stopped talking. "This has been a great party. Elizabeth and I want to say thank you—for the gifts, all of it." He held out his hand to Elizabeth. She rose to stand beside him. "We'd also like to say thank you again for all your hard work over the last year. Because of that hard work, we're planning on expanding next spring. In April." He looked at Elizabeth. "April, is that right?"

She nodded.

"Right. Anyway, as a small token of our thanks, everyone please take the rest of the day off. With pay." Several people clapped and cheered.

Carmine Carapetti rushed in. "What? Did you guys already hear?"

His mother stepped up. "Hear what, Carmine? Where've you been?"

"Nowhere." He raised a hand. "I swear, Ma. I was out back by the storeroom smoking a ciggie, and it came over the radio."

"What? Another bombing?"

"No, Ma. The Japanese surrendered. The war's over."

The room erupted into cheers, with much hugging and kissing.

Dante and Elizabeth exchanged a brief hug and kiss before being swept up in the celebratory atmosphere.

Later, she held his hand as they strode across the now empty parking lot in the late afternoon sun.

"Can you believe it? The war's finally over?" She rested the other hand on her abdomen. "That's the best gift the baby received today."

Dante shook his head. "It's hard to believe, but nothing makes me happier." He paused. "Except one thing."

"What's that? Mrs. Stiles' roast pork?"

He grinned. "No, though it's good, don't get me wrong, it comes in second to spending time with you."

She smiled and then snapped her fingers. "Oh, darn. I meant to grab those financial reports off my desk to go over later."

Dante shook his head. "Not today."

They'd made it to the shade of the giant elms surrounding their house. Elizabeth started up the steps to the porch. "What're we going to do then?" She turned to face her husband.

Dante was still standing on the ground. "We're going to take a nap."

"What? Seriously?"

He nodded. "I've never been more serious. I haven't slept in my own bed or held my wife and baby," Dante leaned forward to place a gentle kiss on Elizabeth's abdomen, "in almost three weeks. It's all I've thought about on the trip home. You next to me. Cool sheets. The birds singing and the breeze blowing in the bedroom windows." His warm brown eyes held a beseeching look. "Please say yes."

Elizabeth held out her hand. "Yes."

They climbed the steps together and entered into the coolness of their home, closing the door on the rest of the world—for this afternoon at least.

Two people scarred by war, but healed by love.

Author's Note

Reviews spread the word of an enjoyed book and are the best way to thank an author for their hard work. Please leave a short review on your favorite book site.

About the Author

C. L. Howland loves creating stories of everyday people caught up in the sometimes extraordinary business of living. When not plotting what challenges her characters will face next, C. L. enjoys life with her family in the Green Mountains of Vermont.

To learn more about C. L., or to sign up
for her mailing list, please visit:
www.clhowland.com

My Mother Grows Wallflowers

There isn't a heck of a lot that doesn't scream target about Mina Mason: her weight, her homemade dresses, even the hoarder's paradise loosely disguised as the Masons' home. Samuel Two Bears Miller reshapes Mina's understated existence with his arrival, his dark skin and long braid exotic next to the Puritan pallor of the local boys. All through high school, Mina conceals her odd home life behind the closed doors of her dilapidated house, even after discovering love with the outspoken boy. Mina must choose between the person who makes her feel alive and the family who relies on her.

Now Available at Major Online Retailers

Legacy of a
Wallflower

C.L. Howland

Flashing blue lights and a pink sandal in the middle of a rural Vermont road mark the end of a dream for Mina Mason as a tragic accident halts her elopement to Sam Miller. No one's ever been allowed inside the Mason's shabby house. That rule isn't about to change, leaving Mina to care for her aging mother amid piles of hoarded possessions. With no respite in sight, Mina breaks her engagement to Sam. He deserves the normal life he'll never find with her.

Now Available at Major Online Retailers

Printed in Great Britain
by Amazon

37000620R00182